Kevin P. Keating

THE NATURAL ORDER OF THINGS

After working as a boilermaker in the steel mills in Ohio, Kevin P. Keating became a professor of English and began teaching at Baldwin Wallace University, Cleveland State University, Lorain County Community College, and Lakeland Community College. His essays and stories have appeared in more than fifty literary journals, including *The Blue Lake Review, The Fifth Street Review, The Mad Hatter's Review, The Avatar Review, The North Coast Review, The Licking River Review, The Red Rock Review, Whiskey Island, Juked, Inertia, Identity Theory, Exquisite Corpse, Wordriver*, and many others. He currently resides in Cleveland, Ohio.

The

NATURAL ORDER

OF THINGS

The

NATURAL ORDER

OF THINGS

A Novel

Kevin P. Keating

Vintage Contemporaries
A Division of Random House LLC
New York

FIRST VINTAGE CONTEMPORARIES EDITION, APRIL 2014

Copyright © 2012 by Kevin P. Keating

All rights reserved. Published in the United States by Vintage Books,
a division of Random House LLC, New York, and in Canada by
Random House of Canada Limited, Toronto, Penguin Random House
companies. Originally published in the United States by Aqueous Books,
New Orleans, in 2012.

Vintage is a registered trademark and Vintage Contemporaries and
colophon are trademarks of Random House LLC.

The Cataloging-in-Publication Data is on file at the Library of Congress.

Vintage Trade Paperback ISBN: 978-0-8041-6927-1
eBook ISBN: 978-0-8041-6926-4

www.vintagebooks.com

Printed in the United States of America
10 9 8 7 6 5 4 3 2 1

For my parents

And now I will unclasp a secret book,
And to your quick-conceiving discontents
I'll read you matter deep and dangerous,
As full of peril and adventurous spirit
As to o'erwalk a current roaring loud
On the unsteadfast footing of a spear.

—WILLIAM SHAKESPEARE, *King Henry IV*, PART I

CONTENTS

PART ONE

Vigil

I

For more than one hundred years, the Jesuit school has been regarded by its students, administrators, and staff as a beacon of uncompromising moral standards, an important symbol of Catholic piety located at the center of a labyrinth of winding boulevards, blind alleys, and crumbling brick lanes; streets that seem to twist and turn and double back on themselves so that even the slavering packs of stray dogs, the most intuitive of cartographers, have great difficulty navigating the chaos of slate sidewalks as they scrounge for rancid gobbets before vanishing like ghosts into the dripping cellars of abandoned houses; a once picturesque quarter of the city now overrun by liquor stores, empty factories, and a small cheerless café that has garnered notoriety as a literary demimonde where uninspired poets squabble with the barista over the price of a cup of coffee; "the old neighborhood" as it is sometimes called—old because the Gilded Age mansions and Depression-era brownstones are in advanced stages of decay; the rooftops leaking, the foundations sinking imperceptibly into sandy soil, the copper pipes waiting to be harvested from the plaster walls and sold for scrap; old because no developer has been willing to risk the necessary investment to tear down these decomposing behemoths—the grand movie palace, the marble rotunda of a failed bank, the famous hotel ballroom with its Corinthian columns covered in gangland graffiti—to clear enough land for a sparkling new shopping center, a high-dollar bistro, a fashionable boutique, a well-lit parking garage.

Of the city's glorious past, little now remains. The school alone endures as a kind of living artifact; a manifestation, depending on one's perspective, of Milton's Pandemonium or Augustine's City of God. With its immense gothic tower of rough-hewn stone and its anarchy of corridors and antechambers and enormous frescoed galleries, the school has grown into a city within a city, a citadel of secrets, one with obscure and hidden geometries designed to keep the curious away from the ancient and forbidden rites rumored to take place inside. And yet this formidable reputation has never deterred a boisterous battalion of prostitutes from marching up and down the avenue in broad daylight.

The brooding, elderly priests, draped in heavy ecclesiastical attire, glare at the women and shake their heads in stern disapproval. Long lines of submissive students, some bearing candles and rosaries and missals, slink across the campus to the chapel where the priests stand guard. Desperate to catch a glimpse of an exposed tit, the boys pause outside the chapel doors until they feel the sharp jab of canes and shillelaghs prodding them into that ponderous reservoir of silence where they kneel in the pews and, with their hands clasped in what they hope passes for prayer, pretend to gaze in adoration at the tarnished statue of the martyred saint for whom the school is named.

The whores find these rites so absurd that they perform a little mock ceremony of their own, twirling in the iron gloom like ecstatic dervishes, their voices collecting into thin, muddy puddles of laughter. The boys wonder at this. Certainly the whores have little to laugh about these days. A madman is at large, preying on the homeless as they sleep in alleys and on park benches, disfiguring his victims with the simple tools of his trade—a bottle of lighter fluid, a book of matches. Despite the danger, business remains steady, and since the whores rarely read the papers or watch the nightly news they go about their usual routine without taking additional precautions.

Few bother to solicit business from the high-strung prep school boys, many of whom, the sons of trial lawyers and investment bankers and successful entrepreneurs, have the means to offer these women a safe haven from night-roaming lunatics. Such boys tend to be idealistic; they believe true love really exists in the world and are convinced, or have been convinced by the propagandistic priests, that a girl of rare and exquisite beauty—and one whose fidelity is beyond reproach—will in due course come along and deflower them, but only after a proper wedding ceremony.

A certain boy of unusual daring, William de Vere has risked eternal damnation by visiting a woman who goes by the name Tamar. Every Friday afternoon he meets her at the nearby Stone Town Café where they sit in the same corner booth, far from the big picture window and the mystified stares of passersby, and split a generous slice of cheesecake draped with thin ribbons of milk chocolate. In addition to being well-versed in the art of love, Tamar also happens to be an accomplished raconteur with a thousand stories to tell, some bawdy, some comic, all hopelessly tragic.

Between sips of coffee she tells Will the story of her name-sake, the infamous lover of Onan, the patron saint of all randy Catholic schoolboys. Will has heard this story a hundred times before and politely reminds Tamar that the Jesuits are, above all else, experts on the subject of biblical harlotry. Besides, it's not her storytelling skills that he finds so appealing. Unlike the other women who walk the streets, Tamar doesn't try to disguise her features beneath layers of garish makeup. She has large dark eyes like pieces of polished black agate and wild hair that hangs loosely around her shoulders and courses down her back and a prominent mole on her left cheek. These are the things he likes about her. He also appreciates her sense of style—the shiny red boots and purple miniskirt and tremendous hoop earrings. Most of all he likes her lean sinewy body, with its dazzling array of bruises and welts and angry scars.

After paying the tab, Will gallantly takes Tamar by the hand and leads her a few short blocks to the Zanzibar Towers & Gardens, a spectacular ten-story flophouse with a cracking limestone façade that rises high above the surrounding hovels like some monstrous, teetering cairn. He rents an apartment there to host weekend parties and practice his bass guitar with the other members of a death metal band he has formed. Naturally, he does this without his parent's permission or knowledge—his father in particular would not approve, not at all—but Will is eighteen now, and there are no laws, at least none with which he is familiar, prohibiting him from having a pad of his own.

Once inside the apartment, the two quickly get undressed and tumble into bed. The uptight prima donnas that Will sometimes dates from an eastside boarding school refuse to do the things he pressures them to do—even an innocent handjob is too much to expect—and he has come to regard Tamar as a kind of secular saint, one who is generous with her body to the point of martyrdom. With an impish grin he reaches beneath the greasy sheets to fondle her breasts, and as he presses his school-boy hard-on against the cryptic emblem branded to her thigh—the letters IHS encircled in sunbeams that look not unlike the daggers Roman soldiers used for their assassinations and suicides—he is suddenly struck by a rare flash of creative insight. He has been suffering from a terrible bout of writer's block and no longer trusts his own ideas, but after giving the matter some thought, he decides to invite Tamar to one of his wild parties with the intention of getting an illustrious classmate laid.

Tamar consents to the plan. She isn't the sort to turn down a job, especially one so close to home. She lives upstairs in a two bedroom flat with her three-year-old daughter, a filthy little madhouse littered with cigarette butts and empty bottles of booze, but she never divulges this information. She is only interested in the work and in this boy's unlimited supply of money. Her professional life may be an open book, but her private life is strictly confidential.

Will kisses her on the lips. He can still taste coffee and chocolate at the corners of her mouth. "You're so sweet," he says. Then he climbs on top of her and in a tireless, mechanical frenzy begins pumping away.

II

Residents of this neighborhood once shared a gleeful contempt for the Jesuits, but after a slumber of one hundred years, the reclusive priests started to buy up the crowded shacks and cavernous industrial plants that encircled the school like the deteriorating fortifications of some ghastly dystopian city. The local government, an ineffectual crew of villains mired in corruption, took little interest in halting the widespread unemployment and subsequent foreclosures that, for the past decade, spread through the streets like an epidemic. Only the priests, who controlled the school's massive endowment, possessed the power and political clout to heal the neighborhood and to resurrect it from the grave possibility of further decline.

Most residents accepted the fair market price for their homes and escaped from under the monolithic tenement buildings and the long shadows cast across the glass-strewn lots. Others were less cooperative. A group of aging and sanctimonious bohemians, unsuccessful at its own piddling attempts to gentrify the neighborhood, went before committees of weary aldermen, insisting that a number of structures in this district were important historic landmarks that should be preserved no matter the cost. The Jesuits attended these public hearings. Though outraged by the insolent tone of these peevish urban pioneers, the priests were not overly concerned. The school was blessed to have hundreds of gifted alumni who were partners in prominent law firms, distinguished men who successfully argued high profile cases before juries in courthouses across the country and who, with great aplomb, could decimate any frivolous lawsuit that used, as the basis of its claim, the tired cliché "historic landmark."

After overcoming the obligatory legal hurdles, the attorneys drew up the necessary documents and had them signed in triplicate by judges and county commissioners, most of whom were graduates of the school as well. A few weeks later, as television news reporters and a small number of dejected protesters watched from behind police barricades, a demolition crew arrived with excavators and bulldozers and a wrecking ball that came arcing across the sky like the pendulum of a celestial grandfather clock ready to strike the death knell. No one put up a fight for very long, and the structures were razed without further incident. The conquest of the neighborhood continued until enough space was cleared for a football stadium, a magnificent new temple for the modern man, a holy of holies that glittered in the night and drew riotous spectators who worshiped at this wellspring of myth and legend and who atoned for their own lack of athletic prowess through the purchase of indulgences—pennants and jerseys and overpriced refreshments.

In recent years the school has earned a reputation as a football powerhouse. Consequently, enrollment soars and fundraising doubles. Impressed by the team's success, philanthropists agree to finance other projects—a science lab, an auditorium, a state-of-the-art fitness center. Now there is pressure to win a state championship. Coach Kaliher recruits heavily, makes promises he has no intention of keeping, ridiculous guarantees of fame and fortune. With the possible exception of the players and their hopeful parents, everyone understands the illegality of these practices, but should some misguided individual raise an objection or leak even the most innocuous bit of information to the press, the Jesuits will gladly unleash their attorneys, who will sort things out with characteristic speed and discretion and hound the traitors to the gates of hell as though partaking in a marvelous blood sport.

III

This season the star quarterback is Frank "the Minotaur" Mc-Sweeney, a strapping seventeen-year-old senior whose shaved head and icy stare intimidate friends and enemies alike. At six feet, three inches tall, he strides across campus like an invincible Goliath, eager to rip the head from David's scrawny shoulders and swing it from his fingertips like a lantern. No one can topple him. College scouts phone his house on game day to wish him good luck; on Sunday they call to find out if he has sustained any serious injuries; on holidays they call to make sure he has received the enormous gift baskets of exotic fruit and French cheeses and big tins of creatine. Local sportscasters, mesmerized by his agility and "monster right arm," feature slow-motion footage of his fifty-yard passes; from high atop the bleachers, thousands of inebriated fans watch him scramble outside the pocket, eluding a phalanx of defensive linemen, to make another incredible play; and in the blustery autumn night, the dreamy-eyed cheerleaders whisper words that have a certain storybook quality to them—Notre Dame, National Football League, lucrative endorsement deals.

Things are going his way, everyone says so, but Frank is starting to have doubts. The team wins its first four games of the season, routing its opponents with ease, but during the fifth game, his offensive line is decimated. The right guard's femur snaps during a routine play. Frank has never heard anyone scream like that before, a high-pitched shriek that continues to echo in his mind at unexpected moments and makes him rub his own leg to make sure it is still intact. During the fourth quarter, the left tackle's fingers are horrifically mangled under a cavalcade of bloodthirsty boys in cleats. More screams. Frank is sacked half a dozen times and the team loses by three points. The next game is a total catastrophe. Without an adequate offensive line to protect him against a blitzing defense, Frank is clobbered, his ribs bruised, his nose bloodied. Another tough loss, and now there is a real danger that the team will not make a post-season appearance.

Lately he has trouble sleeping at night and has even lost his appetite for members of the opposite sex. A passing phase, that's all it is; seventeen-year-old boys are prone to episodes of this kind; it's quite natural, or so his confessors repeatedly assure him. The important thing is not to become distracted. He must concentrate. Tomorrow night is the big game, a rivalry known throughout the city as the Holy War, a must-win situation. The game happens to coincide with the Feast of All Saints, a day of holy obligation for Catholics, an irony not lost on the priests who assure Frank that the faithful will be praying for him. "With God's grace you will lead our team to victory." But before absolving him of his transgressions, the priests advise Frank to say three Our Fathers and a Hail Mary, and though this is not part of their usual prescription for spiritual health, they dole out a handful of black and white pills—the school colors—to help "focus his mind."

On Friday morning the P.A. system snaps on, and the principal's voice, a solemn, disembodied baritone that thunders through the hallways, makes an unexpected announcement: "Men, as you know we face a great challenge tomorrow night, and I would like us all to take a moment to pray for the team and for our quarterback. He is perhaps the most gifted athlete our school has ever produced. In order to set the proper mood for the game, I ask you to keep an all-night vigil. From this moment on, remain absolutely silent. Speak to no one. Save it for the game. At kickoff time I want our opponents to hear you erupt with school spirit. Calm before the storm, gentlemen, calm before the storm. Let us begin our vigil by bowing our heads and saying the words our Lord taught us . . . *Pater noster, qui es in caelis: sanctificetur Nomen Tuum . . .*"

IV

For the rest of the day, Frank tries to keep a low profile, avoids the smiles of admirers, the scowls of detractors, the passive sneers of losers like Edmund Campion and the other hacks who write sports columns for the school newspaper. In vain he searches for a quiet corner, an empty classroom, where he can simply stare into space and clear his head, but the Jesuits shun privacy; boys do wicked things in private, and the school is designed to keep its students under constant surveillance. Somewhere in that mystifying web of gloomy corridors, a spy is always lurking.

This doesn't prevent William de Vere from tracking him down between classes and slinging an arm around his shoulder, not an easy thing to do since he is so much shorter than Frank, a runt really, but Frank would never say this to Will, not even as a joke.

"Hello, Minotaur. Got a minute?"

Frank flinches. Only someone like Will, someone whose pedigree has made him immune to the paranoia that afflicts the middle-class students, would dare defy the Jesuits' edict against speaking. Will is an all-around troublemaker, a wild man, a rebel. As if to confirm the point, he is sporting a black eye, a swollen lip, a bruised cheek. What's the explanation? A fight, a mugging, a domestic dispute? Maybe the wounds are self-inflicted, part of that deranged death metal look Will is always striving for. Frank decides not to ask any questions. Probably his teachers haven't asked either, preferring instead to gloat at Will's suffering, praising God for this small act of divine retribution.

"Are you up for a little soiree tonight, Baby Meat?"

Frank does not possess an extensive vocabulary and finds Will's use of the word "soiree" a bit disconcerting. Will is forever talking in code, hinting at things that are probably unlawful, certainly sinful.

"You're cracking, Slick. It's obvious. The stress is finally getting to you. But don't worry." Will leans in close, speaks quietly in his ear. "You're the guest of honor at my Halloween party tonight. After an hour or two in Zanzibar all of your problems will suddenly vanish. Just like *that*."

He snaps his fingers, and Frank is so startled by the sharp sound in the silent hallway that he lets out a nervous laugh and turns to make sure the priests aren't observing them. "Aw, but I can't. The big game's tomorrow. If the coach ever found out he'd kill me. Hell, he'd kill *you*, Will."

"Oh, come on, Baby Meat, you don't have to stay long. An hour. No, thirty minutes. You won't regret it."

Frank has visited this den of iniquity on more than one occasion and knows Will to be a gracious host. He keeps a keg of beer in the living room for easy access and another in the bathtub in case of an emergency; he owns a large aquarium stocked with red-bellied piranha with iridescent scales ("my Jesus fish," he calls them) that he systematically starves all week and then feeds during the party—scraps of raw meat, slops from the butcher, slimy entrails from factory farms. On special occasions he uses a live animal, a hamster or a white mouse that he dangles by its tail and then slowly lowers into the roiling water. A gruesome display of nature, yes, but one that never fails to get an enthusiastic round of applause from his drunken guests.

Frank is conflicted. This is a complicated matter. Politics are involved. He wonders what he should do: the game plan is unclear, the clock is ticking, but before he can reach a decision, the bell rings.

"Better hurry, Slick," says Will. "We don't want to be late to Pinter's class."

Bobbling their textbooks, the boys dash down the hall.

V

Even adolescent males have some intuitive sense of a caste system, and for this reason Frank does not consider Will a close friend. Though they have known each other since freshman year and often take classes together, they come from different worlds and have very little in common.

Will lives on a forty-acre estate with an infinity swimming pool overlooking the family's private stables and a wooded valley. Every Christmas and Easter, he vacations in Europe—Copenhagen, Brussels, Vienna, wherever the family business takes him. Will has skied the Alps and sipped Beaujolais in Paris cafés and smoked hashish in the notorious coffee shops that line the canals of Amsterdam's red-light district. His father is the CEO of a company that manufactures and exports scales, scales of all types and sizes, scales to weigh fruits and vegetables, scales to weigh newborn babies, scales to weigh portly middle-aged men and women who look down at the fluctuating numbers and sigh in despair, even scales to weigh tractor trailers, the kind Frank's father drives. Frank himself has weighed in at an even two hundred pounds on one such scale; there are five of them in the locker room, gifts of the de Vere family.

Frank's family has never made a donation of any kind to the school. His mother and father can barely come up with spare change for the collection basket on Sunday mornings. Perhaps that is why the Jesuits, recalling the gospel story of a poor widow who casts a few pennies into the treasury (. . . *and Jesus said, "For all the rich did cast in their abundance, but she of her want did cast in all that she had, even all her living"*), offered Frank a full athletic scholarship, without which he would be attending public school with the other working-class boys from the neighborhood. His distinction as a football star has given him rare access to the social ladder, and his parents expect him to climb it to its top rungs.

The McSweeneys live in a plain whitewashed clapboard frame house five blocks from the school, and like most of the other neglected century-old homes in that quarter of the city, theirs seems destined for certain demolition. Within the next two years the Jesuits intend to break ground on a new basketball arena, and soon the lawyers will coerce another dozen families to box up their meager belongings and move from one subsidized apartment to the next like a caravan of ragged refugees doomed to wander the badlands in search of some small, pitiful oasis to call home.

As he steps through the back door, desperate for a moment's peace, Frank is ambushed by his parents, who wait for him at the kitchen table.

"There he is, number seventeen himself!" says his dad, crushing out a cigarette. "The future Heisman Trophy winner."

"Let me have those things." His mother takes his varsity jacket and book bag and hangs them in the closet.

"How'd it go today, Frank? Teachers weren't too tough on

you, were they? They cut you a little slack, I hope. Remember, son, those people owe you, they owe you big time. This is national exposure we're talking about. Enrollment is up, salaries are up—"

"Would you give it a rest," says his mother.

His dad laughs, a little louder than he should in such a tiny house. Normally his dad mutters a quick hello and then disappears into the basement, where he sits on an old sofa and licks his self-inflicted wounds until he falls asleep in front of the TV with a fresh cigarette dangling from the corner of his mouth. Frank has never questioned him about this routine, mainly because he suspects that his dad has secrets to keep, a million private miseries that might come to light if Frank gets too curious and begins to snoop around. It's for this reason that father and son avoid eye contact—neither wants to see the guilt concealed in the other's eyes.

His mother pulls a tray of cookies from the oven. "Frank, a reporter from the school newspaper called. Says he's putting a big story together. He wants to ask you some questions, take a couple of pictures."

His dad glowers. "Jesus, Maggie, he doesn't need to eat garbage before the big game."

"Oh, he can have a few. They won't kill him."

"His body is a fine-tuned machine, and you're tampering with it. All that butter, oil, sugar. It's poison." He searches his pockets for a book of matches, another cigarette.

His mother slams the tray down on the table.

"What do you take me for, Malachy? Do you think I'm some kind of idiot? Do you really think I would poison our son? Do you think I would feed him anything that might harm his body? I know he's a *fine-tuned machine*." She mocks him with a high-pitched voice. "How do you think he got that way? The power of prayer? No! For the past four years I've scrimped and saved to buy only the finest ingredients, only the best. Whole wheat, flaxseed oil, spirulina, green tea, organic raisins, egg whites from free-range chickens . . ."

Frank sighs. What would life be without scenes like this? He's thinking of it now, wondering if these repetitious dramas, now so much a part of his daily routine, are worth rescuing from the bulldozers and backhoes and dump trucks. He walks to the closet and grabs his book bag.

His father gives him a miserable look. "Frank . . ."

"Just remembered, Dad. I have to go back to school to submit a term paper. And then I'm off to a friend's house. Gotta study the playbook, you know." It sounds like a lie, Frank is aware of this, but there is some truth to what he says, and what's more, he *wants* it to be true, he wants to be the responsible member of the household.

"Glad to hear it, son. You study your ass off. I'm counting on you. We all are."

This is nothing new—Frank's father counting on *him*. Long ago Frank had given up on asking his dad for advice, for a way to help him out of these confusing situations he now finds himself in.

His mother presses a plastic container of warm cookies into his hands. "Go on, go on, take them. They're *good* for you. Prickly pear cactus, dragon fruit, wheat grass, soy lecithin granules, mountain bilberry, a handful of walnuts . . ."

Before any serious shouting can begin, Frank takes the cookies and hurries out the door into the swirling October wind. Through desolate alleys that glitter with shattered beer bottles and down brick lanes that permeate with the evil stench

of urine, under clotheslines that stretch from the rusty rail-
ings and trellises of an old apartment building and swing like
an enormous tangled web, Frank makes his way toward the
school and its iconic gothic tower. After traveling a few blocks
he hears panting, padded footsteps, the faint click of nails, a
menacing snarl of animal anger. He can smell filth rising from
wet, matted fur, and when he turns the corner he is confronted
by a large, shuddering mass that bars his path. A dozen yellow
eyes stare at him in stoic solidarity. Frank steps into a pool of
dead afternoon light. In exchange for safe passage he slides
the plastic container of cookies across the ground, but the dogs
know the ways of this neighborhood, they are not so foolish
as to accept gifts from the menacing figures that pass through
its shadows. With a chorus of low growls and a flash of their
teeth, the dogs warn him away. Big as ponies some of them—
mastiffs and Rottweilers—that hobble on legs that have been
twisted and crushed and broken.

Frank quickly changes direction, resigned to the fact that
in this world, violence and charity, like life and death, come in
equal measures.

VI

Later that night, when he arrives at the Zanzibar Towers &
Gardens, he is surprised to find dozens of costumed figures
crowding around the keg in Will's apartment—a cardinal in
flowing red robes, a drunken priest, a pregnant nun, a cheerleader, a soldier in green battle fatigues. It's Halloween, he has
forgotten, and without a costume he feels self-conscious. He
backs toward the door, but someone like Frank cannot enter a
room unnoticed, and before he can make a quick exit, the host
emerges from a haze of aromatic smoke and grabs his arm.

Outside the classroom, Will is a different person altogether. His face is still bruised, his lip swollen, but instead of a black blazer and a striped tie, he is wearing baggy jeans and a T-shirt with a grinning skull.

"I'm a memento mori," says Will. "What the hell are *you* supposed to be?"

"Uh, I didn't realize it was a costume party."

"I'm only *teasing* you, Slick. You don't need a costume. You're the Minotaur, remember? You're the bloodthirsty beast that feeds on Athenian youths." He pushes a pint of beer into Frank's hand. "Drink up, my friend, for tomorrow we die."

Suddenly eager to catch a buzz, Frank drains the beer in one long swig, an astounding feat that leaves everyone breathless.

"Hey, Baby Meat, come check this out." Will leads him through a narrow hall and over to a closet where the stalk of a plant creeps toward bright sodium lights.

"I can buy weed on the street, of course, but there's nothing like homegrown." He hands Frank a joint the size of a small cigar and expertly flicks a match with his thumb. "Here, have a little taste of the creature. That's high-grade stuff, Slick. Harvested only an hour ago. I could probably sell it at school for a hundred dollars a quarter ounce, only I don't grow enough of it. Or maybe I do and I'm smoking too much of it myself."

Frank takes a powerful drag, holds his breath for what seems an eternity, and then lets the thick rings of smoke wobble toward the whirling ceiling fan. The stuff tastes vaguely like fertilizer, smells like horseshit, makes the world instantly dreamy and mellow. Tomorrow's big game gradually fades from memory, and Frank follows the freaky permutations of his mind, the thread of each thought becoming tangled in the next until his brain turns into a big unruly ball of yarn.

"Fuck my old man," says Will, rubbing his bruised face, "and fuck your old man, too, right?"

Frank, who is not quite sure what Will means by this, nods his head and smiles. Beaming with all the lechery and charm of a politician, he drifts into the front room and shakes hands with his classmates, gives high fives, tells a few dirty jokes. "I'm spinning yarn!" he shouts. Everyone laughs. Of course they do. These people would laugh at anything their quarterback has to say, and Frank, eager to impress his adoring fans, decides to perform his legendary animal routine. He stomps his feet, snorts like a bull, careens in cyclonic fury from one corner of the apartment to the next, looking for something to smash. With the exception of a few folding chairs and the slimy aquarium percolating with green water, there is nothing here worthy of destruction. Drooling, panting, turning red with exasperation, Frank crashes against a table, knocking over a dozen cups of draft beer. He hammers his fists against the doors and bangs his head against the walls. Chunks of plaster cascade down the front of his shirt.

The pious invocation soon begins: "We're number one! We're number one!" But Frank hears only a distant buzzing and feels a familiar Friday night blackness gathering between his ears like a furious cloud of bugs. He's had enough, knows he's had enough, but he drinks another beer anyway, and with the fragile bulb in his brain dimming to the lowest possible wattage he peels off his shirt and waits for the girls to descend. Some try to mother him; they call him "dear" and "sweetie" and tell him to sit down before he falls down, but these girls he rudely shoves aside in favor of the more flirtatious ones, the tall, lively, slender-framed girls who kiss his neck and nibble on his ears, but when he begins to grapple with them and says he wants to "take it to the bedroom," they try desperately to push him away and threaten to scream.

Will swiftly intervenes. "Whoa, Baby Meat! Hold on. I have a little surprise for you. This way, this way." Like some scheming carnival owner leading another fool into a dark tent to see the freakish thing he keeps in a dirty glass jar, Will cracks open a door to reveal a woman waiting in bed with only a thin white sheet concealing her naked body.

"This is Tamar," he says. "Lady looks like a goddamn prize fighter, doesn't she, Slick?"

Though he is nearly blind from drink and barely able to register an impure thought, a venial sin, Frank somehow manages to let out an instinctive snarl of desire. At last he has found a kindred spirit. Like him, Tamar is a kind of gladiator and has the bruises to prove it, an angry scar just below her naval from an incision that hasn't healed properly, a missing tooth, a nose that is just a little crooked. She smells, too, like smoke and chemicals and sweat and a thousand other nameless things, each with a story to tell, and after tonight there will be yet another tale to add to her collection.

"I'm so glad you like her," says Will, "because for the next thirty minutes she's all yours."

In the living room the death metal band begins to warm up. The lead singer growls into the microphone while the drummer, the one with the dreadlocks and the lazy left eye, hits the double bass drum with extraordinary speed, a lunatic march written for a marauding army of cannibal corpses, but Frank hears only Tamar's flat and distant voice, a voice that speaks from the bottom of a deep well: "Come to bed, you bad boy . . ."

She lowers the sheet and gets on her hands and knees. Frank doesn't need to be told twice. He's gonna fuck this bitch, yes, fuck her all night long. An all-night vigil.

VII

The following morning brings misery.

A storm has blown in off the lake, and freezing rain pelts the windows like small stones hurled by the tiny hands of angels. Paralyzed by pain and shivering in the drafty bedroom, Frank wonders if he suffered a concussion when he slammed his head into the wall last night. Each fold of his neocortex is a fault line, and each tiny shift of his head brings on tremors and quakes. His moans and the deep, tympanic rumbling in his chest record the seismic activity. A dozen pints of flat beer slosh around his bloated belly. Somehow he must make the harrowing journey to the bathroom, though it seems a hundred miles away. Naked, hunched over, apelike, he shuffles up to the toilet, but when he opens the lid he finds the bowl already clogged with clumps of tissue and strange, floating islands of feces. He gasps, gags, chokes. Suddenly the dam breaks. He drops to his knees, and a great bilious river bursts from his lips, burning his esophagus and coating his tongue.

"That's right," he whispers. "Best to get it all out."

After wiping his mouth on a towel draped over the shower curtain rod, he returns to the bedroom and collects his clothes. The woman is gone, has been gone for many hours now, but he barely recalls spending the night with her. Cringing with dread and embarrassment at the things he may have done, he gets dressed and then heads to the front door.

All over the apartment bodies are curled up on the floor

like vulnerable fetuses. Will sits on a folding chair near the big bay window, sipping a beer and watching a movie. In his hand he holds a letter typed on pink paper.

"Good morning, Sunshine!" says Will. "Care for a little hair of the dog?"

The Minotaur is afraid to shake his head. His skull is cracking right down the middle like a prehistoric egg about to hatch a ravenous, flesh-eating beast. He tries to keep perfectly still, staring at the letter in Will's hand.

"Another eviction notice!" Will says and tosses the letter to the ground. "So how'd it go last night?"

The Minotaur thinks about this for a moment, bites his lower lip. Forming words becomes a struggle.

"Everything went real good," he rasps. "Helluva party."

"Well, I'm awfully glad I could be of service." Will grins. "With Tamar you don't have to worry about catching the clap. It's the *plague* you have to worry about. Ha!"

The Minotaur blinks in dumb incomprehension.

"Hey, Slick, you *do* know what day it is, don't you?"

"Yeah, I know . . ."

"It's the first of November. The Day of the Dead. A day to build altars and shrines honoring the souls of the dearly departed, a day to drink and laugh and join hands in the Danse Macabre. Because no matter one's station in life, the dance of death unites us all. Yes, we all dance to the same tune."

Frank thanks Will for his hospitality and then stumbles out the door and down the stairs. On his way home he stops to rest against a tree and unleashes another pumping welter of vomit into an open sewer.

Luckily no one is awake at his house, and he creeps undetected to his bed. For a few hours he manages to sleep, but peace and tranquility elude him. All afternoon he is besieged by terrible visions, cold classrooms crowded with wizened men in black robes who tie him to a chair and jab him with hot pokers. They wheel out the infamous Brazen Bull, a medieval device used by inquisitors to slow-roast heretics. Its creaking hinges sound like the screams of its previous tenants: "Frank! Frank, you're late! Kickoff is in forty-five minutes! Coach Kaliher just called. He's frantic. He's out of his mind. We thought you left the house hours ago."

Through crusty eyes, he sees his mother and father hovering over him. They tremble with worry and seem to be on the verge of tears. He rolls out of bed, loses his balance, almost falls to the floor. The aftertaste of beer and puke and marijuana has him running to the bathroom.

"Frank, what's going on here? What the hell *happened* to you? Is something wrong? Are you sick? Who did this to you? Who is responsible? Tell us. You have to tell us. The priests will want answers. The coach. The newspapers. For godsakes, Frank, you must protect us. You must give us a story!"

VIII

Through the rain-soaked streets of the city, Frank sprints toward the fiendish, yellow lights of the football stadium. Even from a distance he can hear the crowd pounding, drumming, whistling. The inexhaustible clangor of ten thousand irrational minds. The roar of famished lions waiting to tear the flesh from his bones. For a split second he actually believes he is being led to his death. When he enters the locker room, he finds that his teammates have already made their way onto the field for calisthenics and warm-up drills. Pacing back and forth in front of the showers, visibly sweating through his shirt, massaging his writhen face with powerful fingers, Coach Kaliher turns on him and shouts, "You irresponsible sonofabitch! Get your goddamn ass out there before I shit down your throat!" Frank blinks, not because he is unaccustomed to such rage but because the voice rips into his brain, another rusty railroad spike pounded into his right frontal lobe.

The game begins. During the first half, Frank throws for only thirty yards and leads the offense past midfield only once. Watching helplessly from the sidelines, Coach Kaliher jumps up and down and waves his arms; he spits and sputters and shouts blasphemies. His assistants keep a safe distance. At halftime he grabs Frank by the jersey and slams him hard against the lockers. Again and again he does this.

"My job is on the line, you asshole! *More* than just my job!"

During the second half, Frank can barely breathe. He forgets the count, confuses the plays, stumbles, trips, runs into his own linemen. He hears the constant crack of shoulder pads, the peals of thunder from an advancing infantry, the maniacal screams of zealous fans. While stranded under a writhing heap of stinking bodies, he feels a hand clamp onto his balls and tighten like a vice. An injury time-out is called. For five minutes he squirms on the field, suspecting one of his own teammates. His fans actually boo him, their hero, their savior. When the final whistle blows, the team is routed 28–3. The season is lost. At the other end of the field, beneath the goalposts, the opposing quarterback drops to one knee and gives thanks to the Lord Jesus for blessing him with this miraculous victory.

His knees battered, his back aching, Frank trudges into

the tunnel. Someone shouts his name, and he looks up just in time to see a dark figure dump a cup of scalding coffee on his head. He clutches his face and collides into the cinderblock wall. Edmund Campion, the school's photojournalist, is there to snap a picture to commemorate his suffering. A portrait for the ages. In the locker room, Frank limps to the nearest toilet stall and dry heaves. Hot tears coarse down his cheeks and drip one by one into the bowl. He marvels at the simple beauty of the rippling water.

Stunned by yet another humiliating defeat, his teammates shower, get dressed, and leave the stadium without speaking to him. Coach Kaliher doesn't make an appearance at all.

Alone and trembling with pain, Frank collapses on a bench. The silence is kind to him. He closes his eyes and sees his teachers, the principal, the wealthy philanthropists like Will's father, and somewhere far away, he hears a voice— soft, kind, gentle, just Christ-like enough to lend irony to this diabolical display of commerce. Or is it Pilate's voice that he hears? It's difficult for him to distinguish between the two: "Parking fees, concessions, seat licenses, television revenues, book deals, increased enrollment . . ."

Secretly, Frank is glad he has done this terrible thing, glad he has brought this machine to a grinding halt, but he also knows that he will never get away with it. There are consequences in this life and in the next, or so he has been told, and when he leaves the stadium, he expects to find an angry mob waiting under the luciferian light, but no one is there, not even his parents, and as he walks home through the labyrinth of streets and listens to the brittle leaves scattering along the pavement, he can sense a dark presence.

Behind him the gothic bell tower rises stately and imperturbable above the evening, above the decades and the centuries, and somewhere within its shadow, the eyes of a thousand angry souls watch and wait, never letting him out of their sight.

Box

❧

I

On a Monday morning in early October, three weeks before the big game, Malachy McSweeney paces back and forth on the loading dock of the Burning River Brewery, going round and round with the automated speed of a conveyor belt. The first stinging winds of autumn come whipping off the lake, kicking up dust and leaves and scattering cigarette butts across the parking lot. Somehow the icy air shrivels his already haggard face and drains his cheeks of color like the crab apples that litter the ground. His coffee quickly turns tepid and tastes acidic on the tip of his tongue. To keep warm he pauses beside a steel barrel where he vigorously rubs his hands above the dying embers. His fellow truck drivers huddle beside him, and in an oddly lyrical low-life patois fused from the slang of a dozen different languages and never heard outside the perimeter of these wretched streets, the men grumble about the impending winter imprisonment with their nagging wives, unappreciative children, and disobedient dogs; dreaded months of sleet and snow when an epidemic of cabin fever sweeps through the city, making the

Box 29

men do things so desperate and despicable that many seek the guidance and mercy of the Jesuits.

Like a squadron of soldiers in a defeated army, the men form a disorganized line and await further orders. They fart and yawn and pick their teeth. They cough and wheeze and drum their chests with clenched fists. They stomp their heavy, black boots in time to the rhythmic scuff and scrape of fork-lifts against wooden pallets and the sharp percussion of robotic arms clanking against longneck bottles of beer. Then from out of this cacophonous canticle of machinery comes a booming voice that commands them all to "Shut it!"

Cloggy Collins emerges from the sweltering inferno of his small, windowless office and stares them down. Already chewing his first cigar of the day and perspiring profusely through his white collared shirt, Cloggy trundles across the loading dock, cradling what at first appears to be a large card-board sarcophagus stuffed with human body parts—a jumble of arms and legs, elbows and knees. In a gesture meant to show his disgust and impatience with his sorry crew of driv-ers, he wipes the corners of his mouth with thumb and forefin-ger, flicking a pasty glob into the wind where it seems to freeze in midair before falling to earth and shattering like a delicate crystal of exceptional beauty.

"Here's a little surprise, boys." He drops the box on the platform. "New marketing strategy."

With a wave of his hand and the word "Abracadabra!" he makes a life-sized cardboard cheerleader appear from out of the box. At six feet tall, she towers above these dwarfish men like some colossus of coitus, her long legs and smooth bronze thighs spread in a deliberately provocative pose, her tight tummy and delectable navel partially concealed by a pair of shimmering

pom-poms. Her bright eyes burn with uninhibited and exuber-
ant lust. Her lascivious and dazzling smile encourage all present
to come hither and pay homage to her unique majesty.

The men whistle, ogle, adjust themselves with frostbitten
fingers; they discuss esoteric and vulgar sexual techniques, a
Kama Sutra for the workingman—the Cleveland Steamer,
the Tennessee Snow Plow, the Dirty Sanchez. Here is a clever
decoy guaranteed to lure men by the thousands out of their
comfortable recliners and into stores to purchase inordinate
amounts of ale and to drink as much of it as their diseased
livers will allow. Even McSweeney, the most reserved of the
bunch, can't help but grin. It's a cruel deception, yes, but one
that doesn't deter his cock—that vindictive prick—from
briefly nodding its otherwise somnolent head in the pathetic
void of his trousers.

"Get these out pronto!" Cloggy shouts. "Put 'em on top of
every display. And try not to feel any of 'em up. We don't want
no damaged goods. Now move it, all of yous."

But before distributing the models to the drivers, Cloggy
slides his rough hands around a narrow waist and brushes his
bristly, tobacco-speckled chin against the airbrushed cleavage.
His eyes grow bleary and distant. The wrinkles in his face
deepen. When he speaks, it is as though he is in the midst of a
drug-induced trance.

"This is what we all dream about at night, eh? This is what
we deserve as men, as American men. Yessir, this is what it's
finally all about. What else is there? A winning team and a hot
piece of ass to cheer on the players . . ."

With forced smiles, the drivers collect their share of cardboard women and jump down from the dock, but as they slog
through the leaves that pile up in the weedy lot and make

Box 31

their way to the trucks, they are forced to endure the familiar gales of half-mad laughter that erupt from the gaping maw of Cloggy Collins.

II

Malachy McSweeney's first stop is the Jesuit high school.

With their astonishing ability to discriminate between various types of rich, dried, delicate malts, the priests are acclaimed as connoisseurs of beer, and each week they request (some would say require) a delivery of lagers and stouts and fancy raspberry lambics from the local brewery. Under normal circumstances, they are so delighted to see Malachy McSweeney, their prompt and dependable deliveryman, and are so concerned for his safe passage through the dangerous streets of this once grand city, that they lay their hands on his head and say a quick prayer to Saint Fiacre—he's the patron saint of cab drivers, true, but because the Vatican has yet to canonize a beer truck driver, it's the best they can do.

McSweeney, ever grateful for these humble petitions to heaven, looks forward to his regular stop at the school, but lately he has noticed a change among the priests. They seem irritable and cast accusatory glances in his direction. Some openly stare at him and scowl. At the start of the football season, the Jesuits, who initially had so much to celebrate, doubled their consumption from the usual six kegs to twelve, but in recent days their celebratory toasts have turned into drunken disputes about sacking the head coach and the almost blasphemous suggestion of replacing the starting quarterback with an inexperienced backup. It's still early in the season, but already the team has lost two crucial games, and playoff hopes are beginning to fade.

After he parks the delivery truck behind the main class-room building and starts to unload the kegs, McSweeney can sense the priests observing him from high atop the Gothic tower. Their eyes burn past cloudy cataracts and through classroom windows smeared with the fingerprints of teenage boys frantic to escape yet another tedious lecture on heaven and hell. Though they speak of tolerance and forgiveness, the Jesuits clearly resent the fact that someone so poor, so un-educated, so utterly incapable of managing a crisis can wield such enormous power over them; that a man like Malachy McSweeney, a humble truck driver and inhabitant of the sur-rounding slums, can in some way be responsible for the fate of the football team and thus for the fate of the entire school. The fact that his son is the star quarterback is obviously a divine blunder, a cosmic joke. It goes against the natural order.

Trying to ignore their stares, McSweeney rolls the kegs one by one down the steep incline into the cellar, where he places them in neat rows against the limestone walls. After complet-ing this task, he removes his cap, bows his head, and waits for the customary blessing. He stands there for five minutes, but no one comes to greet him, not even to check the inventory or sign the invoice. Cold air roars through the baffling net-work of musty tunnels and sounds like a priest making a grim proclamation from the pulpit: *Failure in children can always be traced back to the parents!*

The words fly out of the dark like an assassin's dagger; they hit their mark, strike deep, and McSweeney, fearing the mysterious power of the priests, races up the incline, climbs inside his truck, and speeds away from the school's haunted landscape.

Box 33

III

Although the rest of his route is a familiar one, to McSweeney it seems utterly alien and uncharted. The convenient marts and liquor stores are suffused with a ghastly blue light, and the sales clerks regard him with eyes that reflect their deep suspicion of thieving humanity. As morning turns to afternoon and as the white lines in the road begin to hypnotize him, he finds himself driving past his house, which is nowhere near his next stop. He shifts the truck into high gear and turns the volume up on the radio, but still he hears, or at least imagines he does, his wife's voice, a sharp, high-pitched, nerve-rattling squawk that rips through the paper-thin walls of their bedroom, carried aloft on the massive swells of early arctic air. Her duty in life is to remind him of his utter ineptitude and to recite an endless list of repairs—oil the hinges, tighten the faucets, sand and stain the hardwood floors, patch the cracks in the ceilings, clean the storm windows. There is also the small matter of his tossing and turning in bed, his thunderous snores, his peculiar habit of screaming in the night. Her complaints reach him even in the basement, his only refuge, where he spends his evenings on the sofa, watching television and smoking the quality reefer he manages to procure from one of his son's friends. In the basement he can at least *pretend* to be busy changing the filter on the furnace, setting mousetraps, and sorting through boxes of nails and screws. Usually this little pantomime is enough to appease his wife, but it doesn't prevent the house from sliding ever further into decrepitude.

With a heavy sigh he glances at the cardboard model propped up on the passenger seat, his trusty copilot, and like a nervous teenager reeling in virginity, he places his hand on her knee. A sudden urge comes over him. Briefly he considers pulling over to the berm, lowering his pants, and pressing his aching manhood against her leg, but he thinks better of this plan and tries to snap out of his silly fantasy.

After parking the truck behind the Select'n'Save, McSweeney unloads a dozen cases of beer and navigates his squeaky dolly through a maze of shelves. On Aisle 69, he stacks the cases into the steep tiers of a ziggurat, like the one he saw in his son's history textbook, and then places the cheerleader on top like some voluptuous temple prostitute of ancient Babylon. He steps back to examine his handiwork, a master builder with a knack for symmetry and a sense of the numinous, but there is something about this scene that he finds deeply unsettling. He tries to reposition the model but soon finds himself massaging the small tattoo on her right thigh and stroking the faint outline of nipples beneath her half top. She gazes down at him and seems to indicate her pleasure with an almost imperceptible flick of her black and white pom-poms. McSweeney's face goes flush, his knees buckle, his lips form words of reverence and awe.

From the deli comes the sharp sound of mechanized death. An old woman, squinting from behind the thick lenses of her horn-rimmed glasses, stops cranking a hand-powered meat grinder to observe McSweeney.

He scuttles sideways toward the exit with the cardboard girl dangling under his arm. "This one is damaged," he tells her with a sheepish grin.

The woman lets out a long, thin witch's cackle that poisons the air with foul omens, then she returns to her work, stuffing handfuls of bloody scraps deep inside the funnel and cranking the handle until the meat oozes out of the grinder, gray and gristly on the stainless steel countertop.

Box   35

IV

That evening, when he opens the back door of his house, a gust of wind sends a halo of leaves spinning above his head. Standing at the stove, Maggie stirs a pot of chili, the sleeves of her high school football jersey crusted over with tomato paste, her white slippers sprinkled with the crumbs of stale soda crackers. "Hey, there, Malachy McSweeney." She gives him a quick kiss on the cheek and says, "Would ya mind shutting the damn door? I like my chili without maple leaves."

He does as he is told and then tries to ladle some chili from the pot.

She swats his hand. "Did you stop at the hardware store like I asked?"

"Hardware store?"

She shakes her head, slowly, to make sure he registers her displeasure. "You promised to fix the furnace tonight, remember? There's exposed wiring. Christ, if I left things up to you this place would burn to the ground. Maybe I should ask our son to fix it." She turns her head toward the living room. "Oh, Frank!"

"No, no. I'll check it out right now."

"And close the basement door behind you. Smells like a wolf's den down there."

He slinks away, wondering if it's part of the marriage contract, something in the fine print, wherein a woman has the option to put on a pair of slippers every night and treat her husband like a complete imbecile. At the bottom step, he pauses to listen to the creak and groan of the floorboards, and when he is sure that his wife has gone to some distant corner of the house, perhaps to the bathroom to sit on the toilet and read the sports page, he removes the cardboard model that he has folded and hastily concealed inside his winter coat. After smoothing out any unsightly lines and creases, he places the model on the coffee table, where for one frustrating hour, he contemplates her heavenly breasts, ruby red lips, and shiny black hair. Marveling at her statuesque physique and curvaceous wonderment, he vows to understand the inexplicable hold her beauty has on him.

In the end, there seems to be only one solution to the enigma. He lets his hand drift down to his pulsing erection. A natural phenomenon that needs no further explanation.

V

That night, as they occupy their separate territories of the bed and watch the Monday night football game on their new TV (a gift from the Jesuits at the beginning of the season), Maggie reaches across the widening chasm that divides them and strokes her husband beneath the sheets. When he turns to face her, he sees only a nest of curls, bleached white and wiry, protruding from behind her ears and over the pillow. Every now and then he catches the lingering scent of chili powder and spices. The flannel nightgown she wears makes her look square, squat, rigidly geometric. For some time now he has worried about her weight. There is a long history of heart disease in her family, and he often wonders how he'll take to widowerhood.

"Why don't we try something kinky tonight?" she asks.

"Kinky?"

"Maybe you could do something rough. Something really dirty."

He squirms. "Like what?"

"Spank me," she says. "Slap me. Hard."

Box 37

"For godsake, Maggie . . ." He tries to think of a plausible excuse. In twenty years of marriage, she has never shown any interest in naughty games, experimentation, sin. Like him, she is a devout Catholic and shuns perversion. "But Frank is in the next room."

She giggles, pinches his beer belly. "Oh, he's sound asleep by now. He won't hear us."

"Aw, baloney. He stays up all night long, studying the play-book, strategizing, figuring out a way to win the big game."

"Strategizing? You make him sound like Julius Caesar."

"Yeah, well, he's just as smart as the rich kids at that school. Smarter probably. He has real-life experience, which is some-thing they don't have."

She rolls away from him and stares at the ceiling, her face drawn and sleepless. "That's right, McSweeney, change the subject. I know you hate me. I'm a mess, I'm disgusting. The thought of making love to me turns your stomach, doesn't it?" She sits up, resting on one elbow. "Well, let me tell you some-thing. It isn't *natural* for a man to neglect his wife."

Though he half-heartedly denies the terrible accusations she levels against him, McSweeney can no longer pretend to be aroused by her thick shanks and enormous, jiggling thighs. She ceased to be a woman who could make him howl with yearning and deep desire. Marriage has turned her into a shapeless, fleshy hermaphrodite, a doting mother who treats him like a troubled child. He has contemplated leaving her, but like most men who are out of money and out of options, he is afraid to take action. Sooner or later he will need to do some-thing; he cannot continue on this way, but his problems are so profound that rather than try to solve them, he finds it much easier to lock them away in a safe and lonely place where there is little chance of anyone getting at them. After twenty years of concealment, there is no telling how crowded with secrets his soul has become. Maybe he should discuss these things with the priests, get them out in the open, but he can't think about that right now. It's been a long day.

Maggie taps him on the shoulder, and her voice floats across the bed, soft and lilting as a lullaby: "Wake up, Mc-Sweeney, wake up. Look, it's the new ad . . ."

He cracks open an eye and sees a collage of nonsensical images flickering across the TV screen, continuous quick cuts of scantily clad girls and bare-chested boys, their bodies painted black and white, dancing, gyrating, limbs interlocking in the golden sunlight of an autumn day. A football game. The referee blows his whistle. The players take their positions on the line of scrimmage. Long silky legs come into focus. The camera pans up to reveal a tall cheerleader—the cheerleader!—sauntering down the sideline, a gentle breeze sweeping through her dark hair. With libidinous and curious fingers, she fondles a bottle of beer and pours a sparkling stream of ale into her eager mouth. The quarterback, dumbfounded by her beauty, drops the football and is immediately crushed between two stampeding linebackers. The crowd goes wild.

McSweeney's legs tremble. The cheerleader, while certainly no more attractive than a hundred other anonymous models who parade across the idiot box on a daily basis, nevertheless manages to radiate sex with every improbable and exaggerated curve of her surgically altered body and reminds him that he, like all men, is a prisoner of his pecker, condemned by a pitiless dictator, and sentenced to a lifetime of captivity with little hope for parole. In the deep purple fog of flickering TV light, he touches his wife's plump, pale breasts

Box 39

and, closing his eyes tight, dreams of the beautiful model, God how he dreams of her, and within minutes he is panting and thrusting his hips like he really means it.

VI

Something comes over him.

After work one rainy night, Malachy McSweeney scurries behind the brewery and crawls inside a cardboard box where he waits for Cloggy Collins to lock up. One hour later, as the rain intensifies and pounds the sagging rooftop of his impromptu shelter, he sees the lights go out. Shivering in the wet and the cold and fumbling with his keys, McSweeney cautiously emerges from his cocoon and creeps toward the building. Though he refuses to dwell on the possibility of getting caught, it does occur to him that his boss might still be sitting at his desk, waiting for him in the dark with a model perched on his lap and a bottle of beer in his hand, a tire iron, a loaded gun.

"You sick, sorry fuck!" he imagines Cloggy saying. "There ain't no work, not for crazy people, not for head cases, not for *perverts*!"

McSweeney feels short of breath and begins to pant. The world seems like a different place now—less predictable, more chaotic—and as he eases open the loading dock door and sidles through the brewery, he whispers, "I could do your job, Cloggy, I could do your job . . ."

His eyes rolling with fear, he enters Cloggy's office and waits for something to happen. No one is inside. The place reeks of smoke and sweat, and though he cringes at its meaning, the ripe earthy odor of freshly spilled semen. He eases past wobbling stacks of yellow paper that clutter Cloggy's desk and almost knocks over a coffee pot. In the far corner, buried under a mountain of greasy rags, a dozen cardboard women stare into space like girls heavily drugged and imprisoned in a faraway brothel, a bevy of tragic beauty queens captured by a cigar-chomping ogre and forced to pleasure him whenever he demands it. McSweeney's mission has suddenly become one of great urgency: he must rescue these lovely maidens and deliver them from a life of degradation and servitude. He grabs a slew of girls and smuggles them out to the trunk of his car where he stacks them one on top of the other like slices of meat on a sex sandwich.

"You're safe now," he assures them. "Safe . . ."

He brings the models back to his house where, for several nights after the exhilarating heist, he performs what soon becomes a sacred ritual. When he is sure Maggie has fallen asleep and his son has gone to his room to study the playbook, he hurries down the stairs, always careful to avoid the creaking step or two, and there in the exquisite solitude of the basement, he lights three candles, always three, the magic number, and places the models in various spots around the room. Before joining them, he sprays cologne behind his ears and around his shaggy genitals. He pours a tall beer, smokes a fat joint, and drifts away, upward and outside of himself to another plane of existence where he is no longer a daydreaming working-class stiff from a dying industrial city but a randy high school athlete at a wild party, a sophisticated playboy in a downtown nightclub, a movie mogul auditioning nubile starlets for his next summer blockbuster, a vampire summoning voluptuous succubi from his underground lair.

Usually these harmless adventures leave him satisfied and

Box 41

spent, but occasionally, as he stretches naked and perspiring on the couch and listens to the frightening boom of the igniting furnace and catches the foul scent of mildew permeating from the cracks in the cinderblock walls, he suspects that Maggie might be right. Maybe he *is* inept, and maybe he is something far more terrible than that.

Once, while preparing for his midnight rendezvous, he sniffs something rancid and discovers behind a wilted house-plant a heap of gnawed chicken bones. He doesn't remember leaving them there. At such times his mystical visions turn sour, and he imagines things, truly devilish things—the state hospital, padded rooms filled with pleading patients, probing doctors, sturdy and determined nurses brandishing enormous dripping needles—but he tries to assure himself that all married men carry on sordid double lives. Some pop pills, some have illegitimate children, some dress in women's clothing. What difference does it make?

Monogamy is an aberration. No man can belong exclusively to one woman, and it is generally understood that married men, when alone at night, do any number of things that they pretend to frown upon in the light of day.

VII

The ritual continues without variation until Halloween, the eve of the Holy War, and before descending to his sybaritic playground, McSweeney sits at the kitchen table, waiting for his son to come home from school, and puzzles over how he could have sired such a creature, the great muscled Minotaur who, with his freakish physique and arrogant swagger, makes lesser mortals stare in fascination and quiver with dread. Since

Maggie is incapable of cheating on him, he believes a mistake was made at the hospital, that two infants were switched at birth. Somewhere in the world a beautiful couple is mystified by their child's inconceivable homeliness and lack of coordination, an affluent couple who expect perfection from nature because they themselves are perfect—refined, urbane, totally unaccustomed to the horrors of mediocrity: the self-loathing, the hopelessness, the terrible despair. Little do they know that two trolls are raising their son, but soon they will come looking for him and demand restitution, not from the hospital for making such an incredibly obvious and unconscionable error, but from the McSweeneys for bungling the job of raising the boy and not helping him achieve his full potential.

At four o'clock the changeling comes bounding up the back steps and into the kitchen. McSweeney crushes out his cigarette, sits up straight, tries not to slouch. It's important that he speak to the boy, man to man. The football team cannot afford to lose another game.

"There he is, number seventeen himself! The future Heisman Trophy winner."

Maggie leaps from her chair and says, "Let me have those things." She takes the boy's varsity jacket and book bag and hangs them in the closet.

McSweeney, compelled to do the Jesuit's bidding, tries to sound nonchalant, relaxed, but his words feel forced and artificial. It seems he has spoken them before, has rehearsed every line.

"How'd it go today, Frank? Teachers weren't too tough on you, were they? They cut you a little slack, I hope. Remember, son, those people owe you, they owe you big time. This is na-

Box 43

tional exposure we're talking about. Enrollment is up, salaries are up . . ."

"Would you please give it a rest," says Maggie.

He laughs at her, more maliciously than he intended.

She pulls a hot tray from the oven. "Frank, a reporter from the school newspaper called. Says he's putting a big story together. He wants to ask you a few questions, take a few pictures."

When McSweeney realizes the cookies are intended for Frank, he panics. "Jesus, Maggie, he doesn't need to eat a bunch of garbage before the big game."

"Oh, he can have a few. They won't kill him."

"His body is a fine-tuned machine, and you're tampering with it. All that butter, oil, sugar. It's poison." He searches his pockets for a book of matches, another cigarette.

She slams the tray down on the table.

"What do you take me for, Malachy? Do you think I'm some kind of idiot? Do you really think I would poison our son? Do you think I would feed him anything that might harm his body? I know he's a *fine-tuned machine*. How do you think he got that way? The power of prayer? No! For the past four years I've scrimped and saved to buy only the finest ingredients, only the best. Whole wheat, flaxseed oil, spirulina, green tea, organic raisins, egg whites from free-range chickens . . ."

McSweeney watches Frank walk over to the closet and grab his book bag and jacket. Beyond a few simple hellos and goodbyes, father and son are incommunicative. Both have an innate suspicion of sentimentality and can never find the appropriate words to match their feelings. An occasional hand-

shake is the extent of the physical contact between them. Mc-
Sweeney, however, wants to learn more about the rarefied
social circles of the Jesuit school, the parties Frank is always
attending, the study groups, the meetings with teachers and
coaches. For a minute he actually considers following his son
through the streets and alleys, creeping up to a window and
peering through the parted sashes to spy on him. He needs to
see what life is like for a high school quarterback. Is it as glorious as people say? Do the cheerleaders really fawn over him?
Or are girls today just as cold and unapproachable as they were
when McSweeney was a boy of seventeen? He badly wants to
ask his son these questions. He must have the answers.

"Frank . . ." he begins, but the words die in his throat.

"Just remembered, Dad," says the boy. "I have to go back
to school to submit a term paper. And then I'm off to a friend's
house. Gotta study the playbook, you know."

McSweeney tries to smile. "Glad to hear it, son. You study
your ass off. I'm counting on you. We all are."

Maggie pushes a plastic container of warm cookies into
Frank's hands. "Go on, go on, take them. They're *good* for
you. Prickly pear cactus, dragon fruit, wheat grass, soy lecithin
granules, mountain bilberry, a handful of walnuts . . ."

VIII

Shortly before the clock strikes midnight, McSweeney
searches through his son's closet and finds the unique ceremo-
nial garb he so desperately needs. In the basement, he sets up
the models in a semi-circle, drapes them with costume jewelry,
douses them in cheap perfume, and as he whispers the forbidden incantation—one so obscene in its description of sodomy
that he feels nervous just saying the words—he catches a shin-

Box 45

ing vision of himself in the mirror, a man transformed by a football helmet, immense shoulder pads, and a mesh jersey of black and white. It's not the official team uniform, of course, not the one the players wear on game day; no, those things are kept under lock and key in the new stadium; it's only the grass-stained equipment his son uses for scrimmages, but even this scratched and beaten gear works wonders and makes McSweeney feel twenty-five years younger.

He sucks in his gut, stands erect. With a winning smile, he listens to the musical clatter of cleats against the tile floor and endures the discomfort of his engorged penis pressing against the athletic supporter. Invigorated by this image of pure brawn, he lifts one of the girls, brings her close to his facemask, inhales her divine aroma, a singular bouquet that can never be fully appreciated by the uninitiated. The smell of cardboard reminds most people of parcels shipped through the mail, merchandise delivered, gifts received. They care only about the contents of a box—books and beer and blow-up dolls—and recklessly discard the most significant details of everyday life.

Suddenly he wonders if he can actually *eat* a box. All his life he has avoided a healthy diet—he abhors fruits and vegetables—but these girls are probably quite fibrous, good for his digestive system and high blood pressure. With his mouth watering in anticipation of this sumptuous feast, he unclasps the chinstrap and lifts the girl to his eager lips, but before he can chow down on the subtle mound concealed under the skirt, a terrible scream rips through the basement.

"McSweeney!"

Confused by the eerie faces shifting in the shadows, he believes that one of the models has come to life. She stands at the bottom of the stairs, teetering wildly in her high heels, arms flailing in an attempt to balance herself. Something is wrong with her; she must be defective, an aborted mock-up, a rare blunder of mass production. When she does manage to take a step forward and penetrates the sacred circle of candlelight, she reveals her myriad imperfections: her airbrushed tits have turned ponderous and faintly green with a crosshatch of veins; her buttocks bulge from the white miniskirt, the firm musculature now lost forever under an inch of pitted cellulite; worse yet, her lovely eyes, once so full of lust, are now small and pink, almost porcine, and blink with a mixture of alarm and outrage.

McSweeney's stomach tightens, his throat goes dry. "What are you *doing*?" he croaks. "Why are you *dressed* this way?"

"Why am *I* dressed this way?" Maggie cries.

"Yes. What the hell do you think you're doing?"

For a moment his wife is silent; she looks in the mirror, adjusts her breasts, fixes her hair, and when she speaks, her voice has the old familiar tone of admonition, a thing that cannot be denied for very long. "I thought I might surprise you with this little number. I'm not stupid, you know. I see the way you beam every time that infantile ad comes on. Caught you red-handed, didn't I?"

He clings to one of the models, hoping it might offer him some protection from these ugly recriminations. Through clenched teeth, he says, "Why don't you leave me then? The fact of the matter is we can't stand the sight of each other anymore, can we?"

Now her eyes soften, fill with intense pity.

"That's not true," she says. "You need help, that's all. Don't worry, we'll get you some help. I should have recognized the signs. Let's start the healing process. Let's start right away."

Box 47

She grabs one of the cardboard models, breaks it over her plump knee, and like an enthusiastic Girl Scout at a bonfire, she thrusts it into the blue pilot light under the furnace.

To silence the pop and hiss of this erotic conflagration, McSweeney clamps his hands over his ears and wails, "My beautiful baby, oh, my beautiful baby!"

Oblivious to the danger, he slumps to the floor and tries to gather up the sharp cinders. Sparks cascade over cheekbones and bosoms and thighs, flames spread across the throw rug and singe the hairs on the back of his hands, but in the midst of this bedlam, he experiences a startling sense of inner calm that never abandons him, not even when Maggie comes charging across the room with a fire extinguisher and shoots an enormous load of white foam that dribbles down the bridge of his nose and drips from his chin in thick opalescent pearls.

Although it has taken many days to have this epiphany, McSweeney now understands that the model is an indestructible goddess, capable of being everywhere and nowhere, flickering forever in the ghostly light of the television, posing atop a pyramid of beer on Aisle 69 of the Select'n'Save, pressed flat against a convenience store window where homeless men squander their last few dollars on jugs of red wine. For once in his life, he actually looks forward to standing on the loading dock of the Burning River Brewery where, in the cold of another autumn morning, he will wait for Cloggy Collins to roll open the door and reveal the miraculous vision of the model resurrected from the ashes. For as long as he lives he will have her. Again and again he will have her. She will never get fat, she will never grow old, and she will never tire of bestowing upon him the heavenly blessings of physical fulfillment.

No-Deposit Love

I

The Friday before the big game finds Bernie Kaliher broke and desperate for a beer, and he spends the next hour or two—he's not sure how long really; he no longer wears a watch—scrounging for loose change in the pockets of an old winter coat, digging beneath the ragged cushions of a sofa, reaching behind the silent refrigerator (it no longer hums; the electricity was shut off weeks ago), looking under a throw rug, behind the toilet, inside the broom closet, his fingers creeping spider-like into every dark recess and mite-infested alcove, and, though he pities himself for doing something so obviously futile, beneath the piss-and-sweat-stained mattress where, instead of money, he unearths an assortment of dirty magazines, hardened tissues, a sports page with a photograph of his players lined up in front of the Jesuit high school like an invincible Roman legion in battle formation. The team has been described as "an unstoppable juggernaut, a ravening beast," and at the center of this hundred-headed hydra stands the proud coach, grim-faced, steely-eyed, Herculean. The fading letters at the top of the newspaper read more like a benediction than a byline: *May the Good Lord—and this Coaching Genius—Lead These Boys to Victory*.

Kaliher sighs. It's no use. There isn't a single dollar to be found anywhere. With mounting frustration, he crumples the newspaper into a ball and flings it across the apartment. He goes to the bedroom window, both hands buried deep in his empty pockets, and presses his forehead against the cold panes of glass. At this time of year premature darkness bears down on the city like a firm hand closing the lid on a musty Bible box, but in the distance, through the soughing trees, he can make out the hulking structure of the Jesuit school. A yellow blaze of artificial light transforms the building into a scumbled painting of Pandemonium, the bricks glinting with quartz, the spires illumined by lightning storms and lava flows. A dark blur of golden-eyed grackles rockets across the sky. They circle the crenellated parapet of the Gothic tower and roost on its narrow ledges. By closely observing the birds, Kaliher hopes to detect some kind of favorable augury. In fact, he looks for signs everywhere, just to be sure—in the appearance of a black cat, in the passage of a comet, in the arrangement of tarot cards and tea leaves and coffee grounds, anything that might hint at the outcome of tomorrow's game.

Some say he is superstitious, but strictly speaking he doesn't believe in luck; he believes in a sure thing and, up until a few months ago, he always had an uncanny ability for making correct predictions. Lately, however, his instincts have failed him. He can no longer see the future as he once could. Fate shrouds the world in mystery and refuses to give up her secrets. Even now a sharp tingle like static electricity shoots up his spine: an ominous premonition, but one that comes much too late.

Suddenly there is a loud knock at the door, three solid

raps with a pause between each one, a very serious-sounding knock, a knock that says he is in deep shit, the deepest in a long time, and here he is, caught without a pair of boots to wade through it. Using the tough-guy voice he has perfected from a decade of coaching belligerent prep school boys, he shouts, "Go away!" because no one ever knocks at his door except for the obvious reason: money. His ex-wife and her attorneys, his bookie, even old friends and neighbors, they all line up at his door, looking to hit him up and suck him dry, but he knows perfectly well who is out there—it can only be one person—and although his instincts tell him to flee, to scramble down the fire escape, he understands that sooner or later he must face the fire-breathing dragon, not out of choice exactly—what kind of hero yearns for his own grue-some immolation?—but because escape is no longer an op-tion. The entrance to the cave is blocked, the bridge burned to cinders.

Kaliher looks at his ghostly reflection in the window, tests out a smile, the one he uses to captivate audiences when de-livering the keynote address at benefit dinners, but his smile falters; it looks defiant, devious, impudent, maybe even a lit-tle twisted. His eyes are blood-rimmed, his teeth caked with tartar, his tongue dry from another week-long bender. The charms of success have abandoned him entirely—a terrible thing for a man who clings to his fading celebrity as an idola-ter clings to a golden monkey paw. Taking a deep breath, he cracks open the door. In the hallway he hears the sound of a dozen antique keys jangling on a rusty ring, and in a slanted shaft of light he sees a thousand silver strands of cat hair shim-mer, loop, and twirl.

"Why, good afternoon, Mrs. O'Neill!"

"Fuck you, Kaliher. You got somethin' to smile about these days?"

Mrs. O'Neill, the owner and manager of the Zanzibar Towers & Gardens, leans heavily against the doorway, a long pillar of cigarette ash wobbling between her lizard lips. She is a woman with a remarkable gift for cutting through the bullshit, and her demeanor suggests not only anger but sobriety. Not a good sign. She's wearing a green bathrobe and slippers, her Friday night "uniform," and her fingers plough through hair so wild and wiry and bleached of color that her scalp looks like a little plot of curled cornhusks roasting under a ferocious summer sun.

"Something I can do for you?" Kaliher asks.

"Yeah, asshole, pay up. Right now. Or hit the road. Bunch of goddamn infants living here. Helpless parasites, every last one of yous. This ain't no charity ward. And it ain't no brothel neither."

"I beg your pardon . . ."

"Give it a rest, Kaliher. I know all about you. You and that dirty whore down the hall. I've seen her leaving your apartment. I won't have it. I run a respectable place."

She thrusts her nose past the chain, her nostrils puckering and flaring, the bulbous tip covered with meandering tributaries of broken blood vessels that disappear into craters vast and deep and dark.

"That ain't no weed I smell, is it? Cause if it is, I'll call the cops, by God I will. Make my life so much easier. One call, Kaliher, and out ya go."

"Weed, Mrs. O'Neill? Heavens, no!" He unhooks the chain and swings the door open. "Would you like to come in? Have a look around? Join me in a cocktail? Please, I insist."

He takes her by the hand, but she yanks it away and wipes it across the front of her robe. Amazing that *she* is the one to wipe *her* hand! But he isn't about to let a rude gesture get to him, no, that might disrupt his timing, and he has these innocuous little transactions timed to the nearest tenth of a second. He always thinks in terms of a stopwatch, another habit from his years as a coach. He steps aside as Mrs. O'Neill, heavy and compact as a bison, shambles into the apartment, her great, humped shoulders threatening to rip apart the doorframe.

"Okay, whadya got?"

"Um, I have Kentucky bourbon. Irish whiskey. Single malt scotch."

She sneers. "You ain't got jack shit."

"No, I swear it. How about a nice glass of Cabernet?"

She snaps her fingers. "C'mon, c'mon . . ."

He glowers at her, his tormentor, his jailer, and opens the kitchen cupboards one at a time. She isn't particular, she'll drink just about anything: cooking sherry, cough syrup, even rubbing alcohol isn't beneath her, but they both know the truth, know that his cupboards are bare and that the only thing he has to offer her is a glass of cloudy tap water. This is just a preposterous pantomime he performs each month, but even the destitute abide by certain rules of etiquette.

"Yer wife was here a few hours ago lookin' for ya. Musta knocked on your door fer a good ten minutes 'fore I come down and chased 'er off. I can't have some angry cougar makin' a spectacle of 'erself. I don't like troublemakers, Kaliher. Don't like deadbeats neither." She scratches the bristly black hairs sprouting on the back of her calves. They look like pine needles, sharp and shiny and covered in miniscule scales. "What's a pretty woman want with the likes of you anyway?"

Afraid he might break down in front of her, Kaliher hides his face behind the pantry door and whispers, "I'll win her back . . ."

With a loud snort of contempt, Mrs. O'Neill lumbers into the dark bedroom, her imposing silhouette framed against the window. She lets the bathrobe slide from her freckled back. Kaliher shudders. It's like watching a snake shed its skin. The heavy ring of keys hits the hardwood floor with a terrible clatter. The glowing ember of her cigarette hovers in the blackness like the unblinking eye of a cyclops and sinks slowly to the mattress before winking out. His sleeping arrangements are primitive. There is no frame, no box spring, no down comforter, but Mrs. O'Neill doesn't seem to mind.

Kaliher hesitates, cowed by her silence. He thinks of his children, John and Carol, six-year-old twins, and recalls how, during their last weekend visit, they sobbed in their sleeping bags arranged on either side of that same mattress and begged to be taken home to their mother: "Please, Daddy, *please*."

"Time!" Mrs. O'Neill proclaims.

"Yes," Kaliher murmurs, "I'm coming, coming . . ."

II

Mrs. O'Neill actively seeks out male renters, losers one and all, the downtrodden, ruined, addicted, and insane. She usually captures her prey at the Stone Town Café, where the city's luckless gather to drink one cup of coffee after another (refills are free) and stare out the window as if waiting for somebody who once loved them to miraculously appear and say that all is forgiven, mistakes happen, now it's time to start life over again. Most of these men secretly yearn to tell a woman, any woman, about their private miseries, their personal failures, and Mrs. O'Neill delights in playing the role of comforter and confessor. With great patience and understanding, she listens to these tales of woe, nods her head, squeezes a hand in a very reassuring way. She offers a warm smile when it is most needed. Then, moving in for the kill, she brings up the subject of her apartment building, "the property," she calls it, willed to her by her now deceased third husband.

"You come right on over, honey, and see the place for yourself. Maybe we can work out some kind of arrangement. No deposit required to rent a room."

For most of these men this news comes as a great relief, since the only thing they have with which to barter is the worthless currency of a hundred broken promises. Of course a few of them, the more reasonable ones, find her motives suspect, but in the end desperation always wins out. They don't even wait for her to scribble an address on a napkin; they simply follow her back to the building, a never-ending parade of derelicts and fools marching up the walkway—scrawny, scruffy, their faces frozen with expressions of self-pity and stunned disbelief. How many men has she lured here over the years? How many has she cajoled, threatened, and humiliated in this warren of stinking, threadbare cubicles? Some have second thoughts.

Sensing their misgivings, Mrs. O'Neill tries to sweeten the deal by offering rooms on the seventh floor. "Lucky number seven, eh, honey?"

Bernie Kaliher can hardly believe that he has joined the ranks of these losers. Only three months ago the local sports columnists—those hacks who never see eye-to-eye on anything—agreed that his team would crush each of its regular- and post-season opponents with ease and cruise undefeated to the state championship game. No one dared to think otherwise. It was predestined. God had commanded it to be so. How then to explain the slew of injuries to his offensive linemen, the diminishing skills of his star quarterback, the heartbreaking defeats in overtime? God does not abandon the pious. Surely a decisive victory tomorrow night will turn this disastrous season around, but history has shown that even God needs a little convincing, and to appease him the Jesuits have ordered the students to pray on their knees, to petition the Lord of Hosts, the Lord of Armies, to lead their beloved team to victory.

Kaliher intends to do his part, too. As head coach, he has access to the athletic department's bank account for discretionary funds and has already made a sizable withdrawal. His bookie insisted on having the cash up front this time, but Kaliher has every intention of returning the money before the Jesuits even notice the transaction. He has done it before. Sometimes he bets small amounts on professional sports—a hundred here and there, nothing of great consequence. Big bets are strictly reserved for his own team, a thousand dollars on the opening game, thousands more in the weeks to follow.

After tomorrow's triumphant win, he will beg God's pardon for violating the trust of his players—the sheer stupidity of his mistakes, the magnitude of his financial indiscretions. Even when faced with the prospect of eternal damnation, he will not deny his culpability ... with this one small caveat. God must give him an unequivocal answer to a question that has haunted him for many months: why do so many men have an almost instinctual urge to sabotage their own lives?

He can't think of these things now. Only twenty-four hours remain until the big game, the infamous Holy War, and there is still much work to be done, grand strategies to map out, small but crucial tactics to perfect. Defeat is no longer an option, victory the only possible means of escape.

III

No matter how many times he submits to this monthly ritual, he is shocked by the vulgarity of Mrs. O'Neill's bedroom talk and the rough manner in which she shoves his face into the swampy valley between her sloping breasts, down to the impressive rolls of fat that have congealed around her navel, across the rugged terrain of her thorny snatch, ever lower, *lower*, all the while rasping her sinister commands with pitiless glee: "That's right, Coach, go on, work it, *work it*. Now, suck my toes! Suck 'em like you mean it."

Taking direction like a trained seal, he sweeps his tongue over the tough meat of the sole, up and down the swollen arch, heel to toe, heel to toe. He recoils from her foot, trying hard to control his gag reflex, but Mrs. O'Neill digs her claws into the back of his neck. Finally, he opens his mouth to accept the five little piggies and uses his teeth to gently nibble on the thick stumps that look like a man's knuckles—large, hairy, simian.

"That's a good boy . . ."

The apartment smells faintly like a sewer; its rooms are drafty, poorly insulated, the walls cracked and bubbled from years of rain and snow, but these things do not prevent Mrs. O'Neill from sweating through the sheets. Using the advantage of her weight, she pins him to the mattress, parts her legs and slowly envelopes him in her clammy flesh.

Thirty minutes later, the tentacled creature squirts her ink over his abdomen, and the unspeakable ordeal comes to an end. She releases him from her grim embrace, fires up another cigarette, last one in the pack, and says, "Okay, Kaliher, you can stay one more month. But you're a real awful lay, do ya know that? Truly despicable. Now I understand why yer old lady left ya." She coughs, forces up a gob of green phlegm, then swallows it. "A little friendly advice. Either come up with some cash or improve yer skills in the sack."

With that she stands up, pulls the bathrobe around her thick torso, and plunges into a pool of black shadow, Grendel's mother, glutted on warrior blood, diving into the heaving depths of her sinister fen somewhere in the misty moorlands. Kaliher, marveling at the terrible strength of this tusked and taloned tarn-hag, wonders if she ever had children of her own, stillborn things sent straight to Limbo.

Before limping out the door, Mrs. O'Neill turns and says, "Best of luck tomorrow night, Coach!"

"Oh, you horrible, horrible . . ." Kaliher whispers.

In the darkness, without daring to light the candles, he sits cross-legged at the end of the mattress and runs his hands over his head. For a long time he does nothing at all, just stares into space and listens to the lunatic laughter of the other residents, the chanting, singing, crying that comes night and day through the dusty vents. In this madhouse, there is never a moment's peace.

Though he is aching and drained of energy, he somehow finds the strength to get to his feet and staggers to the bathroom. Thankfully, there is no mirror in here, no way for him to inspect the dark circles under his eyes, the new lines that have formed on his forehead and at the corners of his mouth. He hunches over the sink. Using the crusty remnants of an old tube of toothpaste he brushes his teeth, but no matter how hard he scours, gurgles, and spits, he cannot get rid of the putrid taste of toenails, sour and bitter like old lemon rinds, that clings to the roof of his mouth and the back of his throat. When he can no longer tolerate the dirtiness on him, in him, and around him, he stands in the shower under an icy spray of water. There is no soap, no exfoliating scrub, no shaving gel, none of the fragrant lotions he once enjoyed as a happily married man. In fact, very little remains of his old life except the mattress on the floor where Mrs. O'Neill occasionally positions herself and groans with unbridled pleasure.

Reluctantly he returns to the bedroom, but when he tears off the soiled sheet he notices a twenty-dollar bill wedged between the mattress and the wall. How he overlooked it he does not know. With a little whimper of gratitude, he holds it up to the light, smells it, rubs it between his fingertips, and after several minutes of meditation decides that this must be an act of divine providence, irrefutable proof that God is watching over him. Quickly, before some new disaster befalls him, he gets dressed and hurries out into the cold October night. A celebration is in order. It's happy hour at the local brewery. One-dollar pints of lager and stout.

Kaliher shivers and pulls the collar of his jacket tight around his throat. Already the weather is beginning to turn. Forecasters are predicting a hard winter. As he hurries along the sidewalk, he moves aside to let a young man pass, another hapless bohemian, judging from his tattered jeans and T-shirt with a large, grinning skull. Maybe he's a musician or a fledgling poet choking on a bolus of foolish fantasies, the old childish dreams of fame and fortune. But there is something different about this kid, something vaguely familiar. Though he can be no more than eighteen or nineteen years old, he looks world-weary and soul-sick. His left eye is bruised, his lip swollen. He has seen hard times, harder than most perhaps, and in his wake he leaves a long, messy trail of despair.

The kid glances up at Kaliher. There is a flash of recognition between them. Could he be a student from the Jesuit school? The boy looks away, picks up the pace, and disappears inside the building. Kaliher considers warning him away from this necropolis of dead dreams. But what's the use? People never change. Besides, like everyone condemned to stay at the Zanzibar Towers & Gardens, this kid probably has it coming to him.

The city echoes with the wail of sirens. A police cruiser races by, its lights flashing. Gripped by a vivid premonition, Kaliher stands rooted to the street corner, mesmerized by the baffling array of kaleidoscopic color dribbling over the windows of the apartment building. It's almost like someone has knocked over a thousand cans of paint from the rooftop, thick globules that hurtle into space and then vanish in the darkness only to reemerge an instant later in striking new patterns. A sign! While he watches this mystifying cascade, tastes its powerful essence, breathes its eerie energy, Coach Bernie Kaliher feels absolutely certain that his luck is about to change and breathes a long, heavy sigh of relief.

The Deer Park

❦

I

An abrupt rush of cold air whistles through the front window of the cab, wrenching Edward de Vere from his gloomy ruminations. The driver, wreathed in silver smoke, clamps the smoldering butt of a cigarette between his tragic stumps of teeth and makes another small adjustment to the rearview mirror.

"You do not mind?"

De Vere shakes his head. No, the smoke doesn't bother him, not terribly. After the violent confrontation that morning with his thieving son and the subsequent argument with his wife about the family's financial troubles, de Vere discovers that he has become almost completely numb to pain, to pleasure, to the unvarying drone of his own thoughts.

From the pocket of his camel hair coat, he retrieves the flask inscribed with his initials (a gift from an utterly forgettable mistress), and with a wistful smile, takes a healthy swig of absinthe. De Vere has come to rely on the stuff. The effects are strictly spiritual of course, not particularly good for his ulcer or for his reasoning faculties, enemies of the mystical experience, but somehow it makes these evenings a little more interesting, less predictable. The liquor sears his esophagus, ignites the walls of his gut, spreads like a vast oil plume across the surface of his consciousness, illuminating the murkiest depths of his soul with tongues of Pentecostal fire. He relishes the sensation.

"Where are you going tonight, sir?" asks the driver.

"Oh, nowhere in particular."

Because he doesn't want to sound like just another slurring drunk in the back of a cab during the midnight hours, de Vere lifts his chin, purses his lips, and attempts to enunciate each syllable, each hard consonant and nasally vowel, but he stumbles over that last word—*par-tic-u-lar*—and realizes, with some chagrin, that he can no longer disguise his old accent, can't soften the working-class cadences that for so many years marked him as a poseur. Lost is the patrician affectation he has fine-tuned since his days as a student at the Jesuit school. The ruse is finally up: his words lack authority; they carry no more weight than if spoken by any predaceous degenerate born and raised in this blighted section of town.

Deciding it best to keep his mouth shut, he uses simple hand gestures to direct the driver deeper into the city's most destitute and ungovernable quarters, an anxious journey without compass or charts. De Vere probes every garbage-strewn corner, every shuttered window, every dangerous alley. Things are desolate now, but it's only a matter of time before the crazies, decked out in wild costumes, emerge from their shanties and squalid apartment blocks to celebrate under the power lines and behind the chain-link fences crowned with barbed wire. It's Halloween, a night sacred to the unhinged mind, but de Vere now sees a deeper pattern and believes it doesn't matter what day or hour it happens to be. They are everywhere, these lunatics, a never-ending parade of human ruin, a plague cast down from heaven in a way that hints at God's indifference to the world.

"It is unusually quiet this evening," says the driver, his eyes nervously scanning the streets.

De Vere tries to suppress a knowing smile. Soon this little preserve will be positively teeming with game, and the idea—of a hunter and his quarry—makes him wonder if in a former life he had been a gentleman of quality who frequented the private hunting grounds of the king, invited by His Majesty to a country château to spend holidays shooting impressive white-tailed stags and, at day's end, violating young wenches behind a stand of blue pines.

De Vere's wife is convinced that he is an old soul, that he has undergone innumerable incarnations as insect, beast, vassal, and lord. "You're afflicted with the curse of metempsychosis," she explained to him one night.

He sighs and fingers through the dwindling cash in his money clip. If only she could gaze into her crystal ball and divine a simple solution to their financial difficulties—maybe he would be in Paris, Copenhagen, Amsterdam instead of marooned in the city of his birth, riding in the back of a yellow cab that rumbles like a tank in the final cataclysmic scene of some generic wartime melodrama, the rusted muffler scraping along the ridges and fissures in the road, the brakes screeching and grinding at every turn, the radio hissing and crackling and occasionally exploding with unintelligible outbursts from an angry dispatcher. Suddenly de Vere feels not like an aristocrat waited on by a liveried footman but a magician's assistant stuffed into a tiny black box, waiting to be impaled by sharp objects.

From the rearview mirror dark eyes study him. They blink in rapid succession as if trying to untangle his snarled storyline, the profusion of lives he has lived.

"Family troubles?"

De Vere lowers his flask. "Why do you ask?"

"I have been driving this cab for many years now, yes, many years. Women, children, they take their toll on a man. I have come to recognize the symptoms."

"Perhaps you can describe these . . . symptoms."

The driver chuckles and expertly flicks his cigarette out the window. "Well, for one, you have a certain look of resignation. Also, a look of distrust in your eyes. But of course a man can never trust the people he loves. No, not entirely."

De Vere crosses his arms, shifts uneasily in the backseat. "I don't trust anyone. My son is a thief, my best friend is a gullible fool, and I'm starting to think my wife is a borderline sociopath trying to poison me. She's developed a fascination for alternative medicine. Witchcraft." He shrugs his shoulders. "It's a cliché, I know, but only my dog remains loyal to me."

He feels some shame for divulging the details of his life to a complete stranger, but like a lot of people he knows, too many really, de Vere has become more and more involved in his own problems; he cultivates them, multiplies them, makes them deeper and richer than if he left them alone to spin round and round his brain.

The driver nods. "Why do we trouble ourselves over such things, eh? Wives, sons, they are of little consequence. Life is merely something to endure. Like a disease. Repose will come soon enough."

De Vere smirks. "Repose? Yes. Or absolution. I would settle for that."

"You are a man with deep religious convictions?"

De Vere considers this for a moment, notices the small statue of Saint Fiacre on the dashboard. "I thought about becoming an atheist, but then I realized atheism requires more devotion."

The driver laughs, a low gritty sound like the crunch and grind of asphalt beneath the tires. "Indeed," he says, "an atheist must be diligent. There is always the temptation to believe in a fearsome god or in a tempting devil. And any nightmarish circumstance can quickly cure a man of his apostasy."

De Vere isn't interested in advice, if that is what this meddlesome man is offering. No one can convince him that what he is doing is wrong, certainly not the cab driver, who will soon discover the truth for himself; not the abstinence-stricken priests, who listen to de Vere's expurgated confessions on Saturday afternoons and wait for the appropriate moment to beg him for more filthy lucre; not his wife, who suspects him of every kind of misdeed and then attempts to exorcize the demons of infidelity by encouraging him to ingest a hundred different homeopathic potions that are as evil-smelling as they are toxic; not even his perpetually dour best friend, to whom he confides every wretched detail late at night in the disquieting calm of his study.

There are too many moral crusaders in the world, each with an equally improbable scheme to lead a man to salvation, a million cures for a million vices—through prayer, repentance, self-flagellation—but when he looks through the portal that separates reality from the hereafter, de Vere sees not the treasures of heaven but the fiery pools of hell. Having already dipped his toes in the scalding waters, he wonders if he can finally muster the courage to submerge himself fully in what the Jesuits warn is "total depravity." Of course, most people have no way of knowing just how sublime the river of sin can be, how thrilling to be swept away and carried off to a place you never intended to go. Or maybe they do. The world, as de Vere knows from experience, is full of irredeemable hypocrites.

II

Six months ago, when he first embarked on these forbidden excursions, de Vere preferred to use his own car, but then late one evening, while idling at a red light, a group of teenage boys, oozing with adolescent virulence, materialized from the shadows. They made lewd gestures, rapped on his door, spat on his windshield. Phlegm hung in heavy green beads from the tinted glass. An intolerable situation. He wasn't about to let this gang of little brown bastards fuck with his lady. No, that would never do. Aside from an occasional trip to the slums, de Vere's ostentatious European touring car may be the only thing that offers him some satisfaction in this world. He read somewhere that cars are modeled on the female form, and there *is*, he finds, something rather arousing about its sleek and elegant design, the exaggerated curves of the rear end, the heady scent of leather, the breathless moans of the V6 engine. With mounting agitation, he put his hand on the door handle, fully prepared to kick some ass, but from the corner of his eye he caught the flash of a knife blade. De Vere hit the gas hard and thundered away. Gloating with triumph, he opened the sunroof and raised his middle finger. From this incident he learned two invaluable lessons: victory always belongs to the man with the most torque and horsepower, and more important, it's best to take a taxi to and from the hunting grounds.

Of course these monthly outings wouldn't be necessary if he hadn't mismanaged the melancholy business of his marriage. He has grown indifferent toward his wife. Over the years she has become irreparably tarnished, another neglected *objet d'art* in his immense and uncatalogued collection of conquests. Sex with her is boring, pedestrian, another tedious obligation like walking the dog or attending Mass on Sunday morning. He thought about ending things once and for all, getting his lawyers involved, but a messy divorce right now would only hasten his destruction. He is already on the brink of financial collapse. Until the economy picks up, he must bide his time, explore other avenues.

To his surprise he finds that company parties and gala dinners aren't exactly conducive to casual encounters with members of the opposite sex, especially when the tiny breasted ladies, with their taut puritanical faces and severe prudish frowns, waste so much time droning on and on about disgustingly conventional subjects: their learning disabled children, their lazy and inadequate husbands, their terminally ill parents, their insipid duties as accountants and business analysts. He manages to seduce a college intern or two, but even they insist on old-fashioned gentleness and solicitude, and he quickly learns that a comfortable lifestyle doesn't necessarily entitle a man to possess a secret harem of pretty girls (or even a few plain ones for that matter). Though he wants no entanglements, he has an acute understanding of the rules of the game and, for a little while at least, he abides by them, purchases a few extravagant gifts, vials of perfume, diamond tennis bracelets, spa treatments, reservations for wine and cheese tastings, and in exchange for these creature comforts, he expects his mistresses to submit to his modest desires and then to vanish once he tires of their shrill voices.

But things never work out this way, certainly not in suburbia, where all eroticism is crushed to a fine powder and scattered in the wind like ashes from a funeral pyre, the burnt offerings of impetuous youth, and any lingering impetuosity in a man de Vere's age is regarded as perversion, plain and simple. Unusual delights, if they are to be found at all, must come from these midnight hunts through the streets of a post-industrial wasteland. This haunt of sweet sin does not discriminate: here every man is welcome, and sex remains a constant fount of miracles. Although he is somewhat familiar with the terrain and can still recall the forsaken avenues and narrow brick lanes from his days at the Jesuit high school, he is keenly aware of the dangers all around.

III

After circling a particularly dismal block for the third time—three, that charming number—de Vere glimpses a pack of stray dogs trotting through the tempered light, wretched curs bred in brutal haste in slimy culverts and under the skeleton tracks of a rotting train trestle. In their tireless quest for food, they topple a trashcan outside an apartment building, the vaguely familiar Zanzibar Towers & Gardens, and fight over a hunk of putrid meat, a sheet of greasy wax paper smeared with red juices, a container of cookies, a headless doll. Snarling their disapproval, the brindled mongrels watch the cab roll by. De Vere feels a close connection to these animals, admires the purity of their instincts. Nature has conferred upon them some special power for reading the minds of men. He wonders if they can sniff out the stench of desperation that drips from his pores and clings to his shirt, his cashmere sweater, his indispensable silk boxers.

"Mongrels . . ." the driver mutters, swerving to avoid the beer cans that clatter into the street.

Something catches de Vere's eye. With a tantalizing mixture of eagerness and dread, he sits up, adjusts his collar and sleeves, glides a practiced finger across his professionally whitened teeth. "Stop the cab," he orders.

"But, sir, there are troublemakers about."

"I said stop the cab!"

"Very well."

De Vere rolls down the window, clears his throat, and boldly addresses the woman who has just emerged from the apartment building. "Excuse me, miss!"

Through the partition, the driver whispers, "Sir, she is chattel, a loathsome thing. Vile."

"Miss, a moment of your time."

"I beg of you, sir, I cannot possibly . . ."

With an almost regal bearing, the woman struts across the street in a pair of incredible red boots. A pickup swerves to avoid her. In the bed of the truck several young men shout with malice. "*Puta! Mujerzuela! Almeja!*" Spellbound, de Vere watches her and wonders what has gone wrong in her life, why she doesn't work in an office building like the rest of the women he knows; it takes next to nothing to sit in a cubicle and pretend to be busy for most of the day. In the business world, one's appearance means everything, and she can't very well show up to an important meeting dressed in a purple miniskirt, her cheeks smeared with rouge, her eyes ringed with mascara like warm, wet ash.

"Hey, sweet thing," she says, leaning against the cab. "You lookin' for some company?"

"As a matter of fact . . ." Feeling almost amorous, he offers the woman his flask.

"Oh, that's some good shit, baby," she rasps after taking a sip.

"Remarkable," says de Vere, stroking the woman's hand. "A woman who appreciates the green-eyed monster. I think I'm in love."

She suppresses a belch. "Green-eyed, one-eyed, it's all the same to me."

"Marvelous! What's your name, darling?"

"Name's Tamar, baby."

"How unusual. You're not busy this evening, are you, Tamar?"

"Just finished working a big soiree. Right up there." She points to a window crowded with silhouettes at the Zanzibar Towers & Gardens. "But I'm free now. Well, maybe not *free*."

De Vere opens the door and moves over so the woman can slide in beside him.

The driver hisses. "Sir, I will not be a party to this kind of thing."

De Vere clicks his tongue. By now his response has become automatic, a maddeningly predictable exchange between master and servant. He passes the customary amount of money through the partition and watches the driver count the bills one at a time. It always surprises him how readily these men of conscience transform themselves into purveyors of pleasure, how willing they are to implicate themselves in his crimes and to share in his guilt.

"Very well then," says the driver. "But one day, sir, one day soon, when she can no longer serve her purpose, this woman will be discovered in an alley with her throat slashed. No questions will be asked. No investigation will be conducted. Among these people, life is a brief visitor. It's just as well. More time on this earth would bring little in the way of happiness to such a creature."

As the cab rolls away from the curb, de Vere becomes aware of the driver watching him in the rearview mirror. He has gotten used to this, too. They always watch, these drivers; they are depraved, the whole damned world is depraved, and so he decides to give the man a show, the standard pornography. He unzips his pants, bunches the woman's black hair in his fists and forces her into a syncopated rhythm. She stinks to high heaven, reeks of chemicals, lighter fluid, formaldehyde, an odor he can't quite place. She probably hasn't bathed in days. This in itself doesn't bother him. In fact, there is something erotic about her filthiness. It makes his knees tremble. Besides, he always comes prepared to deal with unpleasant details. From his coat pocket he produces a bottle of eau de toilette and spritzes the back of her neck.

She lifts her head. "The fuck you doin'?"

"Shut up and keep going."

"Why you gotta talk that way?"

"Finish the goddamn job."

The woman resumes bobbing up and down in de Vere's lap, her movements so wild, so relentless, so crazed, that he is afraid she might tear into him with her chipped teeth. He groans, rocks his hips back and forth. Then he feels the taxi shudder violently and almost stall.

He opens his eyes, knocks on the partition. "What the hell is it now? Why are you slowing down?"

"I think they're following us," the driver tells him. "Yes, there is no doubt about it. They are definitely following us."

"What are you talking about?"

"You see, this is what they do. Like hunters they lurk in the shadows and then trounce on their prey. Ruthless."

"Who?"

"The police."

De Vere turns his head, sees a cruiser riding the back bumper. "Dammit, your taillight is out."

"Nonsense."

"I noticed it when I climbed inside this fucking tin can."

The driver scowls. "They obviously spotted you luring that slut into my cab. I cannot afford to go to jail again. Please, ask her to stop."

But de Vere can't do that, not now, not even as the cruiser pursues them through the absurd serpentine streets, not even when the siren starts its terrible piercing wail, and the blue-and-white lights blind him. He digs his nails into the seat and lets out a rapturous cry: "Oh, God! Maybe this is my road to Damascus!"

The driver hits the breaks and puts the cab in park. "Drunken fool, keep your mouth shut. Or I promise . . . things will not go well for you."

An officer approaches the cab, hitches his belt, but instead of interrogating the driver, he opens the back door, grabs the woman by the wrist and drags her over to the sidewalk. She wipes her chin with the back of her hand and pulls the hem of her skirt down so her panties don't show.

"Still turning tricks, eh, Tamar? Funny. Thought we told you we didn't want to see you around here anymore. Didn't we tell you that? You gonna answer me? I know you ain't deaf, Tamar. Stupid yes, deaf no."

A German shepherd, teeth bared, bounds toward the cab, a long rope of saliva swinging in a wide arc from its snapping jaws. Another patrol car arrives. Radio scanners screech and croak and erupt with high, thin whistles. The officer turns his flashlight on de Vere, who is so overcome with dread that he can only sit there like a bewildered toddler, pants around his ankles, a look of drooling incomprehension on his face.

"Whatcha doing in this neighborhood, pal? You like coming to this part of town? You a regular?" Impatient with de Vere's infantile sputtering, the officer yanks him from the cab and pushes him against the trunk. "Christ almighty, pull up your pants, you animal! Now, put your hands behind your back." He slaps on the cuffs, reaches into de Vere's camel hair coat, confiscates his flask, his wallet, the bottle of perfume.

"Wait a minute," says de Vere, "this isn't the road to Damascus . . ."

"Damascus? No, buddy, we're taking you downtown."

"You're making a grave mistake. I know people, important people. They'll tell you. I'm a reputable businessman, a loving husband and father."

De Vere's voice is shrill, manic. He struggles, thrashes his legs, but the officer slings an arm around his neck and squeezes tight until de Vere begins to gasp for air.

"Just cooperate, okay, bud? You don't want an assault charge tacked on, do ya?"

As chapel bells begin to chime the witching hour, a raucous crowd spills from the gaping double doors of the Zanzibar Towers & Gardens. Apparently the cab has been going in circles, and now de Vere must endure the laughter of priests and pregnant nuns and a bloated Lazarus wrapped in rags. They drink and smoke and dance, some of them grinding violently against each other, feigning copulation. On the sidewalk a man whirls round and round, his dreadlocks rising above his head like the tentacles of some fabled sea creature. Last to emerge from the building is a tall figure in the bloodred robes of a grand inquisitor, a sagacious and unreasonably cruel arbiter of the laws of God and man. With a subtle flick of his wrist he silences the discordant howls and jeers of his grotesque entourage.

De Vere lurches heavily, falls to his knees, and humbly pleads his case before his fellow darkness worshippers. "Listen to me. Would you please *listen*? Tomorrow morning I'll go straight to the chapel. I'll light a candle before a statue of the Virgin. I'll make a vow before the Lord to live a life of celibacy . . ."

His head starts to spin. The absinthe percolates in the pit of his stomach and suddenly surges up his throat, a hot green sludge that splatters the officer's polished black shoes and the cuffs of his pants.

"Mother*fucker*!"

The other cops laugh. "Hey, Caddigan, have fun cleaning that shit."

"Fuck you. I ain't touching it."

De Vere gasps and sputters, "I'm sorry, so sorry . . ."

Then he feels a sharp crack against his spine, a quick spasm of pain that shoots down to the tips of his toes, and things go dark for a little while.

IV

Mumbling piteous oaths, fighting against the cuffs that dig into his wrists, de Vere drifts in and out of consciousness, and for one incredible moment, he feels himself turn to vapor and slip through a small crack at the top of the back window. With a covey of fractious grackles, he flies high above the church spires and spins around the Gothic tower of the Jesuit school. Out over the lake a storm rages, and the gathering clouds drape him in the bruised colors of high autumn—cadmium reds and yellows. A strong gust of wind transports him over the great steel bridge that spans the crooked river and hurtles him along the city streets. He slides down a sparkling glass atrium and lands in a bustling emporium of fashionable restaurants and nightclubs where stunted boys, wearing sandwich boards, blunder among a group of portly men in pinstriped suits and emaciated women in skimpy cocktail dresses.

De Vere's eyes flutter open. He is pulled from the back of the police cruiser, lifted to his feet, and dragged into headquarters. At the front desk he is made to stand at attention. "Another dirty married man," someone quips. Boiling white light seeps behind his eye sockets and scalds his brain. He waits there for hours, it seems, but eventually, mercifully, he is booked for indecent exposure, public intoxication, solicitation of prostitution, a long recitation of trumped-up charges. He hears the words, but they do not make any sense to him, and at this point he doesn't really care what they mean. He is photographed, fingerprinted, his body searched for contraband. Manacled and moaning like an idiot that lurches from some horror movie dungeon, he is led through a series of endless corridors that echo with tortured screams, like someone being stabbed over and over with a penknife.

An alarm sounds. A clanking steel door rolls open, and he is shoved into a large holding cell swarming with flies. He collapses beside a mysterious yellow stream that trickles toward a drain. After a few minutes he becomes dimly aware that he is not alone. Other men, dozens of them, each indistinguishable from the other, materialize like shades from the underworld. All suffer the afflictions and burdens of anonymity, their faces transformed into primitive masks, wooden idols with wooden scowls.

The men close in, their eyes unwavering. Unlike the police they do not ask him to cooperate. They taunt him, playfully at first as children sometimes do with a puppy or a kitten to see how it will react, and once they determine he is harmless, they begin to slap him in earnest, jab him in the kidneys, stomp on his fingers, yank him by the hair. He doesn't struggle for long. They force him to his knees, tell him to open wide, not to bite.

"Gonna get me some slop on my knob."

"Mmmm, yeah, get my salad tossed, that's what I'm talkin' 'bout."

"You like that, don't you, bitch?"

"Do a good job now, or they gonna carry your ass out in a body bag."

With this warning, they line up ten deep, some massaging themselves in preparation, spirits of the dead eager to douse him in ectoplasm. He lifts his head and recognizes the small, feral eyes of the man standing at the front of the line.

"Good evening, my friend," says the cabdriver. "Life, as you know, consists of little more than the ebb and flow of excessive pleasure and pain, wave upon wave of joy and sorrow. Unfortunately, you have found yourself in a deep trough. But do not fear. It will not always be so for you. Fate is ever-changing. Oblivion alone is imperishable."

Then the driver unbuckles his belt and, with a smile that reveals those unsightly gray stumps, whispers, "And now, if you please, there are many men waiting . . ."

In the Secret Parts of Fortune

༄

I

Halloween, season of sorcerers and black magic, and once again Elsie has allowed Claude to visit her bed, but first she commands him to chase the dog from the house, mainly because she can't stomach the animal's crude pantomime of their monthly romps. It stares at them while they make love, panting to the irregular rhythm of the bedsprings, swabbing its genitalia with a dripping, lolling tongue of magnificent reach and precision, growling and gnashing its teeth whenever Claude clutches the sides of the mattress and unleashes his ridiculous yowls of ecstasy into the luxurious eiderdown pillows. Sensing a conspiracy, Elsie springs catlike from the bed to lock the door and confides her fear that the Great Dane is not merely playing the part of a voyeur; its real intention is to carefully observe everything that goes on in the house while its master is away on business and then to reenact it all for him upon his return.

"They have a mysterious way of communicating with one another," Elsie whispers, her voice colored by panic. "I think they may be . . . *telepathic*." Soft indigo notes whistle from her ruby-red lips, the captivating aria of a woman, still gorgeous at forty, afraid of being found out. There is a small gap in her teeth that makes her look like the Wife of Bath—saucy, licentious, calculating.

"Don't be ridiculous," Claude says.

"I swear it. There is an unholy covenant between them. They each know what the other is thinking."

"Rubbish."

"That damned animal provides Edward with precise and accurate information. Okay, I'm not sure how it works, but it's truly disturbing. Maybe Gonzago taps out Morse code with his claws."

As he listens to these outrageous hypotheses, Claude wonders, not without some exasperation, how the perversions of a dirty old dog and the delusions of a half-mad woman, whose bookshelves are crammed with paperbacks on astrology, ESP, and self-hypnosis, can continually thwart the sad little ritual of a middle-aged man suffering the pangs of disprized love, but at this stage of his life Claude has come to accept the fact that when enormous sums of money are at stake, paranoia becomes an almost palpable thing, a shivering sentinel standing guard outside the door, waiting night and day for signs of a possible invasion.

As if to confirm this point, Gonzago begins to bark under the bedroom window.

Elsie gasps. "Do you hear that? He's *laughing* at us."

Despite Claude's protestations, Elsie sits up in bed and pulls the sheet over the warm treasure trove between her legs that Claude has lovingly christened Graymalkin. A positively criminal act, concealing these things from him. Elsie's purpose on this earth is to remain forever naked. Nudity suits her, she was born for it. Though the scar from the cesarean has faded, it stands as a stark reminder that she is the mother of a teen-aged son, heir apparent to an enviable fortune, scion of a distinguished family.

With a deep sigh, Claude tramps across the room, bare-assed, dong dangling, and slams the window shut. He stands there a moment, watching Gonzago sniff around the flower-beds and scratch at the last of the wilting columbines and pansies that struggle to survive the first frost. Though he has his doubts about what Gonzago does and does not know, Claude is certain of one thing: the dog's telepathic powers do not work on Elsie; if they did, the dumb, slobbering beast would have the good sense to dash into the woods behind the house, never to return. Maybe like Claude (indeed, like many males in general), Gonzago cannot understand the meaning of the heavy, crepuscular clouds rising from the long-dormant volcano that is a woman's soul, and certainly Elsie's soul is more inscrutable than most; in fact, it's the only modest thing about her, veiled from top to bottom like an ashen-faced novitiate—solemn, austere, impenetrable.

"I have an idea," she says as though in a trance, her voice small and distant. "We'll poison it. No one ever performs an autopsy on a dog."

She assumes the pose of a prioress deep in meditation, hands resting on her knees, palms facing up so the energy of the cosmos can filter through her fingertips and seep into the claustrophobic confines of her brain where her thoughts pulse and flicker in an interminable Dark Age. Claude knows her capacities, her limitations. Love has not deluded him that much.

"Why don't you take Gonzago to the vet?" he suggests, reaching for the pack of cigarettes on the nightstand, grateful as ever for her insatiable oral fixation. "Have him put to sleep. Easy. Done and over with."

"No, the dog must be buried in the backyard."

"Just ask the vet for the remains after the job is done."

A vein pulses on her forehead. "You don't know anything about animals, do you? The vet won't hand over the carcass. There's a city ordinance. It's illegal for taxpayers to bury pets on their property."

"Cremation then. Give Edward a decorative urn when he gets back from his trip. He can keep his beloved Gonzago in the study. On the mantel. Below the portrait of your son."

"Cremation? Never. Edward would consider it a sacrilege. He's attended elaborate funeral services for animals. Secret rites. Pet cemeteries, fancy caskets hand-carved by Cistercians, enormous marble headstones, string quartets playing a dirge, even a priest to consecrate the grave. Edward would want something solemn and formal for his best friend."

Claude bristles at the phrase. "Best friend . . . Well, I hardly think a priest would consent to that sort of thing."

"You're wrong. Edward knows important people. He has a lot of pull in the Church. He helped to finance a new chapel at the Jesuit school."

Now Elsie is being deliberately cruel.

"Yes, our alma mater . . ." Claude murmurs.

"I think we both know what needs to be done."

In her voice, he detects something sinister, vindictive, an unspoken command to fulfill her darkest desires. She lowers the sheet, reveals her splendors. Like an enchantress before a bubbling cauldron high in a castle tower, she saunters across the room and sits at her vanity, where she consults her dog-eared books of black magic. Using a red pen, she scratches a cryptic formula on a notepad—($(CH_3)_3SiCN$)—and then, murmuring some mumbo jumbo over an amber vial, she mixes several packets of powder together with a small silver spoon. That she keeps poison on her nightstand doesn't surprise him much, and he dares not ask how she obtains the stuff—beautiful women have their ways, he is content to leave it at that—but he is a little concerned for his own safety. What if, prior to a night of passion, she accidentally mistakes the poison for perfume? Should his rapacious lips taste the deadly distilment dabbed behind her ears, between her breasts, and around Graymalkin's soft coat, he will be sent on a one-way trip to the undiscovered country.

Her work complete, she turns to Claude and asks, "What is the very worst thing you can do to a man?"

Unable to suppress an impudent smile, he reaches down and tries to part her knees.

She pushes him away. "Fool. Kill his dog."

"I'm not so sure about this, Elsie . . ." He takes a step back, uncomfortable with the way she dares to thumb her nose at death and danger.

"Darling, just think of it." She leans forward to kiss his chest, darts her tongue over his ever-expanding stomach and around his hairy navel. "With Gonzago dead and cold in the ground we'll finally know tranquility, spiritual release. *La petite mort.*"

Eager to pour forth an abundance of his love and adoration, he gently lifts her chin, glides his thumb over her moistened lips and then steps closer until he is fully enveloped in the luxurious warmth of her mouth.

He shudders. "Oh, you beautiful woman . . ."

She is incredibly skillful, knows exactly what he likes.

She slurps, gags, makes funny quacking sounds, a lusty soundtrack that has him rocking on the balls of his feet and doing a dance to Eros. The finish comes quickly. He pumps, grinds, and groans, but just as his eyelids start to flutter, he happens to glance out the window and sees the dog imitating him, prancing around on its hind legs like some bizarre animal act at a roadside carnival. Perhaps sensing another opportunity to make mischief, Gonzago begins to howl with maniacal laughter, a single extended note that starts as a banshee's moan and ends as a deafening siren that oscillates with horrific madhouse harmonics.

Elsie tenses, bites down hard, her jaws snapping shut like a spring-loaded mousetrap.

Squealing like misfortunate Abelard de-cocked for his grievous sins, Claude writhes on the floor, and through his tears, he resolves to take a swift and murderous course of action.

II

Wearing only his friend's terrycloth robe, he steps out into the bitter October night and pads across the vast grounds in his bare feet. Trying hard not to make a sound, cringing every time the wind shakes the tall grasses, he slides behind one of the giant ghoul-faced topiaries that ring the property like the gargoyles on the cornices of a great cathedral. In the grotto behind the tall hedges, he spies Gonzago circling a statue of Francis of Assisi. Along with sorcery, Elsie is also a confirmed believer in superstitions of a more conventional nature, and she often lights candles here, hoping the revered saint will intercede on her behalf.

Claude creeps ever closer but now worries that he doesn't

have the *cajones* to carry out the job. To assassinate the dog when its back is turned seems a cruel and cowardly thing to do, but it is the watchful stare of Saint Francis that makes the deed especially wicked. The saint's serene eyes belie his outrage. He loves all animals and looks unkindly upon anyone who may wish them ill: "Those who exclude any of God's creatures from the shelter of compassion and pity will deal likewise with their fellow man."

Claude would never harm an animal, not intentionally at least, not unless he had an excellent reason for doing so. In silent prayer, he tells this to the cowled friar. He tells him other things as well: as a boy he owned a one-eyed cat named Hecuba (his mother was a professor of mythology), and when the cat died (tractor-trailer, rush hour) he barricaded himself in the basement of their Victorian house and wept for hours among the stacks of moldering textbooks and discarded term papers. Maybe a good father-son talk would have straightened him out, given him some perspective on this minor tragedy, but Dad was no longer in the picture, and Mother was so unnerved by his inconsolable blubbering that she insisted he receive professional help. With her arms firmly crossed and foot drumming against the cold white hospital tiles, she seemed prepared to bully the therapist into diagnosing him with a whole slew of disorders.

"Fifteen-year-old boys shouldn't cry when the cat dies. What's Hecuba to him? He's not homosexual, is he?"

To Claude's ears, the question sounded like a rhetorical one.

The therapist, tugging nervously at the tip of his Vandyke beard and wanting to be rid of this woman and her overgrown child as quickly as possible, said, "Perhaps he suffers from emotional dysregulation . . . as the result of low self-esteem?" Surely the standard diagnosis for boys of that tender age, but Mother wasn't satisfied. She wanted to hear the word "abnormal" and spent the better part of Claude's emasculated pubescence shopping around for a doctor who wasn't too proud to use it.

Now, as he massages the angry teeth marks beginning to show on the shriveled shaft of his penis, he starts to think that maybe his mother was right and wonders, not for the first time, what Elsie can possibly see in him, a pathetic pencil pusher in her husband's employ, who for fifty weeks out of the year toils away in a small windowless office near the airport, writing operating manuals for scales manufactured in Europe and distributed around the world, a mindless job that has turned him into a stammering, slovenly misfit with coffee stains on his shirtsleeves and a dusting of dandruff on his shoulders. He seldom socializes with people outside the office and has become so utterly incapable of meeting single ladies that he has turned to his best friend's wife for consolation.

As if to remind him of his total incompetence, Elsie now calls his name from the bedroom window. "Claude! Claude, is everything alright?"

"Yes, yes, everything is fine."

"Well, please hurry. We have to wake up early."

A terse reminder that tomorrow is a day for country matters, a day for white magic rather than black. Elsie wants to leave at daybreak and drive along the lonely roads that wind through forgotten mountain villages so she can ransack the novelty shops for antique volumes of forbidden lore and visit those squalid frame houses hidden deep in the woods where, for an exorbitant fee, she can purchase glass jars of tannis root, cat's claw extract, fennel fruit. The weird sisters who toil in the sinister basement labs claim their medicines can reverse the aging process and that they themselves are much older than they appear. He once asked Elsie why she bothers with such obvious chicanery. "Because," she snapped, "men don't look at me the way they used to." His heart started to pound with jealousy. "Men in general or just your husband?" he wanted to ask but lacked the courage to speak the words.

Claude closes his eyes and tries to stop the flow of distracting thoughts. He must focus on the task at hand, visualize the dog obeying his command ("Sit, boy, sit"), but when he turns around, he finds that Gonzago has disappeared. From the corner of his eye, he glimpses the beast bolting across the yard to the house.

"Son of a bitch!"

His heart pounding again, Claude remembers that he left the back door ajar. If Gonzago races upstairs and leaps into bed with Elsie ... well, he doesn't want to think about the consequences, the terrible penalty he will pay. Celibacy for one month? Two? There is no telling how long she will make him suffer, how long he will need to find solace in dirty magazines and masturbation.

He dashes toward the house, but before he can reach the door and put the leash around the dog's neck, he feels his toes sink into a lumpy pile of warm shit. He cries out in revulsion and despair, furiously scraping the ghastly black crap from the bottom of his feet.

III

To his great relief, Claude tracks down Gonzago in the den. Panting from all the excitement, the dog sits next to the master's leather armchair and slurps water from a shiny new dish. Careful not to make any sudden gestures that might startle the animal, Claude removes the amber vial from the pocket of his robe and twists the cap off. His hands start to shake. A bead of sweat rolls down the bridge of his nose. He must not pollute his fingertips. Holding the vial at arm's length, he pours the poison—one, two, three drops—into the dish. He almost expects to see an explosion of color, a small plume of pink smoke, a magnesium flare shooting across the room, but nothing happens, and Gonzago, after giving the fatal toxin an experimental sniff, laps it up like a king drinking from his favorite chalice.

Gazing pitilessly down at the dog, Claude whispers, "That's right, drink deep before you depart." Smoothing back his hair, he goes to the liquor cabinet and helps himself to a generous glass of absinthe. "Ah, now that's wormwood," he says, smacking his lips and sinking into the armchair.

Ironically, it was here, in this very room, that Edward de Vere, before leaving on his latest business trip, invited Claude to join him for a drink by the fire, two old friends, smoking cigars and nursing tumblers of green liqueur. As usual, Edward had a burning need to brag about his devious plans, the next forbidden excursion, the impending molestation while in Paris, or Copenhagen, or wherever he claimed to be conducting his shady business transactions. Edward frequented exclusive bordellos and other high-dollar dens of iniquity recommended by the smarmy black-market racketeers who offered him a choice of freshly deloused nymphets imported from the desert wastes of developing countries.

"Paris is lovely this time of year. Oh, it's not Amsterdam, of course, but the girls are exceedingly professional . . .

though they do tend to be a bit picky. They detest obesity. Sometimes they refuse to service fat Americans." He walked over to Claude and patted his belly. Claude glared at him, his nemesis.

Edward was wearing a poplin dress shirt with French cuffs, a silk tie from Hermes, handcrafted shoes from Milan. His nails were manicured and his teeth were bleached bone-white. From the looks of it, he must have had his stiff curli-cues and massive swoops of dark hair sculpted by Rodin, a great pompadour modeled after the Gates of Hell. His soul was sheathed in barnacles, his eyes black and empty as infinite space, his pupils so large and lifeless that they seemed to suck in light like a singularity.

"In some ways I actually prefer the Parisian whores," he went on. "Maybe one day I'll take you with me. I know a won-derful spot at the Place de la Contrescarpe. Best *maison close* on the Left Bank."

Claude rolled his eyes at the way Edward gave the words a nasally accent. It seemed odd that he could speak the lingo at all. He had no talent or appreciation for languages. As boys at the Jesuit high school, they were subjected to hours of grueling college preparatory coursework and innumerable fire-and-brimstone exhortations on Cain and Abel, but while Claude succeeded at his studies, graduating near the top of his class, Edward proved a complete mediocrity, always struggling to earn "a gentleman's C." Somehow he cheated his way through Latin, which was compulsory for all students. His lack of in-tellectual curiosity was seen not as laziness or stupidity but as a personal affront to the Jesuits' love of learning, and for his constant and intentional butchery of Virgil, the priests made Edward stay after school to translate entire chapters of *The*

Aeneid, to no avail. He couldn't understand a word of it, didn't know Pyrrhus from Priam, a hawk from a handsaw, and like a lot of frustrated adolescent boys, Edward vowed to get even with his teachers.

To his credit, it didn't take him long to amass an enviable fortune and to lord it over those same penniless priests who, in the days to come, were always looking to kiss the feet of some generous benefactor. By the time he was thirty, Edward owned a heavily wooded forty-acre lot in Avon. He conscripted a European architect with a dubious past to design a house of glass and steel that looked like a cross between a medieval castle and an iceberg, his very own Fortress of Solitude. On a promontory overlooking a dale, he built an infinity swimming pool, a tennis court with a red clay surface, a putting green and, some distance from the house, the pretty little grotto where, at night, his wife could light candles and prostrate herself before Catholic statuary. On the north end of the property, he constructed two large stables where he kept six impeccably groomed Danish Warmbloods that he showed on special occasions—state fairs and parades and children's birthday parties. In short, he created a suburban fiefdom and crowned himself petty dictator . . . but a dictator whose throne could easily be usurped. For years Claude has been laying the groundwork. He knows this tyrant all too well, knows he is a man of many weaknesses. Now well into middle age, Edward is still very much a child, a sensualist blinded by the degenerative disease of narcissism.

"These trips abroad have become a necessity," Edward said with a baleful smile, sinking into the chair where Claude sits now. The king's throne. "You have no idea what I've been through this year. My wife has become a terrible burden. She burns through my money. *Burns* through it." He takes a long, contemplative puff on his cigar. Above the rim of his glass and through the sheen of blue smoke, he stares at Claude and after a pregnant pause says, "Maybe it's time I finally got rid of her. I can only pray someone will take her off my hands, someone more suited to the job . . ."

IV

How much time elapses before Gonzago actually dies, Claude cannot say; the animal makes no sound at all, no strangled cries of torment, but at some point in the night, after finishing his third glass of absinthe, Claude notices the dog sprawled across the rug, motionless, eyes bulging from its skull, tongue hanging heavy and wet from the corner of its mouth. In that alien silence devoid of the dog's demonic laughter, Claude feels the alcohol cascading into the deep fissures of his brain. Though he is not a superstitious man and has always made a friend of reason and logic, he decides that it is probably best to bury Gonzago before joining Elsie in bed and sating himself on love. To let the dog rot in the open air seems an invitation to allow its stupid, slavering spirit to haunt his dreams.

After dragging the mangy carcass across the yard, Claude chooses a nice spot near the grotto where the earth is soft, and warm, and the worms look particularly eager to do their work. He finds a shovel in the tool shed and then begins to build a doghouse that will last Gonzago till doomsday. Like some infernal gravedigger, he tunnels into the loamy soil, uncovering the bones of the luckless squirrels and rabbits that Gonzago has brutally mangled and then buried with the jittery backward glances of an assassin. As he digs deeper, Claude uncovers a million subtle odors locked away in the earth, the fleshy green leaves transformed over the years into a brown soup that sends up fingers of steam into the evening air, eons of carnage artfully concealed by the moribund bouquet of nature.

Even after more than forty years on this cursed planet, Claude cannot comprehend the fact that one day he, too, will belong to that corrupt odor, his lingering stench the last trace of an existence that has failed to leave a more lasting mark. The maggots will have at him, and his sullied flesh will melt into the rich alluvial mud. Ultimately, his bloated carcass will make a fine meal for some wayward fiend like Gonzago. It's for this reason that he plans to be interred in the deepest cat-acombs of a monastery where, despite the anonymity of his jumbled bones, there might at least be a small chance that his skull, polished smooth by the dripping limestone walls, will become a *memento mori*, a paperweight for the manuscripts of some future literary genius who decides to smuggle it out of the tomb and place it on the edge of his desk next to an hour-glass, a vase of red roses, a glass of amontillado.

Exhausted and dizzy from the absinthe, Claude rolls the corpse into the pit and then begins to fill the hole. He wonders how his old friend will take the news of Gonzago's passing. Edward has been behaving rather erratically of late, and there is a distinct possibility that in his unbearable grief he will dig up the corpse and rock it back and forth in his arms, trying to grasp the enormity of his loss. "Why?" he might whisper, "why?" Because asking why—why this course of action and not some other—well, those are the kinds of questions men of his station often ask, men who have grown accustomed to suc-cess and balk at any event that veers radically from the script they have meticulously crafted. How they abhor change and deplore the ubiquity of life's impermanence. But erosion takes its toll on all things, reveals complex rows of strata and sub-strata below the surface, so that over the slow course of time, the souls of these men, petrified like fossils encased in layers of stone, are finally exposed, extracted, put on display for all to see. Change is inescapable, it unites rich and poor alike, the mindless cosmic constant that converts all things into uniden-tifiable heaps of dust and bones.

Claude taps down the dirt, throws the shovel aside, and returns to the house, but before heading upstairs to join El-sie in bed, he pauses in the den, takes one last look around. The bottle of absinthe and the vial of poison are still on the table beside the armchair. A peculiar feeling comes over him. The branches of the elms and maples clatter against the win-dowpane, the moon drifts behind a cloud, the wind whispers its secrets and then goes silent; in short, the globe continues to spin in its usual manner, but Claude has the sensation, an acute *awareness*, that he is not, and perhaps has never been, the protagonist of this drama but is merely a supporting player, one who appears briefly onstage to recite a few modest lines before retreating to the wings to wait for the spectacular, daz-zling, grisly finish.

He pours three drops of poison into the bottle, not enough to do any harm really, just enough to course through the sinis-ter alleys of Edward's soul and make him a little light-headed when he gets back from his "business trip." Then quietly, almost reverentially, Claude returns the bottle to its proper place in the liquor cabinet, and in a voice solemn and clear, he speaks the little Latin he can still recall from his days as a schoolboy with the Jesuits.

"*Consummatum est.*"

For in truth it is a consummation devoutly to be wished.

Zanzibar

I

It's Saturday morning, the Halloween party ended only a few hours ago, and dozens of costumed figures, nuns and priests and a red-robed inquisitor, are sprawled across the dirty hardwood floors. In time they will all come back to life, stagger to their feet, ransack the bathroom cabinets for bottles of aspirin, and thrust their pounding heads into the sink to gulp warm water straight from the tap, desperate to dilute the draft beer swirling inside their stomachs, anything that might alleviate the agony of another crushing hangover, but of course no medicine can ever match the anesthetic of deep, death-like sleep.

William de Vere tiptoes around their inert bodies and, in the first portent of light, discovers a note that the landlady has slid under his door. He reads each line with growing unease and, because he is a musician, is able to detect a lunatic cadence in the words, something manic and vulgar, like lyrics set to a grotesque polka played on a rusty squeezebox, "Who Stole the Keeshka" sung by a corpulent hobgoblin in a ratty, green robe who yearns to dance with him, feverish with lust.

The demented melody, sung in Mrs. O'Neill's orotund voice, rings in his head and makes his two-bedroom apartment seem like a demon-haunted music hall, complete with squeaking hinges, hissing radiators, inexplicable pockets of icy air that whistle through the bare rooms. Unlike the other notices that demand immediate back payment of rent, this one simply informs him that he has twenty-four hours in which to vacate the premises—the police will be summoned otherwise—and at the bottom of the note, scribbled in red ink, are the explicit and unalterable terms of an offer that will allow him to stay on for another month.

Like a morose child, Will slumps on a folding chair near the front window and gazes at the street below. Hard bullets of freezing rain strike the dirty panes of glass. Dead, yellow leaves gather around the twisted trunk of a chestnut tree, their coarse-toothed edges disintegrating into muck. Above the nearby shipyards, coppery clouds of coal-fire soot circle the sky and then, like the practiced fingers of a magician, jab suddenly at a row of abandoned brownstones. But in this forsaken quarter of the city, where the luckless denizens have resigned themselves to the maddening routine of minimum-wage work, the only real magic comes in the form of a pint of strong IPA at the local brewery or a double shot of espresso at the café where the lovely and exotic barista anticipates a stunningly horrific demise—or is it a blessed cessation?—to all of her woes.

Will smashes the note into a ball and considers holding a match to it, but he is a showman, an entertainer, and no matter how foul his mood he must always wear a cheerful smile just in case his guests begin to stir. To ease his nerves, he opens a warm beer and turns on the TV. A marauding band of B-movie mercenaries appears from out of the wobbling dust spouts of a vast desert plain. With the creak and clink of saddles and the high, wild cries of pillage and slaughter, the horsemen sweep through the shimmering streets of a post-apocalyptic city. The camera zooms in on a machete-wielding maniac with large yellow eyes like corona flames, his teeth filed to sharp points. Murmuring a deliciously foul prayer to the gods of war and conquest, the man pursues a little girl down a dark alley and, urged on by her screams, hacks wildly at her scalp. He seizes the child's limp body, raises the bubbling chalice of the skull to his dry, leathery lips, and slakes his desperate thirst on blood thick and black as crude oil seeping from the cracks in the earth.

Though he finds these images repellent, Will cannot turn away from the TV, but at the sound of approaching footsteps, he jumps with alarm. He peers into the pale morning light and sees the figure of the great muscled Minotaur coming through the hallway, a fabled creature that no filmmaker could ever dream up. Like so many of Will's acquaintances, the Minotaur inhabits a parallel universe where there rages an intellectual Dark Age absent of books and music and challenging ideas. His head has been bashed and battered so many times, his brain has sustained so many contusions, that he barely responds to anything other than the harshest external stimuli, the most severe forms of pain and pleasure.

Eager to have a bit of fun, Will decides to torment the beast. "Good morning, Sunshine! Care for a little hair of the dog?"

The Minotaur, ashen-faced and sweating, manages to shake his head and points to the letter in Will's hand.

Will tosses it to the ground. "Another eviction notice! So how'd it go last night?"

The Minotaur rubs his temples, blinks back his pain and stark incomprehension of the world, but before he can summon the willpower to stumble down the stairs and into the freezing rain, he leans heavily against the doorframe and takes several deep breaths.

"Everything went real good," he rasps. "Helluva party."

"Well, I'm awfully glad I could be of service." Will grins. "With Tamar you don't have to worry about catching the clap. It's the *plague* you have to worry about. Ha!"

The Minotaur blinks in dumb incomprehension, his hand drifting down to adjust his balls.

"Hey, Slick, you *do* know what day it is, don't you?"

"Yeah, I know . . ."

More screams from the TV. A cackling bandit decapitates a one-eyed cat and devours its dripping innards.

"It's the first of November," says Will. "The Day of the Dead. A day to build altars and shrines honoring the souls of the dearly departed, a day to drink and laugh and join hands in the Danse Macabre. Because no matter one's station in life, the dance of death unites us all. Yes, we all dance to the same tune."

The Minotaur gives him a look of terror, sputters something unintelligible, and then bolts out the door.

Will leans forward on the folding chair to watch his guest stumble through the desolate streets. Along the windowsill, the tawny soot and grit of the city collect into shallow pools, tinting the world with what looks like long trails of blood spilled by the movie mercenaries who drag their prey back to a lonely desert hideout where the gruesome feast continues with wild abandon until the film's final frame.

II

The apartment at the Zanzibar Towers & Gardens has become Will's last refuge. After months of what he thought were empty threats, his mother and father have kicked him out of the house once and for all and, maybe because they are so fond of melodrama, have even vowed to disinherit him, their only child, just for good measure. Not that there's much left to inherit anyway. Like many members of the *nouveau riche*, they enjoy the finer things in life and seem to derive a kind of perverse satisfaction in impressing sycophantic "friends" with their largesse—holiday parties, benefit dinners, annual galas; it's paying for it all that gives them so much trouble. His mother's fashion sense, faux *haute couture*, and weekend shopping sprees to downtown boutiques, not to mention his father's fondness for absinthe, hand-rolled cigars, and occasional peccadilloes in lavish hotel suites with distraught divorcées and young, money-hungry strumpets have made them big believers in debt management and the holy sacrament of confession, but if they attend Mass on Sunday mornings, murmur "forgive us our debts," it is only because they have confused their prodigal spending with piety. To atone for their sins, they help finance a new chapel and commission a local artist to design its giant stained glass window of Jesus, the boss's son as it were, who looks with indifference upon the ruined city where drunks, whores, and madmen wait their turn to get into Paradise.

For years his parents sought happiness in these petty status symbols. Will has seen the bills and bank statements piled high on the kitchen counter, a Mount Vesuvius of delinquent loans with the whole works about to go up in one great cataclysmic bang, threatening to suffocate them all under an ash cloud of lawsuits and criminal investigations. The phrase "misappropriation of funds" is one that he has heard with increasing regularity from his father's den. Since the outstanding balances are so insurmountable, Will feels no guilt about "borrowing" (as he later tries to explain it to them) one of their credit cards. He takes out a hefty cash advance to rent this modest apartment for weekend parties and to sleep with an occasional prostitute; treats himself to the steel-string guitar made of Brazilian rosewood that he has had his eye on for a few months now; buys a dozen shots of top shelf tequila for the band after a gig one night; purchases sodium lights and bottles of mineral solution in order to cultivate his little garden of hydroponic dope, bright green and fragrant as a meadow at the height of summer, the kind of shit that makes you forget your troubles for a while, provides inspiration for your inner genius. Writing songs for a death metal band requires loads of inspiration, after all. Will has to consider tempo and key changes, at what measure to include tremolo picking, blast beats, alternating rhythms, grunts, growls, snarls, wailing harmonics. There are subtleties, techniques of composition; craftsmanship is required, and super-strong weed helps assuage the serious bouts of writer's block that have started to afflict him of late.

His parents find his musical aspirations contemptible; liturgical music is what they like best, a mollifying melody strummed on guitars by two Poor Clares and after they discovered his larceny, his parents flew into a rage. Using her ferocious claws, his mother clamped onto his mop of greasy black hair and shook his head with such force that she chipped a nail and dislodged from the prongs of her ring the two-carat marquise-cut diamond—the envy of the parish ladies. Letting out a panicked snarl, she crouched on the floor and pawed mindlessly at the carpet.

"Well, don't just stand there! Help me, damn you!"

This argument erupted just as his father was leaving on another "business trip." From the old man's suitcase wafted a fragrance so alluring that it must have belonged to a woman many years his junior, perfume so expensive that it had to be bottled by the ounce and dispensed with a medicine dropper. Why his father never bothers to disguise these gifts remains something of a mystery to Will. More mysterious still is why women find him so appealing. Maybe it's because he has an authoritative presence that intimidates subordinates, especially those confused and emotionally distraught assistants who shudder as his corrupt fingers dance like the legs of a millipede along their naked flesh. Though outwardly kind in the presentation of gifts (or bribes, depending on the circumstances), his father is also capable of inflicting pain, and at the sight of his son brazenly smirking at him, the old man tightened his fists and lowered the boom.

"You're no son of mine!" he shouted with each blow. After awhile his mother joined in the refrain until together their voices sounded like a church choir belting out a deranged kyrie.

Will cowered on the floor and through his swollen eyes could see the family portrait hanging above the mantle in his father's den. Unlike his parents, Will is not lithe, tall, athletic, statuesque. In fact, he is quite plain, homely even. He has a weak chin and a thick lower lip that makes him look like a fish in profile, a wounded walleye flopping around in life's cold waters. His legs are short and stocky, his nose flat and wide and speckled with blackheads. The photographer tried to disguise these unfortunate features with the dramatic use of chiaroscuro light, but anyone with a discerning eye could see through the shadows and fog, could distinguish between the freckles and unsightly acne scars, and Will, spitting blood and choking back tears, understood that he did not belong among those fine people, had never really belonged. He was not a part of the family. He was a bastard child, a monster, a freak of nature.

III

Before Mrs. O'Neill can either chase him from the apartment or seduce him with an offer of rent-free accommodations, Will hastily collects his things, stuffing whatever he can into his book bag: his favorite T-shirt with the grinning skull, the rock wool and plastic trays he uses to grow his weed, a faded show bill tacked to the wall with the word "Zanzibar" printed in bold black letters set against a background of blue and green. There is nothing striking about the poster or about the band of the same name. Dozens of death metal bands compete for the same five or six hot spots in town, and many club owners insist that Will's band, in order to distinguish itself from the competition, come up with a gimmick to draw larger crowds.

"You should wear masks and capes," suggests one club manager from behind a makeshift desk of plywood and saw-horses. "Run around the stage with chainsaws dripping with blood. And you should definitely think of a new name. Zanzibar. Sounds a little fruity to me."

Things may be bleak now, compromise can't be far down the road, but regardless of his desperation for cash, Will still clings to his vaguely defined sense of artistic integrity. He is unwilling to turn his music into a ridiculous circus act to appease some smarmy manager, and he is too attached to the band's name to change it. He believes there is something auspicious about the solidity of its syllables, the repetition of its hard consonants, Z, that superfluous letter, "Thou whoreson Zed," mathematical symbol of unknown variables. He recalls hearing an ad on the radio, the narrator's baritone, soothing and earthy like cinnamon and cloves, beckoning him to escape to an island paradise: "Zanzibar, home of Sufi mystics, munificent sultans, wise viziers." When he found an apartment at the Zanzibar Towers & Gardens, he knew right away that it had to mean something.

Because no one will book them in a big venue, the band settles for playing in small, concrete pits that smell of urine and beer, dreary places conducive to hard drinking, gambling, fighting, quick drug deals in filthy toilet stalls. His most recent gig is at the local brewery, where a dozen or so customers, merchant marines on leave and longshoremen just getting off the night shift at the nearby shipyards, heckle him as he screams into the microphone. After the band finishes its last set, the ruddy Irishman tending bar slinks over to the stage and, smiling sheepishly, doles out a few dollars, slips Will a couple of joints, a handful of big black-and-white pills. "Horse tranquilizers," he says with a wink.

Sitting alone at the end of the bar, a man in coveralls and steel-toed boots turns to Will and says, "I been there, friend."

"Where is that?" Will asks, not really caring.

"Island of Zanzibar. Real fucked up place these days. Islamic fundamentalists run the show."

Blinded by the stage lights, his eyes stinging with sweat,

Will finds it difficult to tell what the man looks like, whether he is tall or short, fat or lean. His voice has a certain richness and depth to it, like the low chords of an old church organ that has survived an air raid and is now in need of careful restoration; it's the voice of someone who has participated in the nightmare spectacle of the world, has used his wits on some occasions and fled in naked terror on others. Before speaking again, the man gulps down the rest of his beer and then wipes his mouth with the back of his hand. He drums his fingers on the bar, and Will notices that his right index finger has been sawed away with what must have been a dull blade.

"Let me tell you. I once seen a group of clerics in white robes take this poor sonofabitch out to the public square and hack off his cock and balls with a machete. Don't know what he did to deserve that kind of treatment. Probably tapped someone's old lady, I'm guessing. Well, that's the order of things these days, ain't it, brother?" The man stands up and moves closer to Will. "Hell, you look just like Freddie Mercury. Anyone ever tell you that? He was a Zoroastrian or some crazy shit, wasn't he?"

Furious that anyone would dare compare him to a homo pop star, Will sneers at the man and says he has to take a leak. He gathers his share of pills and dope and then storms away, refusing to return until the man has left the bar.

IV

Now with nowhere to call home, Will takes to the streets.

During the course of his wanderings, he sometimes thinks of himself as either a runaway from a particularly cruel Dickensian workhouse or the sole survivor of a long-forgotten war, an exile bound for a glorious but still unknown destiny, Aeneas in search of his Latium. He has his doubts, of course, especially during the dreary November afternoons when his friends have gone off to their part-time jobs at the fast-food restaurants and rendering plants. Like everyone cursed to live in this dying city, he worries that he has no talent for rising in the world, that he expects more from life than is reasonable, but because he prefers self-righteousness to self-pity, he becomes convinced that only by living like a nomad on the brink of total destitution can he find the elusive Truth he has been seeking ever since he first picked up a guitar, and so homelessness becomes just one more part of his burdensome quest, another kind of suffering, sublime in its ability to wreak havoc with his already eroded confidence, but one that offers the potential reward of adoration from millions of fans willing to wait in long lines to see him play in stadiums and arenas. Everyone loves a good rags-to-riches story, and on that glorious day when he grants *Rolling Stone* an interview, he will proudly boast of his misadventures on these wicked streets, how he survived on cans of cold soup and bottles of warm beer, and how he turned down solicitations in public restrooms from nervous, middle-aged men in suits and ties.

For a few days he crashes with the lead singer, then with the bass guitarist, who staggers through the back door drunk and irritable and slaps his girlfriend until the police show up with their truncheons and tasers. Those who offer him shelter don't want him around for very long, maybe because, like a highly contagious pathogen, there is something viral about homelessness, more abhorrent than the medieval plague. Every time he passes a mirror, he sees angry pustules of defeat spreading across his face, leaving an indelible mark like the acne scars that cover his cheeks.

you were born in kc missouri to a girl that wasn't married after you... she brought you to the nursery... kissed your head and told you not to worry then... she turned and slipped away

Will quickly commits to memory a new list of rules that, for pure soul-stifling masochism, surpass all of those pages of thou shalt nots from Leviticus, a turn of events that he finds ironic since he has spent the better part of his eighteen years circumventing rules of any kind. Regardless of where he stays, the rules remain the same: never take food from the refrigerator unless you're invited to do so first; the same goes for beer, pills, and dope—don't touch them or you'll soon find yourself back on the streets; and if anything goes missing, anything at all—a comb, a guitar pick, loose change scattered on a kitchen countertop—suspicion immediately falls on you. Not that Will is beyond petty theft. Around every corner, new temptations lurk, and he must continually remind himself that there are consequences for disobedience.

Then one day he has a confrontation with the drummer over an empty pack of cigarettes.

"Hey, man, you still got that credit card?"

"No, I already *told* you," Will answers, a bit embarrassed by how shaken he sounds, "my parents are tight with a dollar these days. They're delusional, they're like children. They think they need trips to Paris to visit the catacombs. Excursions through the Belgian countryside to buy cases of beer from Trappist monks. Hell, just give me a little mystic and my guitar, and I'm cool, I'm doing alright."

The drummer tosses the crumpled pack of cigarettes at his chest. "You and your personal problems. Where's your dedication, man, your goddamn *dedication*? When are you gonna find us another gig? We haven't played a decent joint in weeks. And you haven't written any new music in months. Stop your bitching and get us some work, man, some fucking *money*."

V

He spends most of his time at the Stone Town Café.

Sitting in a far corner near the fireplace with his back pressed against the exposed bricks for warmth, struggling to write new material for the band, Will strums random chords on his guitar. Despite his intense concentration, he can't discover an original melody, a satisfying rhythm, a memorable riff. He's beginning to think that he has finally hit rock bottom, but while things look pretty grim right now, he fears there are still greater depths of despair and misery yet to be explored. Unless Fate intervenes, and does so soon, he may find himself plummeting down an inescapable mineshaft of mediocrity. He considers walking next door to the pawnshop, getting whatever he can for his instrument, but he is prevented from doing so by a group of overserious poets who force him to listen to their rambling monologues on art and God and their own unrecognized talent.

"The muses cannot be summoned through sheer willpower alone," they tell him. "Patience defines the true artist. You may have to wait for years, for decades, and even then you may never garner accolades from the unlettered herd."

They are positively committed to self-deception, these failed scribes, always inventing clever excuses to put off their writing for another day while they wait for Inspiration to reveal her grand metaphysical vistas. They bide their time by lecturing Will, their sole pupil, in tones so utterly patronizing and devoid of insight that their voices, like the voices of all teachers and solipsists the world over, begin to sound like the steady hiss of the gas fireplace.

Only the barista treats him with respect. Each day she brings him unusual drinks and confections, "on the house."

The poets resent him for this. They have never been offered a free drink, not even a discounted one, and they see it as yet another form of injustice, another slight against their fierce genius. Some of them are so offended that they refuse to speak to Will again.

"That's espresso cubano," the barista tells him with a little laugh when Will's eyes widen at the taste of its sweetness. Later she makes him a cup of ristretto, which is bitter, and a café coretto with two shots of cognac. She keeps a bottle hidden behind the counter, "survival gear," she calls it, and sometimes pours the cognac straight up into his empty mug.

With the approach of evening, Will locks himself in the restroom, fires up a joint, the last of his stash, inhales deeply, and with the same black magic marker he uses to jot down forgettable and poorly arranged chord progressions in his notebook, he draws abstract patterns on the toilet stall, pretends he is charting his way through a treacherous maze of strange, cyclopean dimensions. When he emerges from the restroom, he finds the barista standing in the doorway, blocking his path.

"The odor," she says, peering inside. Her eyes remain incurious and distant. When she speaks her lips barely move. Will doesn't know if she is angry or amused. He finds the atonal quality of her voice mysterious, her thick accent difficult to read. "I just painted the walls," she continues. "That is why the odor. Maybe you noticed? Chartreuse. Sounds very fancy. But still it looks green to me. Except it's not. No, not quite. There is a little yellow in there. Maybe I am color-blind. The paint was on sale so I bought it. I don't know why I bother. How many men notice the color of the walls in the restroom? Of course I have my fair share of critics. They always find something to complain about."

Although he is a bit paranoid right now and has never been especially courageous around women of a certain station— pretty, reputable, demure—Will manages to focus his blood-shot eyes on the barista's fine features and studies the tattoo of a brightly colored bird on the side of her neck that she play-fully conceals with her long hair and small lively hands.

"My name is Salme," she tells him.

"Will," he croaks. His throat is dry, raw. He can't re-member the last time he drank a glass of water. For five days straight he has been living on espresso and weed.

"You attend the Jesuit high school, don't you?"

He shrugs in a noncommittal way. He hasn't been to school in weeks and has no intention of returning. He is eigh-teen now, and no one can make him go back.

"You play in a band? Zanzibar?"

"Yeah, from time to time. Right now things are a little slow."

"There must be a connection between us. I knew it when I first saw you." She moves her hair aside so he can get a bet-ter look at the tattoo of the red and black bird on her neck, its head cocked, its eyes shining. "You don't recognize it, do you? I thought maybe you would. It's called a Zanzibar bishop. Its song is mysterious and beautiful. Like your music."

Will, who isn't used to compliments, feels his cheeks begin to burn.

"Would you have any interest in playing here? I can pay you. Forty dollars a day. Under the table. I wish I could give you more, but it's all I can afford."

Will listens carefully to her proposition. He is down to spare change, a handful of nickels and dimes, but what if this woman, with her immigrant schemes and duplicitous smile, is up to no good, what if she is luring him into some sort of trap? He understands that she isn't simply offering him a job; she's reporting the facts, and the facts are these: he lacks the talent and persistence and, most important of all, the luck to become a successful musician. A gig at a coffee shop is the best he can do, another proving ground, another clear indication of his creative paralysis.

"You have big dreams, yes, but you should give my offer serious consideration. Please, come with me. I wish to show you something. It may intrigue you."

Off they go, past a swinging door, through the tiny kitchen, then down a creaking staircase into the basement. Above them, a twisted highway of groaning, clanking galvanized pipes hangs precariously from exposed iron beams. Brown spiders and silverfish scurry into dark recesses. Swirling tempests of dust shimmer through a shaft of opalescent streetlight that struggles through the glass block window. A single bulb dangles from a frayed wire and swings back and forth like a man from the gallows, casting a faint yellow glow across dozens of wooden crates stacked one on top of the other.

"This is my husband's domain," she explains, brushing away a skein of cobwebs and stepping gingerly around a pile of mouse droppings. "As you can see, he has turned the basement into a warehouse for his plunder."

"You're married?"

She nods. "For ten years. Ever since I was a young girl, younger than you are now. I was very naïve when we met. He is a merchant marine, a free spirit, and sails the world on a cargo ship. He will never change. And I do not possess the power to persuade him to settle down." She runs her fingers across the tops of the crates. "Twice a year he returns home with odd things, items he finds in bazaars and opium dens and brothels. I have warned him. One day I will toss his treasures onto the street. But I cannot drag these crates up the stairs on my own."

Will sighs. He knew there would be a catch, a reason for the free drinks, but it's too late to think of an excuse.

"Okay, which crates do you want me to haul to the curb first?"

"*Usipime, baga sosi*! If I actually did something like that, my husband would kill me. He would kill us both." She slides against him, touches his shoulder, squeezes his hand. "Do you live nearby? Do you have a place to stay? If you do not mind the mess, there is more than enough room down here for you. An extra bed over there in the corner . . ."

But Will barely hears her. When it comes to matters of chance and coincidence, he has always been a skeptic, but suddenly he sees an irrefutable sign that his life is about to change yet again. Like a genuflecting penitent before the sacristy, he kneels down in the dust, glides his trembling fingers across the splintered wood of a crate, and though he has never had the ability to interpret omens and doesn't really know what this one means, he whispers the improbable name that has been seared with a hot iron into the slats of wood.

"Zanzibar, Zanzibar, Zanzibar . . ."

VI

The following afternoon he starts on the job.

Eager to attract a mainstream audience, he forgoes the death metal riffs and plays the bouncy pop tunes one might expect to hear in a small café, standards and ballads from Tin Pan Alley, jazzy numbers by Michael Franks and Billy Joel, but he learns that success is just as elusive in a small coffee shop as it is on the big stage. After each song he is greeted not with polite applause but with the rude slurping of cappuccino and the low contemptuous rumbles from the poets.

He is grateful when Salme closes the café for the night and he can retreat to the basement. Despite its gloom and solitude and faint odor of chemicals, a sour smell that reminds him of those high school lab experiments he once slept through—the fleshy bull frogs, pale green to the point of translucence, bobbing around in big glass jars of formaldehyde like things half-remembered from childhood dreams—the basement becomes a kind of sanctuary, shielding him from the whirlwind of disappointment and failure and his own needling ambitions that await him at the top of the stairs each day.

In the corner, there is a utility tub with running water where he brushes his teeth, washes his face and armpits, what the street people call a whore's bath, and below the window, there is an end table with a lamp and a pile of travel magazines, the print faded, the pages brittle with age like the delicate parchment of an ancient codex. And of course there are the big wooden crates stacked three and four high like the turrets of an ancient fortress protecting him from any possible intruders who might slink through the darkness and do unspeakable things to him.

For weeks he has wondered what might be inside the crates, and now, out of sheer boredom and simple curiosity, he randomly selects one and pries it open. Initially he is baffled by the curious artifacts buried beneath the straw—peculiar wooden idols with grotesque leers, tin canisters packed with spices, leather-bound volumes written in indecipherable and ancient tongues, waxes and oils and fragrant sandalwood boxes filled with dust. The ashes of forgotten kings, revered mystics?

Inside the crate marked Zanzibar, he finds a glass hookah pipe with a half dozen hoses that reach out like tentacles to caress his cheeks and a canopic jar made of alabaster depicting an Egyptian god—Aten? Horus? Ra?—stuffed with hashish the color of desert sand at sunset. He packs the bowl, lights a match, and takes in the curative smoke that coils in thick purple plumes around his head. The stuff makes him feel disembodied, divorced from reality, in a vague state of turmoil. Spectral shadows dance along the basement floor. His mind is adrift in an incalculable waste; his thoughts gather like the heavy drops of moisture that collect and fall from the banging pipes, thoughts so small and scattered that they quickly evaporate and merge into the mossy cinderblock walls.

He removes his clothes and waits for Salme to join him in bed. Will attributes their affair to the obvious—she is lonely. But her eyes hint at something deeper. They are enigmatic, shrewd, ringed by dark circles that make her appear weary and excited, clever and naïve, intelligent and dull, creative and destructive, reasonable and unhinged.

"Oh, it has been such a *long* time," she whispers, stroking his chest and flat pale stomach. She straddles him with the ferocity of a famished she-wolf about to eviscerate its prey, and if she has any thoughts of the merchant marine, whose ship even now may be sailing through a perilous strait that divides hostile lands, she gives no sign. They spend many nights ensconced in the warm cocoon of musty blankets. It's an arrangement that pleases them both.

VII

During that long, brutal winter, business slows to a crawl, and with the worsening weather Salme starts to worry that she won't be able to keep the café afloat for much longer, that the IRS will audit her, that the authorities will deport her to Zanzibar. Ignoring the ornery poets' insinuations about their beloved barista and her new "boy toy," Will sets aside his guitar in the afternoons to help her with the day-to-day chores—he mops the floors, washes the dishes, and even scrubs the toilets. He refuses to accept any more of her money, but Salme never fails to show him her gratitude in other ways.

Then during the night of the Great Blizzard, when the snow piles up so high that it seems to absorb the ghostly blue streetlights so that the world is immersed in perpetual darkness, day and night indistinguishable from one another, Salme locks up early and instructs Will to wait for her in the basement. He stretches out on the bed and reaches for the hookah, but Salme doesn't come down to join him.

For one troubling hour he shivers alone in the cold and listens to the shrieking wind that sounds more and more like a heated exchange. He props himself up on an elbow, his body tense, his teeth chattering. He attributes the noises to the raging storm and potent marijuana. Paranoia tends to get the best of him, that's all. Besides, Salme is a smart woman, tough, experienced; she can probably handle any trouble without his help. He would only get in the way. But at the approach of midnight, he decides to investigate. Quietly he creeps up the stairs and presses an ear to the door. A deep voice demands to see the thing that she keeps penned up in the basement, the sniveling creature, the worm, the insect.

After a long silence, Salme says, "The café is now closed. Permanently. Gone out of business. No one is allowed inside. You must leave. You must—"

But her words are abruptly cut off. There is a struggle, a

boom of shattering glass, a terrible gasp of strangulation, a piano wire pulled tight around tender flesh, a final desperate plea for mercy and forgiveness.

Will considers screaming for help, but in this neighborhood, who would dare come to his rescue? At this hour, even the police are reluctant to get out of their cruisers. He races down the stairs, stumbles over his own feet, nearly cracks open his skull on the claws of a pry bar. He searches for a closet, a crawl space, an alcove, but there is nowhere to hide. He turns off the lights and crouches behind a stack of crates. He tries not to breathe, not to think.

The door creaks open. A wedge of white light slashes across the cement floor. The heavy thud of steel-toed boots resounds in the basement like the slow, steady beat of a kettle-drum. At the bottom of the stairs stands a man whose shaved head and pronounced cheekbones remind Will of those B-movie bandits that slobber with inhuman malice, a man who has known exile, driven from civilization time and again like a thief and forced to hide from marauding warlords in wadi-channels and cliff-hollows, burying his stool in the sand, burning scrub-brush for warmth, slitting the throats of pack-animals for sustenance, slipping across porous borders by the light of a gibbous moon, disappearing into towns reduced to ashes where children feral and skittish observe him from the shadows of mud huts, an ancient culture acting out the final cataclysmic scene of its long history, and he the last observer of the drama.

The man narrows his viper's eyes and stares at the crate marked Zanzibar, sees that its lid has been ripped open, its contents scattered around the room. Calmly he lifts Will's guitar from the corner of the bed, plucks a string or two, and with one mighty swing shatters it against the cinderblock wall. Tiny shards of wood fly in a hundred directions.

"Come out," says the man.

Will raises his head. "Please . . ." he whispers.

"So, it's you. Freddy Mercury." The man smiles with grim satisfaction and tosses the busted guitar neck to the floor. He takes a measured step, then with a languorous wave of his hand motions not to the crate exactly but to the black and depthless dimensions inside.

"Get in," he says.

Will backs away. "What do you mean?"

"You know what I mean."

"But why?"

"You know why."

"I haven't done anything wrong."

Rubbing the stump of an amputated finger across his lips and angled teeth, the man says, "I'm not a very patient person."

Will knows it is useless to deny his culpability. If experience has taught him anything it's that guilt is malignant and unconquerable, something from which no one can ever truly escape. Like death, it never tires of stalking its prey. He accepts his fate, resigns himself to it totally, and to his amazement all of his fears vanish, in an instant, and he feels a sense of morbid tranquility. He climbs inside the crate, crouches down, tucks his knees against his chin, curls into a tight ball.

The man goes to work. He slams the lid down, hammering it shut with a pry bar and a handful of rusty nails. The wood splinters at the corners of the crate and gouges the back of Will's neck. Grunting and cursing, the man drags the crate across the floor and up the stairs. Will's head bounces violently against the sides. He cradles his legs, rocks back and forth. The café door opens, and through the thin slats of wood, he feels a sharp stab of icy air and sees pins of indigo light. The hinges of a tailgate open, a truck engine rumbles to life. In a reassuring voice the man speaks to him, tells him that the loading docks of the shipyard are not far from here. "All shall be well, and all manner of things shall be well . . ."

VIII

Will sleeps and dreams of a new melody in the dissonant twelve-tone musical scale. There is no middle C, no starting point from which to center his consciousness. He envisions himself writhing on his deathbed, suffering from some un-named affliction, one that utterly baffles a group of doctors, who with perfect impassivity listen to the final beats of his heart and watch his body go limp; the plaintive motif turns into the lamentation of his grieving parents as they stand be-fore an open casket at the funeral parlor to view his corpse, his eyes glued shut, his lips wired together, his broad features dulled by the artless application of makeup, his fingernails manicured and positioned in an unconvincing imitation of repose. "What a misguided boy," they say, "what a terrible disappointment." During the funeral at the Jesuit chapel, the band members reunite a final time to play a dirge, transform-ing the motif into an insidious Danse Macabre, but they shed no tears for their fallen comrade. For them this is just another gig, another way to buy more dope and booze. Their perfor-mance is rushed; it lacks passion and conviction. Out in the blizzard, two grave diggers wait by the door, whistling the tuneless melody, shovels at the ready.

At some point, Will opens his eyes, though he can never

be entirely sure if he is finally awake or still dreaming. In the darkness of the crate, it's hard to tell. He hears the crashing surf and the demon piping of birds heralding a new day and sees seeping slowly from his lips the wraithlike quarter notes of his dream song. He breathes the stale air and worries that he will be forgotten in this box, just another amusing curio, mummified and leathery like a thing dredged up from a haunted bog, but in time the lid of the crate will surely fly open, and instead of the overcast skies of home he will see the bright blue sea that surrounds the faraway island of Zanzibar.

PART TWO

Hack

꩜

I

The Jesuits place a high value on the written word, so much so that they hire an outsider to run the literary magazine. Under the direction of Batya Pinter, *The Millstone* garners recognition as one of the finest publications produced by any high school, private or public, in the United States, its stories and poems one step removed from the divine Logos, its contributors destined to achieve great things, heirs to the throne of Carver and Cheever, tutelary gods that guide the pens of these fledgling scribes and lead them toward the sweet promises of alcoholism and sexual dysfunction.

With the release of each issue, agents and publishers pore over the journal, hoping to discover and capitalize on the most original voice of a new generation, some *enfant terrible* who will gleefully stir up trouble on the literary scene, but *The Millstone* has, at least so far, produced only well-mannered boys who dwell on mainstream subjects almost hagiographic in their depictions of common people. According to these young men, the world is populated not by cynics and miscreants, but with unrecognized saints who feed the hungry and provide shelter for the homeless. While many of these teenage boys fall prey to the shameless sentimentality of conventional storytelling, some of them do recognize the sad fact that life is not without its tragedies and injustices, and occasionally they compose poignant pieces about the unexpected loss of a beloved parish priest or a loyal family dog. With whatever protection pseudonymity affords them, they publish even the rare ribald story, chronicling the secret liaisons of an unconventional couple whose forbidden relationship ends, depending upon the temperament of its author, in either comedic or catastrophic circumstances.

Despite the journal's repetitive themes, the small but loyal readership remains strong, even passionate, and Edmund Campion invariably picks up the latest edition. Copies are scattered around campus like stale breadcrumbs left for the screeching grackles that swoop from their roosts high on the Gothic bell tower. Glancing left and right to make sure no one sees him, Edmund stashes the journal in his book bag and then scampers off to the palatial library where he passes through untold numbers of hexagonal galleries until he finds a cozy alcove behind a shelf of neglected books. Safe from the ridicule of his philistine friends, he holds the magazine close to his nose, takes in the heady perfume of glue and ink, strokes the glossy cover page, and for an entire hour, he immerses himself in the stories, his eyes growing misty at the splendor of the imagery and the slightly discombobulating effect of the parataxis style of the prose, the journal's trademark.

As he races through the final pages, his admiration turns to envy. They make it seem so easy, these writers. They possess an uncommon ability to translate their experiences into words that continue to confound and evade him, and he finds it hard to believe that those same blundering boys who walk the halls with him are capable of such sophisticated insights. How do his classmates intimate suffering without sounding puerile and self-serving? How do they describe the mystical without coming across as lunatics and zealots?

Ever since his sophomore year, when he discovered the dazzling wordplay of Vladmir Nabokov, Edmund has had ambitions to become a serious writer, a member of *The Millstone*'s revered pantheon, but his fiction is consistently rejected, the manuscripts often returned without comment and accompanied by a terse form letter printed on thick gray paper. The words look like they've been etched with hammer and chisel into a heavy stone tablet; there is a kind of finality about them, but to question the judgment of the editor would be more than merely impertinent, it would be tantamount to blasphemy, and Edmund knows better than to provoke the wrath of a redoubtable god like Batya Pinter.

He settles for working on the school newspaper as a sports photojournalist, an unremarkable position that comes with a number of mundane responsibilities: he dashes off puff pieces about the refulgent reign of the mighty football team, conducts long interviews with the forever fuming head coach, and photographs the dim-witted and narcissistic quarterback. In this new Dark Age of short attention spans and almost total disdain for the printed word, Edmund suppresses his imagination and uses raw, whittled-down prose to grab his readers, but he assures himself that he can rise above the mediocrity of reporting and craft a story so beautiful, so subtle, so profound in its unflinching examination of the human heart that the editor of *The Millstone* will surely read it with bated breath and regret over having declined his previous submissions.

Greatness is close at hand—he can sense it—but lately, whenever he stares into the void of a blank piece of paper, he finds himself reeling from a lack of inspiration, and though he is reluctant to admit this to anyone, even to himself, it has been months since he has set pen to paper. No matter. The life of any young writer is essentially one of self-deception, and the tenacious few who persist in their aspirations have simply learned to make their delusions work for them rather than against them.

II

Even though he is unable to gain a foothold on the trackless slopes of creative enterprise, Edmund has no problem turning out enthusiastic term papers for English class, detailed fifteen-page analyses of *The Catcher in the Rye* and *Lord of the Flies* that he hopes will impress his teacher, but whenever he tries to engage her in a conversation before class begins, he cannot summon the right words to describe his love for literature. He rambles from one topic to the next, his arms swinging erratically like a marionette jerked around by an amateur puppeteer. He forgets to pause for breath and feels his face turn bright pink, then dark purple. His lips start to twitch. He's making a fool of himself, he's aware of this, but he can't help it—his adoration for his teacher isn't something he can easily disguise.

As is the case with the other instructors at this august prep school, Batya Pinter has mastered the indispensable arts of insouciance and Schadenfreude and can wield them about with great cunning. She never attempts to conceal her boredom with teaching or contempt for her pupils, doesn't lift a hand to cover her mouth as she lets out a long leisurely yawn; she merely points to his desk and asks him to take a seat. Most disturbing of all, however, are her cold blue eyes, which have a supernatural power that trumps that of the conjuring priests with their tiresome trick of transubstantiation.

Edmund submits his essay and then slinks to the back of the classroom.

The Minotaur, who sits next to him, shakes his head and laughs. "Shit, man, you actually get a hard-on for that crusty, old cougar?"

Edmund is genuinely puzzled by this remark. Old? It's impossible to determine her age. She might be thirty-five or forty. She looks youthful, and it's obvious, to him at least, that she spends as much time working on her appearance as she does editing the award-winning journal. She primps and preens, plucks and polishes. She selects her outfits with utmost care, tight skirts that accentuate her muscular thighs, scandalous button-down blouses that reveal far too much of her supple, honey-hued cleavage, but if her sex appeal is hard to mistake, so is her aura of inquisitorial wrath. With her hands clasped behind her back and chin thrust forward to slice through the rumbling heat of adolescent desire, she paces up and down the rows of desks in her shiny black boots and demands that her slouching students sit up straight and pay attention. Hypnotized by the rhythm of her sashaying hips, Edmund squirms in his chair, crosses his legs, and uses the fig leaf of his notebook to hide the embarrassing bulge in his pants.

Only the Minotaur dares to ignore her. He falls asleep with his textbook propped open under one shaggy elbow, drool trickling from the corner of his mouth, forming a shallow pool around his chiseled jaw. He farts and belches and picks his nose. Sometimes he scribbles football plays in his notebook—a sweep pass roll out, a trick split end pitch. Edmund observes him as a primatologist might observe the behavior of a Bonobo chimp in the wild while it scratches in the dirt with a pointed stick to capture termites. To his amazement, Batya Pinter doesn't reprimand the Minotaur for this crude and disruptive behavior. Instead, she treats him like an adorable circus bear, gently taps his head, yearns to smooch his enormous muzzle, deliberately drops pens and pencils beside his desk and then bends over to retrieve them, giving him a tantalizing flash of her sequined-studded bras and a better vantage point of her cloven ass.

Though he knows it's an absurd idea, Edmund becomes more and more convinced that Batya Pinter is smitten with the Minotaur, but if she has feelings for that doltish, drawling meathead, it isn't because of his imposing physique or devastating good looks or incontestable virility; no, it's because she is impressed by his *mind*, his *intellect*, his surprising ability to write exceptionally erudite essays. Little does she know that Edmund, for a modest but non-negotiable fee, has been composing all of the Minotaur's term papers, a morally dubious enterprise, true, but one he is able to justify since he uses the cash to buy paperback editions of the classics he admires.

A magician with words, Edmund is able to take the Minotaur's violent jumble of declarative sentences and transform them into miniature masterpieces on *Pnin* and *Pale Fire* and *Lolita*. These papers are so insightful that it almost seems a pity to give a cretin like the Minotaur any credit, and Edmund can't help but drop subtle hints and clues about their true authorship. He cites Charles Kinbote and Claire Quilty in the footnotes, quotes Vivian Darkbloom at length.

Edmund prides himself on his clever deception until, as class ends and the bell rings, a suddenly cantankerous Batya Pinter turns her eyes to the back of the classroom and shouts, "Remain seated, gentlemen! I have an important announcement to make."

Edmund turns white with fear. Even the Minotaur seems nervous and slides a little lower in his seat. The two boys exchange worried glances. Their teacher marches across the room and stands at the lectern, her mouth tightening into a severe smile, her long nails tap-tap-tapping against the burnished wood. Has she discovered their crime? If so, the consequences will be dire. Not only will it result in Edmund being permanently blacklisted from *The Millstone*, it will mean automatic failure in the class and almost certain expulsion from the school. Edmund cannot understand academia's peculiar obsession with plagiarism. All of existence is a form of plagiarism; everyone is more or less a fraud, stealing thoughts and ideas and identities. Why, even the Bard himself is said to have—

"Your attention please! I wish to inform you that *The Millstone* is holding its first annual fiction contest. The winner will receive one hundred dollars and have his work showcased in the next issue of the magazine. I will personally judge the finalists. The deadline? October thirty-first. Season of the witch."

No one has the nerve to laugh at this joke except, of course, the Minotaur, who slaps Edmund hard on the back. "Holy shit, man," he whispers. "I thought we were caught for sure. Turns out to be good news, huh? Here's your big opportunity, your one shot at fame and fortune."

But Edmund feels no sense of relief at all. In fact, he begins to tremble even more violently. His heart palpitates. Sweat trickles down his spine. Competition is something he abhors. There are too many cutthroats at this school, too many cheats, too many unscrupulous, blue-blooded boys willing to do just about anything to pad their résumés so they can get into the best universities. The contest won't be fair, that's a given, but at this stage in the game, he has no other options. He is a senior now; time is running out. Action must be taken. No sense dreaming about things. Sooner or later he must find out if he is to be one of the chosen, the anointed, or if he is to be dismissed, forgotten, tossed aside, just another anonymous loser destined to live out his best years in an office cubicle while editing copy for a small town newspaper.

If he wants to make a name for himself, he must learn the secrets of narrative, the techniques of plot and pacing, and somehow, someway, he must get an acceptance letter from Batya Pinter before he graduates.

III

Traditionally the newspaper has always appealed to the less promising students, the ones of middling intellect who have yet to prove themselves worthy of ascending the treacherous steps of the extracurricular hierarchy. Serious writers, those whose philosophical meditations and deft, ironic tales of middle-class despair are featured in *The Millstone*, shun the paper for the derisive tone of its editorials, a critique not without justification. Since truly compelling stories are so scarce at a boy's prep school, Edmund Campion and his colleagues resort to writing cruel reviews—of the annual musical, of the garish décor at the homecoming dance, and especially of the foppish and effete authors who contribute to the literary magazine, but if these budding reporters and columnists succumb to the temptation of leaden sarcasm, it's only because sarcasm is cheap and easy, an indispensable tool for a writer with a limited palette of ideas and a strict deadline.

Each Friday afternoon, when school lets out for the day, the boys promptly gather for a weekly editorial meeting, but Edmund Campion, hard at work on his short story for the fiction contest, plods into the office nearly one hour late. His friends glower at him. By nature they are a peevish and inquisitive lot; they're journalists after all, and Edmund must remember that no question they ever ask is innocent.

"We have to go over the layout tonight," they say. "Did you forget?"

"No, I didn't forget. I was . . . busy."

"Sure you were. Pulling your pud."

"I was writing a term paper. For you know who."

Yes, they know, they are in on the secret, but Edmund hopes they don't notice the way he shifts his eyes and fidgets with the pens in his shirt pocket. They are experts at detecting a lie and are ready to exploit it to their advantage. If they uncover the truth, they will mock him without mercy; they'll call him a fool, a dreamer, a turncoat. Though most of them are only seventeen, they already know something about professional jealousy and long to see him fail. When the results of the fiction contest are announced and his name is not among the list of honorees, they will be waiting for him, unforgiving tormentors eager to apply the screws to his inflated ego. They will publish the names of the finalists and make a special point of mentioning how Edmund Campion submitted a story but failed to garner any recognition. Never again will he be al-

lowed to set foot in this office. He must watch his step. Without the newspaper, he would have no social life at all.

Grudgingly, they make room for Edmund at the table and
tell him the Jesuits want another full-page feature about the
Minotaur for the next issue.

"You must be joking," he says in exasperation.

His friends laugh. "Yes, this will be the sixth story you've
written about that animal. Oh, the cruel reality of crass com-
mercialism!"

For the first time since taking the job as sports journalist,
Edmund feels a real sense of helplessness and despair. It's like
the priests have condemned him to a semester-long detention
and have cast him into a kind of intellectual purgatory. He
has grown to hate the sewage-y smell of the newspaper office,
located in the dank subbasement of the main building, "The
Bunker" as his fellow reporters fondly call it. Mayhem lurks
at the fringes of this reinforced concrete vault. Duplicity and
paranoia lurk in the eyes of its surly, sallow-faced inhabitants.
A firestorm of death metal opera thunders from the portable
stereo—*Die Walküre*, *Siegfried*, *Götterdämmerung*. The heavy
crash of cymbals drowns out the constant whistle of the radia-
tor and loosens the cracked paint from the ceiling and cinder
block walls.

At an oval table, under the glaring white light, the boys sit
as if awaiting the Final Judgment and study a brigade of plastic infantrymen staged for a horrific siege. Dozens of small,
green toy soldiers stand at the ready, bazookas on their shoulders, grenades in their hands. In a little game of war, the boys
move the figurines around the perimeter of the table. Edmund
Campion, never taking his eyes from the make-believe battlefield, slides away to observe the onslaught from a safe distance.

Is it bravery, he wonders, or insanity that inspires certain young men to join in the fray and face life's brutalities and hardships? Whatever reasons they may give and whatever regrets they may have once the fighting begins, some of them learn the meaning of self-sacrifice, what the priests call *agape*, which is the highest form of love, and the lucky few who survive the terrible ordeal come away with compelling stories to tell.

Edmund is a coward; he's willing to admit as much, and he's beginning to worry that he may never have a story worth telling. As he gathers his equipment for the photo shoot, he remembers what the history books have taught him—that cowardice and the decadence of art will, sooner or later, lead a man to a grim and violent end.

IV

As football season gets underway, Minotaur Mania infects the entire city. Hundreds of avid fans line up outside the doors of the school to buy season tickets. The cafeteria staff names a series of gruesome dishes after the beloved quarterback— Minotaur Meatball Subs and Minotaur Meat Pies. Edmund, obligated to photograph these steaming piles of inedible mush, holds the plates aloft to better attract flies, which dive like fighter pilots and bounce off the grease-splattered glass partitions of the buffet.

On Friday afternoon, before the team begins its scrimmage, Edmund snaps several photos of a bare-chested Minotaur running laps and doing calisthenics. In the golden sunshine, the Minotaur's grotesquely defined pecs and abs glisten with sweat, the fibrous muscle tissue rippling like chain mail under his taut skin, the great dome of his shaved head shining like a gazing ball. The pictures seem almost pornographic in nature, homoerotic even, and Edmund makes sure that the Minotaur poses in such a way that his fingers appear to be grasping the mighty shaft of the bell tower in the background.

"If things don't work out with football," says the Minotaur during the interview, "if the agents don't come pounding on my door with endorsement deals, I'll just become an English teacher. That way I can coach high school football. Big money these days in high school football. Look at Coach Kaliher. Guy's gotta have, like, a hundred grand in the bank by now. Or I might study journalism, become a sports columnist. Like you, right? I can give readers an athlete's perspective of the game. There's money in that."

Edmund smiles but doesn't bother to explain that in the writing profession, if such a raffish activity can be considered a profession at all, money is nearly impossible to come by. Why *should* he explain any of this? What does the Minotaur know about the nuances of language? He has never read the great books, and while it is true that Edmund has never read most of them either, not from start to finish, he has made a concerted effort to *try* to read them—*Moby-Dick, Ulysses, Gravity's Rainbow*—monumental works of the human imagination that demand a mediator stand between them and the common reader, a self-appointed priesthood charged with interpreting the avalanche of words that make as much sense as certain passages from the gospels, Gnostic or canonical.

The Jesuits do not consider reading an especially spiritual exercise. They are practical men who believe all intellectual endeavors should have practical applications. Only geniuses, schizophrenics, and schismatics experience the numinous and transcendent while reading books. Ah, but the thrill of witnessing physical punishment on the holy ground of a football field can send true believers into fits of ecstasy. For this reason, the principal frequently asks students to get down on their knees and pray on the Minotaur's behalf.

Can the man be serious, Edmund wonders? Does he actually think the creator of the universe will answer such prayers? What the principal doesn't seem to understand is that prayer, like reading and writing, is a solitary pursuit. In his feature column, Edmund includes a passage from scripture: "But when you pray, go into your room, close the door and pray to your Father, who is unseen. Then your Father, who sees what is done in secret, will reward you."

His pen drips with special contempt for the Minotaur, who as the Jesuits continually like to point out, "is blessed with supernatural talent and ability." But herein lies a conundrum that Edmund is quick to expose. "Is talent really a *blessing*," he asks his readers, "a *supernatural* phenomenon bestowed upon the pious, the humble, the meek, by a compassionate God? Or is it a purely *natural* phenomenon, inherited from selfish, battle-hardened genes and exploited, often by the least worthy among us, to attain goals that are less than admirable? The Church seems to hold contradictory views on the subject."

The Jesuits express their consternation with this pabulum, particularly the garrulous principal, who suggests that with a little more Christian servility Edmund might one day be blessed with a special gift of his own: "From piety comes wisdom and from wisdom comes greatness."

Edmund bows his head and endures this tedious tongue-lashing, but he can detect a note of insincerity in the man's voice. Though he never tires of saying that everyone is equal in the eyes of God, the principal clearly favors some boys over others. After all, the principal would never dream of interrupting class to ask his flock to hold an all-night vigil for an aspiring writer, especially one like Edmund Campion, a humble child of God quietly toiling away in the shadows, forging a dangerous work of art that will expose the hypocrisies of this school and its antiquated priesthood.

<h1 style="text-align:center">V</h1>

Like a monk charged with the illumination of a manuscript, Edmund spends many lonely afternoons sequestered in the library, but despite his hard work and dedication he makes very little progress on his short story for *The Millstone*'s fiction contest, and when the deadline finally arrives, he is left with a pile of hastily revised drafts, each one worse than the one before. In fact, he has revised "The Lady Who Loved Lightning" so many times that it no longer makes much sense to him. Maybe like his vigorous jack-off sessions, it never made any sense to begin with, and yet a long time ago someone pondered the sad and ridiculous life of Onan and made even *that* a sin. Our most desperate attempts at distraction are said to be evil, and Edmund is surprised that the priests haven't yet condemned creative writing as self-abuse, the spilling of intellectual seed, the murder of a million sacred ideas.

In frustration he signs the smudged and crinkled manuscripts with a series of preposterous non de plumes—Pink E. Vintage, Kit Van Peeking, Kate E. Kingpin—but he knows that a serious and discerning editor like Batya Pinter will see through the ruse and recognize his distinctive style.

Oppressive thoughts of failure begin to weigh heavily on him, but he persists with this hopeless enterprise until he has a neatly typed final draft free of spelling and grammatical errors. While the mechanics are flawless, the story itself is trash, there can be no denying this. The prose is mannered, the symbols obvious—white doves, red roses, gently ringing chimes. The plot concerns a seventeen-year-old boy who over the course of the semester becomes so infatuated with his teacher that he boldly makes a pass at her. She resists his advances, but the principal, who happens to be snooping outside the classroom, sees the clumsy kiss, misinterprets the situation, and has the woman sacked.

Edmund tries to conquer his self-doubt by imagining a luminary like Nabokov submitting one of his own stories to a silly contest. Had he been a young man today, Nabokov would probably need to enroll in a creative writing seminar, forced to listen to the inane comments of his fellow students, those sensitive and easily offended part-time scribblers who complain without end that they don't *feel* the story, that it's well written, yes, but that it's still missing something, that it's nasty, malicious, hurtful, all under the direction of an indifferent instructor who pinches her chin and silently ponders her own successes and failures.

He wonders why any reasonable human being would want to write for a living, why anyone would do something so egregiously masochistic. He comes to the conclusion that, at least for those with an artistic temperament, life needs to be unnecessarily difficult and unpleasant; artists yearn for anguish, and when misery cannot be found, they simply invent anguish for themselves. It keeps things interesting. And that's a writer's main obligation to the reader, isn't it? To keep things interesting?

When the library closes at six o'clock, Edmund gathers up the pages and tries to prepare himself for his fate, but before he makes the arduous climb up the stairs to *The Millstone*'s office, he must first visit the Bunker to retrieve his camera, lenses, and several rolls of film. Tomorrow is the Holy War, the most important football game of the entire season, and he is responsible for chronicling the team's inevitable victory, a contest that will guarantee the Minotaur's status as a legendary sports figure.

When he descends into the subbasement, Edmond is relieved to discover that his friends have already cleared out for the night, presumably gone to their various parties. It's Halloween, he almost forgot, a night of mist and clouds, a night of black and gritty winds, a night when mischievous boys are transformed by the ripe breath of autumn into dumb, lumbering beasts, howling and leaping in anticipation of the moonrise. But Edmund, left alone in this dank, dripping pit to ponder his inferiority as a writer, feels that he has become a ghost—invisible, insubstantial, utterly insignificant.

VI

The offices of *The Millstone* are a honeycomb of six interconnected rooms, each one guarded by a set of gargoyle bookends squatting on cluttered shelves, their unblinking eyes scanning the stairway for any unworthies who dare enter that sanctum sanctorum. They are the devourers of uninspired tales, shitting them out in hard little pellets on the windowsills and leaving them to freeze against the frosted panes of glass. Edmund imagines the gargoyles fluttering down from these shelves late at night, creeping through the crackling maple leaves to whisper their secrets in the ears of those who have the gift to decipher their cryptic tongue and to transcribe it for readers who will then tremble at the power of their singular vision.

Hoping to slip his manuscript under the door and hurry away, Edmund reaches the landing and is surprised to see the door wide open. The walls dance with dappled blue moonlight that seems to blur the edges of things. He pauses. Behind a massive oak desk cluttered with dog-eared manuscripts sits Batya Pinter, a dark presence extracted from a beautiful body. She drinks one cup of tea after another, shaking her head, snickering, scowling, murmuring unholy things under her breath. In her hand she holds a red pen the way a butcher holds a serrated knife before a steaming carcass on a slaughterhouse floor, and she uses it with skill and precision to slash sentences and to scribble hostile comments in the margins. She tears out entire pages and feeds them to a shredder, conveniently located next to her chair.

Edmund backs away from the office, cringing every time the floorboards creak and echo through the desolate archways. He decides to leave the building without submitting his story. He cannot face his teacher, cannot in good conscience show her this insular schoolboy melodrama he has written, but when he hears the word "plagiarism" he is forced to stop and listen closely to the sibilant whispers inside. Batya Pinter, he realizes, is not alone. Beautiful women rarely are.

"There's no work on your part," she assures a figure standing just outside Edmund's line of vision. "None whatsoever. Just relax. Relax and enjoy."

"What if someone catches us?"

"No one visits this office. Least of all the Jesuits. It's six flights up."

"I don't know . . ."

"Trust me. Here, let me help you with that."

"I'm not so sure about this."

"You want to pass my class, don't you?"

"I guess so."

"Plagiarism is a serious offense, my boy, and you don't really expect me to believe that you've written this essay all by yourself, do you?"

"Oh, hell."

"Wait. Let me take it out. That's no *petseleh* you have there, *gunsel*."

"Huh?"

"Nothing, nothing."

"This won't take long, will it?"

"That's all *up* to you."

Batya Pinter laughs at her own pun, but she is so mesmerized by the monstrous thing pulsing before her that the laughter dies deep in her throat. She wheels her chair forward, positions her head, opens her mouth. The Minotaur steps forward, stamps his feet, grinds his pelvis against her puckered lips. His eyes roll back until they are white. He runs his fingers through her shining hair.

Shaking with outrage, feeling betrayed in a million different ways, Edmund gasps and staggers against the wall. His fingertips go numb, and he almost drops the pages of his manuscript to the floor. He forces himself to count backward from ten, takes a deep breath. He can easily imagine the awful things the Minotaur will do to him if he is caught. He turns to leave but then has a sudden flash of inspiration, an idea so vulgar, salacious, and unambiguously American that it cannot but change the course of his life. Suppressing his misery and heartache, Edmund opens the camera case, carefully loads the film, and attaches the telephoto lens.

The Minotaur gasps. "What the hell was *that*?"

But Batya Pinter can only gurgle, and choke, and try to reassure him with her bulging blue eyes. Her head never stops bobbing.

Edmund focuses the camera as best he can. It's a low-light situation—the pictures will be a little grainy, that's to be expected—but he has an unwavering faith in his abilities as a photojournalist. He may not be a great writer of fiction, but he can take a damn good picture, and he has just stumbled upon the story of the year, or at least the story of the week (stories rarely last much longer than that these days), a scene of complete and total depravity. It will almost certainly lead to an arrest, criminal charges, a drawn-out legal battle. The media jackals will salivate at this simple story of a scarlet woman who has robbed a vulnerable boy of his innocence and reduced a mighty empire to ashes.

Edmund smiles. Soon he will be the master, the person in total control of the situation, and it is he who will dictate the terms. The sensation of triumph is so alien to him that, for one terrible second, he feels nauseous, but he controls his stomach long enough to snap several pictures in quick succession, one after another until the inevitable, hideous finish.

VII

The Jesuits have their spies everywhere; this is something every student understands implicitly, and when Edmund races from the main building, he is hardly surprised to see a half dozen figures smoking cigarettes under a streetlamp like a cadre of secret police. In the dread silence they walk toward him, the entire staff of the school newspaper.

"Where have you been, Campion?" they ask.

"Up in Batya's belfry?"

"Tell us, has the bitch gone batty yet?"

"Were you busy reciting from your masturbatory magnum opus?"

"Drowning her in the roiling river of your powerful prose?"

"Plundering the putrid pink petals of Pinter's pussy?"

"Or is it purely platonic between you and the supreme priestess of poetry?"

As they unfurl their gaudy banners of alliteration, his friends snicker, but beneath the rush of words there is real venom.

"We've been observing you, Campion."

"You can't hide from us."

"We're the press, the paparazzi."

"We know what you've been up to."

"You lust for accolades and awards."

"And the favors of the quintessential literary slut."

Edmund turns away without answering them. He must escape this wicked labyrinth of hunger and ambition. As he passes the chapel he hears voices. The priests are holding their vigil for the football team. He wants to cast stones at the stained glass window of Jesus, who dares him to do it with His sweet mocking eyes. If it's true that God punishes talented people for their hubris, what does he do to the mediocrities of the world when they behave in the same way; how does he rectify their arrogance? But Edmund knows the answer to this, has always known. He has the uncanny sensation that the whole universe is just a thin sheet of paper, a delicate piece of parchment, and that at any moment it can be ripped apart, and everything—every word, every letter, every trace of meaning—will slip from the page and tumble into the void.

Things that now seem imperishable are no more real than some poorly told story composed in vanishing ink.

"Why do you look so pale!" his friends shout from a distance. "Guilt is written all over your face!"

Edmund opens the carrying case slung over his shoulder and examines the camera. Clutching his head, lurching along the slick cobblestones, he bemoans his nightmarish fate, that for the rest of his life his own unceasing stupidity will follow him around like a curse. He concedes defeat, and though his friends fail to understand the meaning of his words, he repeats them over and over again.

"The lens cap!" he cries. "The lens cap! It's still on the camera!"

Ghost Dance

❧

I

Unlike the other faculty members, Batya Pinter doesn't live in the city but in a cottage of timber and stone located at the end of a long stretch of gravel road far from the violent protrusion of the school's Gothic tower. Late at night, alone in her bed, her head pounding, her back still aching from her peripatetic strolls up and down the rows of desks, she leafs through the latest batch of term papers and drinks her medicinal tea. So far only one essay has captured her attention. The prose is more than merely refined; it's positively Nabokovian, and she finds herself laughing out loud at many passages. In the empty house, her soft sardonic laughter sounds a bit sinister, slightly loony. It can't be helped. She knows plagiarism when she sees it, twenty years as an educator have sharpened her powers of detection, but this student is so bold and so utterly contemptuous of her abilities that he has cited Claire Quilty and Vivian Darkbloom as his sources. At the bottom of the cover page, in big block letters, Batya gives the boy this ultimatum: "If you wish to pass my class, you must submit a new paper!" Here is the bait, the lure. Tomorrow there will be a reckoning.

She sets aside the essay and, before turning off the lights, forces herself to swallow the dregs from her third cup of tea. At what point, she wonders, does medicine become poison? When does it pull the fretful insomniac down a dark tunnel of sleep, dreamless and black as oblivion? She won't have to wait long. The stuff makes her lightheaded and a little queasy. Her breathing becomes shallow, her skin slick with sweat. Her body is in revolt. The bedroom walls slowly converge and seal her inside a tomb that alternately gleams with hoarfrost and glows with embers—cold and hot, hot and cold. She throws off the blankets and listens to the insistent scratch of branches against the windowpane, the faint rustle of dead leaves tumbling across the ground, the quavering howls of coyotes in the valley.

The coyotes—outsiders, interlopers—are foreign to these parts, and have trekked vast distances, some from the pine forests in the southern part of the state, others from the lonesome prairies further west. Now, as the moon crests the treetops, they bound up the steep slopes to spar under the gas lamps in the village square and to plunder the nearby farms, where they feast on abundant livestock—goats, alpacas, and bleating long-haired sheep. Police warn residents to keep their pets indoors after sundown, but their advice often goes unheeded. Little remains of the unfortunate Pomeranians and toy poodles. Along the edge of the sandpit lake the police find scattered bits of bone sucked of their marrow and hides so bloody and mangled that no one can identify them with any certainty. Trying to keep their burning guilt at bay, the owners lead their sniveling children into backyards where they place simple stone markers next to hastily dug graves. From the window of her den, Batya sometimes watches these rites, such as they are, but feels no sympathy for the mourners. What do they know of loss?

The coyotes are very close, but their infernal baying is abruptly silenced by the banshee shriek of a siren, the crack of a gunshot. Batya sits up, her hands shaking. She reaches for her tea but knocks the empty cup off the nightstand. It hits the hardwood floor without shattering. She leans forward, her mind suddenly clear, more focused than it has been in weeks. The hinges begin to squeak, and the bedroom door swings slowly open. She catches her breath, bunches the blankets in her fists. A spectral figure hovers at the threshold, filling the room with a smoldering lavender light.

Batya knows why he is here and can sense his deep displeasure. She *tries* to reason with him, tries to explain how she needs the heat and hunger of a young man, how she still aches for something tactile, raw, carnal. It has been over two years since that horrific day when she found him slumped over his desk in the den, and it's time he stop haunting her, let her get on with her life, but her husband remains unconvinced, incommunicative. His eyes are hooded with indifference, his injuries vast and eternal.

He floats into the room and lingers near the bed, the scene of so many crimes of passion, but he does not speak to her. In life he was always a stoic man whose passions were confined to and restricted by his compulsion for the most arcane books on botany. In this regard he hasn't changed much. Nothing, not even the boundless rewards of the sweet hereafter, can alter the monumental edifice of his brooding demeanor. Only the sad exterior remains—the stooped shoulders, the weak chin, the wrinkled houndstooth sport coat, the paisley bow tie, the black flannel slacks. He refused to wear the things she bought him in the city—cashmere sweaters, colorful dress shirts, mother-of-pearl cuff links—but if he had no sense of style, he certainly had no pretensions either. Few men were more genuine or more stubborn. She adored this about him; she also found it infuriating.

Overwhelmed by grief, she reaches out to embrace her husband, but before her fingertips can caress the angry wound where the bullet blasted through the right side of his skull, she feels him recoil from her touch. He places the teacup on the nightstand. Then without warning, without saying goodbye, without delivering some ominous portent, he vanishes into the moonlight, and once again Batya finds that she is stranded in this house, frustrated and alone. Where does he go when he leaves her? To some celestial theme park? To a fiendish pit of suffering? Or does he simply retreat to that cold mahogany box in the ground, his head still wrapped in cotton gauze? And why, she wonders, are the dead permitted to haunt the living and not the other way around?

But these mysteries do not trouble her too terribly because she has learned that to vanish, whether by slow degrees or all at once, in an instant, is the only enduring and natural fact of the world.

II

An hour before daybreak she pulls on her jeans, a fleece jacket, a sturdy pair of hiking boots that she laces up to her ankles. She grabs a full bottle of tea from the refrigerator and then takes out her husband's .38 revolver from a kitchen drawer. She glides her fingers along the handle of polished ivory. Made from the tusks of African elephants. Harvested by poachers of unimaginable cruelty. A gun of devastating political incorrectness.

With flashlight in hand and cigarette clamped between her teeth, she stumbles along the trail that she and her husband cleared with hatchet, rake, and hoe two summers ago. Now overgrown with giant hogweed and big clumps of bluestem flowers, the path winds between boulders glittering with quartz and curious glacial formations until it reaches the valley floor. Along the way, Batya traverses a narrow ledge of soft gray shale and walks beneath a precipitous wall of bog iron and jagged siltstone bejeweled with sea lilies and brachiopods and mysterious things yet to be named by the scientists who come here to excavate the great armored fish and razor-toothed leviathans, monsters imprisoned in these rocks for eons and all but erased from the memory of the world and the imagination of man.

After battling her way through the brush with her walking stick, Batya finds the partially uprooted stump of a sycamore where her husband carved their initials in careful Gothic script, the B and P of her name now beginning to fade, the letters almost indistinguishable from the whorls of wood. The massive tree that once stood here was an ancient one. The rings indicate that it was already two hundred years old when the Whittlesey Indians briefly settled in this valley in the seventeenth century. After walking around the stump three times, the magic number, Batya sits down, crushes out her cigarette, and uncorks the bottle of tea. Through the creaking limbs of oaks and elms she can make out Venus and Mars rising just before this Halloween dawn.

Across the river, in the rough grass at the edge of a meadow, a dozen eyes stare at her with curiosity and desperate hunger.

Batya turns the alien lance of light on them, but the coyotes do not scare easily. They stand their ground and paw at the dirt and clay. She recognizes them for what they really are, medicine men and shape-shifters, still reeling from their magic potions. After many centuries of exile they have returned to this spot to perform their sacred ghost dance.

When they lived here in this river valley, the Whittlesey would emerge from their wigwams after nightfall and form a sacred circle. To the accompaniment of drums, rattles, and flutes, the shamans would whirl before the evening fires and chant tales about the trickster Coyote: obsessed by his painfully engorged penis, Coyote devised clever schemes to penetrate the nubile and slick-skinned maidens who bathed in the beaver marsh or in the clear waters of the rushing river. Standing perfectly still in the swaying yellow reeds, he would wait for the maidens to float by and then suddenly pounce. Few girls evaded capture. Although he initially enjoyed numerous conquests, Coyote soon encountered trouble. For not everyone approved of his dalliances. Deep in the forest, there lived a lonely old crone who spent her days gathering wood and fetching water from the river. Though cursed with poor eyesight, the old woman had a keen sense of smell, and whenever she sensed Coyote lurking about, she clubbed him over the head with her cane of polished hickory. With a sharp cry of pain, Coyote jumped into the brambles and retreated to the safety of his small hollow. As he licked his wounds and pulled thorns from his backside he chuckled at the woman's brave spirit and planned a most malicious revenge. On a moonless evening, amidst the flutter of bats and the chirping of crickets, he sidled into the old woman's tent while she slept and, letting out a howl of unbridled merriment, slid between her withered legs. The next morning, the old woman awoke with a vaguely familiar sense of fulfillment. She laughed and sang, not unlike those beguiling maidens, and for many nights after this encounter, she left strangled hens and geese outside her tent, hoping these prizes might lure Coyote back to her bed. But he never returned. Indeed, he ignored her altogether, delighting in her solitude and desperate yearning, and in the years that followed, the woman faded away into bitter old age without ever again experiencing the pleasures of youth.

Batya knows the tale well, a fragment of a much larger storytelling tradition that by some miracle survived the expurgation of the Jesuit missionaries who conquered this land for Christendom. Legend has it that in the early seventeenth century the Pope's foot soldiers, bearing shields emblazoned with gold crosses, battled their way through the unaxed wilderness to this very spot, but the Indian holy men, by drinking magic tea and transforming themselves into various woodland creatures, managed to evade capture, conversion, slavery, and death. Mesmerized by the sound of the river, Batya daydreams of such liberation—to dissolve into a green vapor, to metamorphose into a black rat snake, a red-tailed hawk, a fat waddling opossum . . .

Above the rim of the valley, a thin band of steely October light stretches across the eastern horizon and turns the leaden clouds into hazy pink ribbons that look like chalk gently smeared on a blackboard. She finishes the last of her tea, but before making the arduous climb back to her house, she draws the .38 from her pocket. She unlatches the safety, lifts the gun above her head, and fires once into the air. Across the river, still watching her from the meadow, the crafty coyotes yelp and bolt into the woods.

III

In a halfhearted attempt to get her head straight before leaving for work, she stands in the shower under a spray of scalding water until her fingertips prune and her skin turns red, then she changes into the most conservative ensemble she owns—a sleeveless ruched top, wool pencil skirt, gray blazer, maroon silk scarf. The priests do not approve. They frown as she marches through the halls in her platform shoes, but she is a committed teacher, a brilliant and ambitious editor of the school literary magazine, and they pity her, the disconsolate, childless widow, but this at least puts them on equal footing since she pities them, too, especially when she catches them lingering in the doorways, their eyes moving dreamily across her plentiful breasts.

At seven o'clock, she drives to school. Already the bisecting contrails of a hundred jets obscure the sky like the crisscrossing telephone cables and the tangled grid of electric lines suspended above the neighborhood streets, corralling her within this gilded pen like some mindless beast of burden and inspiring her, as it does every morning with ritualistic inevitability, to light her first official cigarette of the day. She inhales a gratifying lungful of smoke, the one and only drag that tastes any damned good, the rest merely a form of habit and imprisonment like much else in life. The idea of ritual pleases her, however, because it suggests something communal—an agreed-upon set of beliefs, values, collective grievances—and it gives her great comfort to know that all across the country, thousands of addicts are simultaneously taking that first puff with a fanaticism that is, if not exactly religious, then certainly sacramental.

For nearly thirty minutes, she sits in the faculty parking

lot with the engine idling and wonders if the exhaust pouring from the broken tailpipe might kill her once and for all, making quick work of what the cigarettes will take another decade or more to do. Scanning the plaza to see if anyone is observing her and feeling not unlike the *femme fatale* in the final scene of a film noir, she removes the .38 from the glove compartment. A fine weapon. Short recoil. Good accuracy. The Jesuits would be aghast if they knew of it, but Batya has a prepared response should they discover her secret. This neighborhood is a dangerous one, the streets are teeming with lunatics, and at the beginning of the semester she wrote a letter to the editor, arguing that teachers should have the right to carry a side arm into the classroom. Full-time faculty only, of course. Substitutes are clearly too inept, not to be trusted. When they read her op-ed, the priests laughed at her candor, thought she was joking. A splendid work of social satire! No one took her seriously.

She checks her watch. Almost time. She flicks the smoldering butt out the window and places the pistol in her purse. For a moment, she stands in the parking lot, breathing the noxious air. The blast furnaces of the nearby steel mill taint the city with ammonia and coke dust. She looks up. A flock of ugly blackbirds, common grackles, slide feverishly between the telephone lines and, before disappearing into the yellow sky, drop their heavy white payloads on the hood of her car. With fury and revulsion, she stares after them but somehow stops herself from taking aim and firing.

IV

It's just a short walk to the main building.

With its pointed arches and sandstone sculptures depicting the Devil tempting a group of foolish virgins, the building looks not unlike a cathedral, smells of incense and candle wax and cigarettes, echoes with the imagined sounds of vows yet to be broken. Batya bounds up the creaking stairs two at a time to her office on the sixth floor. Because most of its windows face west, the nicotine-sodden hallway is encased in an umber gloom, and she fumbles against the wall until she finds a light switch. The sound of a hundred fluorescent bulbs buzz like things alive, agitated, angry, seconds away from showering her in white dust that stings and burns, choking her with a cloud of argon and mercury. Someone once told her that florescent lights cause certain people to have seizures. Saint Paul, they say, was afflicted with seizures ever since witnessing the blinding light while on the road to Damascus. Funny that God would prefer fluorescent lights to some other, but then God torments his slaves in the unlikeliest ways.

She, for instance, is burdened by the spectacle of dozens—maybe an even hundred, who knows, she never bothers to count them—World War II army soldiers, plastic men in green fatigues lobbing grenades, firing howitzers, hoisting bazookas on their shoulders. Some crawl on their bellies, others shout into walkie-talkies. All are assembled in a wide arc around her door so that she is forced to tiptoe between them like Gulliver among a maniacal horde of Lilliputians. They look as though they might storm her office, pillage her shelves, pin her to the wall, and one by one commit heinous acts upon her before filling her torso with a million rounds of tiny ammunition.

She has never been the victim of a prank, not on a scale like this, and she feels unsettled by its sick immaturity. Perhaps she has made the mistake of being too political in class, of having said some disparaging things about war, the ridiculous myth of manifest destiny, upsetting the more unendurably ideological and reactionary students. "Mind you," she tells them as they shift restlessly in their chairs, "I've always considered myself a true patriot." The sincerity of this statement is not to be questioned. There is the gun after all—can anything be more American than that?—and she has a permit to carry it, even to conceal it on her person. To her the law still means something, even if it doesn't to the delinquents who straggle into her classroom each semester. She is also a staunch believer in self-reliance and cringes at the idea of calling campus security, that bumbling band of retired patrolmen better suited to writing parking tickets than dealing with an unstable and potentially dangerous seventeen-year-old stalker.

With a broom and dustpan, she sweeps up the army figures, tosses them into a trashcan, then locks her office door. After adjusting the mirror that hangs on the wall behind her desk, she begins her regiment of facial exercises. She smiles, frowns, pulls the skin taught against her cheekbones. She tries to ignore the faint lines at the corners of her eyes and the way her makeup seems to accentuate rather than camouflage her age. In the soft light, she still looks almost youthful, certainly younger than her forty-three years, but there is no way to disguise the roughness of her sun-damaged hands, the flat brown patches, the veins and tendons that stand out through the thin skin. She applies another daub of lotion and works it vigorously over her fingers and wrists.

Today she is determined to look her best for the confrontation that has now reached a boiling point.

V

"Good day, gentlemen!"

Rarely does she greet her class with such mawkish enthu-

siasm. Usually she snaps terse commands ("You will now turn
to page 101 of your text!"); this has always been her way, and
the more diligent students, the handful of overachievers, the
ones with an instinct to sense trouble, hide behind their books
as if for protection. A few of them ogle her with smoldering
lust, their bodies steamy fumaroles oozing musk and sweat.
They dream of a torrid love affair that ends in madness and
death. Most of the boys, however, are crass and guileless. They
take no interest in her at all. With folded arms, they sit at their
desks, their chins drooping, their eyes puffy and crusted over
with sleep. Among the latter is the culprit, the plagiarist. He
slouches low in his seat, yawns, sighs, snorts with derision. His
boredom she can understand. It's his lack of respect that she
finds so irritating.

"I finished reading your essays last night, gentlemen. The
majority were adequate. Others were quite disappointing . . .
to say the least."

She shoves the paper at the culprit and searches his eyes for
that defiant glimmer of the psychotic, a quick flash of seething
fury, a glimpse of the wild animal that thrashes around inside
his skull and yearns to feast on her bones. They call him the
Minotaur, and for good reason. His shoulders are enormous,
monstrous really. Too much time pumping iron at the gym,
not enough time studying at his desk. A child with no pri-
orities and overactive genitals. She has watched him from the
bleachers, has seen the carnage he leaves behind on the football field, has heard the shocking screams from his opponents
as they are trampled under his powerful legs. Now she waits
for him to grab her by the throat, strangle her, toss her body
beneath the floorboards, brick her up inside a wall. No, he
isn't so imaginative as that. When it comes to death, Ameri-

cans prefer their guns. Guns are simple. A quick bullet to the head, and it's all over. People have no sense of the romantic anymore, a flair for the exquisite details of murder.

After handing back the essays she begins her normal routine, pacing up and down the rows, reciting a long passage of antiseptic prose from a composition textbook. Though it has taken her many months, she has finally learned to accept the dreariness of the new curriculum. The Jesuits, after much "soul searching," as they described it, have decided that because the majority of their students are primarily, and often exclusively, destined for the worlds of business and law (or, with God's grace, the clergy), there is no need for them to "analyze Shakespeare's Seven Ages of Man monologue. Our students require *practical* writing classes, a refresher course on grammar and mechanics. You understand. The poetry of Emily Dickinson and Elizabeth Barrett Browning seems a bit . . . superfluous."

Yes, she understands. Remediation is what they need. Instead of teaching the great books, she finds herself analyzing the hastily written essays and editorials of partisan hacks. It makes no difference to her anymore. She isn't naïve enough to think she can cure these prep school boys of their indolence by injecting them with a douse of intellectual curiosity. School has cretinized these boys. They are immune to learning. Regardless of the topic, most students pay no attention to what she has to say. Their intellects have shriveled and turned to dust, like dog feces baking on the pavement under a blinding white sun. Their interest in academics extends no further than seeking new ways to cheat on exams and essays.

As the hour comes to an end, the students grab their bags and scramble into the hallway, relieved to survive another excruciating hour with Batya Pinter. But she won't allow the culprit to leave, no, not before she lustily chastises him.

"Mr. McSweeney!"

The Minotaur sighs. He lifts his hands, feigning innocence, and with a swagger approaches her.

"I trust you read my comments?"

He nods.

"I'll give you until six o'clock to submit a new paper."

He shakes his head. "I can't have it done by six o'clock."

"Then I suggest you enroll again in this class next semester. At this point, you cannot possibly pass."

"Give me until Monday, okay?"

"No, that won't do."

"You don't understand. The big game is tomorrow night—"

She crosses her arms. "Mr. McSweeney, when *I* was in high school, we had a thing called standards. *My* teachers weren't so accommodating, especially with students caught *cheating* on their term papers. No, I had to submit my own work, and in a timely fashion, or face harsh disciplinary action. Plagiarism, as I'm sure you know, is the worst kind of crime. Expulsion is not out of the question."

Why is she boring him with this? She's starting to sound like a stern headmistress, rattling off a string of clichés. There was a time, and not so long ago either, when just by sitting at the corner of her desk, crossing her legs, adjusting the hem of her skirt, lowering her voice, and batting her eyes in a certain way, she could manipulate a boy like Frank McSweeney and make him do almost anything she wanted.

"But I can't lose my scholarship . . ." His voice cracks a little, betraying his cool exterior.

"Then do as I say, and bring your essay to my office. To-night. After school. You have until six o'clock. No later. It may surprise you to learn that I have a life outside of this class-room."

"But I have to study the playbook and—"

"That's my final offer, Mr. McSweeney. Well?"

As he leaves the room and walks through the long tunnel of pale blue light, he seems to shudder. This boy doesn't see deeply enough into life to understand that she is still a force to be reckoned with. To him, aging is a myth and beauty eternal. He will never wear on his handsome face the hardened scowl of defeat and resignation that he sees on the faces of so many other men. For the young, there is no future, just as there is no past. How easily they shed their memories, these boys, like snakes shedding their skins, but life soon leaves an awful and indelible mark, and experience is the most uncompromising teacher of them all.

VI

Rather than visit the teachers' lounge at the end of the day, Batya Pinter retreats to the gray silence of her office on the sixth floor, where she stands at a window overlooking the city's scarred industrial valley. There, sitting on the dusty sill, she drinks her tea, smokes a cigarette, and watches the ghostly flames dance atop the tall vent stacks of the steel mills. Fire singes the sky, turning the low gray clouds black with ash.

Ever since taking this position at the Jesuit school, Batya has generally shunned the company of her colleagues. There are invitations, of course, to parties, to gallery openings, to the symphony, but she has no real desire to socialize with her fel-low teachers at the quaint coffeehouse crowded with eccentric poets from the old neighborhood. Orchestral music, especially the unceasing bombast of Wagner, makes her nauseous, and Impressionist seascapes with small purple men in wooden dinghies bobbing along on rough brushstrokes of thick vermillion bore her to death, as do those ancient Greek serving bowls with unexpurgated depictions of pederasty between sinewy boys glistening with oil and their erect wrestling coaches wearing only lecherous coyote grins.

Most conversation she finds tedious, especially since the small talk these days centers around which aging faculty members have been whisked away to the clinic because Death has dropped by for an unexpected visit, perhaps not with glimmering scythe and hooded robe, no, but with a sly "Boo!"—just enough to put the fear of God into them, make them sink to the floor with a minor stroke, leaving them with a noticeable slump to their shoulders, an angry downward scowl to their mouths. To everyone's relief, the clinic employs a battalion of overpaid and self-important quacks who know their trade just well enough to keep Death temporarily at bay, oblivious to the fact that Death will wait good-naturedly for the inevitable, silently paring his talons and stoking the fires of hell in preparation for the multitudes who have failed to seek redemption before the final hour.

Perhaps by harping on the ubiquitous nature of suffering and loss, the Jesuits hope to alleviate the anguish she has experienced these past two years, but if they fail to cheer her up, it's because beneath their gentle words of consolation, they secretly despise her and feel that some form of cosmic punishment has been meted out. But how can she begrudge them for having these feelings? Batya is an alien among them, a stranger, an exotic creature from an ancient bloodline, and she has, at least so far, proven herself completely immune to their priestcraft and medieval scholasticism. They are forever talking of the mysterious workings of God, but to these men, God isn't a mystery at all. God they can explain with the greatest confidence, and they often wax poetic about what happens to a person after death. It's *life* that perplexes them; it's life that they cannot explain. "Only through divine revelation," they say, "can humanity hope to comprehend this vale of tears."

The irony doesn't escape Batya. All religious experience, she believes, is a matter of concealment, not revelation, and faith is merely a metaphysical game of self-deception, a way to disguise deep-rooted fears and weaknesses.

VII

At precisely six o'clock, there comes a hesitant knock. The hulking monochromatic form of Frank "The Minotaur" Mc-Sweeney fills the doorway. He steps into the light, looking a bit disheveled, out of breath, his shirt clinging to his back and bulging biceps. He holds the essay out to her.

"Please," she says, "come inside. You look parched. Would you like anything to drink? Some tea perhaps?"

Her voice trembles when she asks the last question. She doesn't want to know how ridiculous she looks right now and is careful to avoid passing in front of the mirror. In the top desk drawer, she finds two dirty mugs and the essential bottle, all prelude to the ritual men and women have been performing through the ages. Only the gun is new to this otherwise ancient rite. Not that she needs it, of course, but these days one can never be too sure. She strokes the handle and closes the drawer before he can see it.

The boy comes into the office, a bit reluctantly, and stands near her desk. He fidgets with his hands, doesn't seem to know what to do with them.

"The great books tell us that intoxicants are beneficial to the soul. They have transformative powers. Nectar of the gods, manna from heaven, nepenthe, opium." Batya pours him some tea and points out the window. "A long time ago, before the white man came and built his dark satanic mills, Indian tribes lived in this valley, and they brewed a tea made from a plant whose scientific name is *Pedicularis densiflora*. It's not actually a plant at all but a parasite that attaches to the roots of other plants. The Indians claimed it had magical properties and could turn men into birds and coyotes. During our hikes in the valley, my late husband and I occasionally came across a few specimens growing at the river's edge. We made batches of the tea. It's absolutely sublime. Excellent for one's spirit and stamina."

"Oh, yeah? That's kind of cool."

He's not really paying attention to her, she can tell. Trying to restrain her anger, she pushes a mug across the desk toward him. He lowers his nose and sniffs it like a dog. Eventually he picks up the mug and drinks the tea, and she watches to make sure he swallows it all down, a good little boy taking his medicine.

"My husband was a botanist. He taught at the university for fifteen years. A brilliant man. Misunderstood, maybe. The students never much cared for him. Most had their eye on the professor's wife, I think." She laughs.

The boy glances at the clock on her desk. "There's this party tonight. I sorta have to be there . . ."

"Oh, then we better drink our tea quickly. I have a party to attend as well. It's Halloween, isn't it? I nearly forgot."

After only one cup, the boy's pupils are big and bright, like shiny, black marbles wobbling around a concrete bowl. She pours him another cup. This time he gulps it down, and Batya is startled by his rapid transformation. Suddenly the boy won't shut up. He leans against her desk, tells her all about his cowardly father and his overprotective mother, both of them completely oblivious to the fact that their son wants to do something unique with his life. "They think I'm a dumb jock. But I'd like to become a writer one day, a real Renaissance man. Maybe I can study journalism, work as a sports columnist, give people an athlete's perspective of the game."

Batya pretends to be interested. She nods her head at all the right places and pats his knee. This is the part of the charade she hates most, listening to yet another chronicle of wasted time and playing shrink to these misfits who vomit up all of their inconsequential problems and yearn for someone to dissect their souls, unraveling the tangled threads of character and conflict, one from the other until their lives are a heap of nonsense piled on the floor at her feet, words without greater context, bled of their significance. At moments like this, Batya truly misses the tactics of a more experienced man—naughty movies flickering on the television screen, lubes, gels, battery-operated toys. Cheap and tawdry, that's how she likes it. Dirty. Vile even. Deviance turns her on; it always has. Of late, the men she has been involved with are excruciatingly polite, overly cautious, terrified of life. Too much like her husband. The Jesuits have yet to hire a fallen theologian or a mad scientist who yearns to conduct radical and lascivious experiments on a middle-aged female subject.

She is running out of patience. The boy is just *standing there*, blabbering on and on about nothing at all, another amateur of intimacy unwilling to make the first move. It isn't natural for a seventeen-year-old to be so timid. But why should this surprise her? Most of these schoolboys are a little too tidy, too polished, their lips too prissy, their hands too dainty, their eyes brimming with too much vulnerability. Despite their claims to be otherwise, she suspects they are not sexual absolutists. Even the most heterosexual man is capable of buggery, and she often wonders how many of her students are closeted homosexuals.

Batya decides it's high time to take matters into her own hands. She must either face the brutal emptiness of another lonely night or seek consolation in the unlikely companionship of her pupil. For her the choice is an easy one. Celibacy has never been a realistic option. Emboldened by the tea, she finds that she is willing to live with the consequences of her actions. She brushes up against the boy's legs. He doesn't withdraw from her touch, and this she takes as a good sign. She touches him with her fingertips, then begins to massage him through his pants. Without stammering or turning his eyes away, he presses up against her hand, another good sign, and lets her unbuckle his belt. She sits in the chair and pulls down his zipper.

"There's no work on your part," she assures him. "None whatsoever. Just relax. Relax and enjoy."

"What if someone catches us?"

"No one visits my office. Least of all the Jesuits. It's six flights up."

"I don't know . . ."

"Trust me. Here, let me help you with that."

"I'm not so sure about this."

"You want to pass my class, don't you?"

"I guess so."

"Plagiarism is a serious offense, my boy, and you don't really expect me to believe that you've written this essay all by yourself, do you?" She can barely hear herself speak the words, her heart is racing so fast now.

"Oh, hell."

"Wait. Let me take it out. That's no *petseleh* you have there, *gunsel*."

"Huh?"

"Nothing, nothing."

"This won't take long, will it?"

"That's all *up* to you."

She marvels at his size. It's like a king cobra charmed from its basket with a few erotic licks on a flute. Initially, he is nervous, wooden, almost cadaverous. With the exception of the rigor mortis that sets in below his waist, the boy remains motionless, his hips frozen, his legs shackled by the pants around his ankles. Even his face has a look of mute absence.

"What the hell was *that*?" the Minotaur croaks.

But she is too consumed in her work to notice anything at all. After arousing him, she opens her blouse and lets him have a look at those things the sculptors, painters, and poets have either avoided or ignored altogether.

As the first beams of moonlight filter through the window, the boy becomes aggressive. He hoists her effortlessly from the chair and tosses her onto the desktop with more force than she would like. Flashing a crazed grin and with a mouth ravenous and eager and almost dangerous with its snapping jaws and gnashing teeth, he lifts her skirt and starts tasting every inch of her, his wet tongue lapping at her navel and thighs and perineum, that patch of no-man's-land her squeamish husband called the Devil's Half Acre. He turns her around, stretches her across the desk so that her legs are splayed. She shudders with gratitude and remorse, caught up in the thrill and pandemonium of his unrelenting punishment.

"Oh, hurt me!" she cries. "*Hurt* me!"

As they both near climax, he tarnishes things by shouting out her first name. Despite the intimacy of this encounter she prefers to be addressed in a formal manner, and after he is finished, and they both collapse panting on the desk, she makes a point of correcting him on this matter in a voice that is at once breathless and stern.

VIII

A man's presence often lingers long after he is gone, and sometimes it is best to erase all evidence of him. She intends to feed the boy's essay to the shredder the moment he leaves her office. Even to use it as kindling would be taboo. She studies his face and finds that he looks not unlike those clean-cut college boys who used to enroll in her husband's botany courses, but then again all of these young men look alike—the same simian forehead sprinkled with acne, the same unintelligent eyes that cast a hubristic gaze over the world. Uncouth children who snort and cough and scratch themselves and unleash pestilential clouds of stale breath. But ghosts of the living as well as the dead haunt the imagination, so it's only natural that she sees her former lovers everywhere she turns.

At least this boy has enough sense to pull up his pants and start making excuses.

"The party . . ." he murmurs.

"Yes," she says, "I must be going, too. People are expecting me."

He slinks toward the door, but instead of hurrying away, he stops at the threshold, his shirt untucked, his belt dangling between his legs, his rosy red cheeks suddenly drained of color. He looks back at her, terror in his eyes. Something is out there, something that frightens him. Her husband's ghost? Has he followed her here? Has he been watching the entire time? The boy steps into the hallway, stumbles over his own feet, and presses his back against the wall as though afraid of falling into a black pit. Letting out a little bleat of alarm, he dashes down the stairs.

Batya laughs. Fully aware that she's been ensnared in some kind of trap, she checks her makeup in the mirror, the mascara, the royal-blue eyeliner. She buttons her blouse, straightens her skirt. No need to rush. It's not quite eight o'clock, still time for a little more tea. Drinking straight from the bottle, she stands at the window and looks out over the quad. Several boys stagger like zombies, arms outstretched, clothes in tatters, faces painted goblin green. Others are dressed as priests and grand inquisitors. A solitary figure with a mangy tail and pointed ears comes bounding across the jumbled cobblestones and howls up at the gothic tower. Off to their drunken masquerades, no doubt. Buffoons, one and all, with no sense of decorum. She finds it puzzling that the Jesuits tolerate this sort of mischief. Don't most clergymen regard Halloween as an abomination, a mockery of their most cherished beliefs?

She puts the bottle down on her desk and from the drawer retrieves the .38. Only then does she walk to the door. What she finds there makes her smile. In fact, she is so impressed by the menacing stagecraft that she wants to applaud and shout, "Author! Author!"

Like an infestation of scuttling green bugs, the plastic soldiers swarm the hallway outside her office, a hundred battle-hardened men, wounded, scarred, disfigured, their bodies weighed down by heavy belts of ammunition, their eyes fixed on a distant point in space. They have been sent here on a secret mission and are determined to achieve their objective. But what exactly *is* the objective? To hunt down and exterminate the ravenous cougar that prowls these corridors at night and feasts on innocent boys? Since the Church can no longer use coercion as a tool, it must rely on intimidation. It's just as well. After all, it is not violence but the threat of violence that has proven so effective the world over. People are driven by fear and self-preservation, and powerful men know how to exploit this weakness to achieve their own wicked ends. But Batya refuses to be guided by these base emotions.

Though her husband left behind no note to explain or justify his actions, he did leave her this fine gun, and she puts the steel barrel to her head now. She has contemplated squeezing the trigger many times before, and never once has she experienced even a fleeting moment of mortal terror. In this regard, the gun has been very instructive, a pedagogical tool unmatched by any textbook; it's a way to test her willpower, her soundness of mind.

She counts backward from ten and then lowers the barrel. The test complete, she puts the .38 in her purse and grabs the broom and dustpan. This has become standard procedure for her, sweeping up these toy soldiers, and after she dumps them in the trashcan, she turns off the lights and leaves her office for one more day.

The Distinguished Precipice

I

On the afternoon of his eighteenth birthday, Tom Wentworth is summoned to the principal's office, where there awaits a quorum of priests, eleven in all, faded men in high-backed chairs whose arthritic fingers fumble with the books of matches piled high in ashtrays stationed at every corner of the room like bowls of holy water at the entranceway to the school chapel. The office is a precise space—tidy, carefully curated, scrupulously scrubbed and polished—and the priests sit hunched and pensive in the tapering shafts of prismatic light like stone icons, their eyes fixed not on the door but on the branches of the ancient elms and sycamores that scratch at the windowpanes like shunned souls contending with one another to claw their way into Paradise.

Whether from advanced age or the bitter cold, or maybe because they simply haven't bothered to wear their dentures to this meeting, the men look gaunt, hollow, their faces taking on an appearance of concavity not unlike the pumpkins left to rot on the front porch stoops of the crumbling, clapboard shanties that crowd the narrow brick lanes of the blighted neighborhood. In subdued tones, they make oblique references to their colleague, the twelfth member of their group, a man who seemed touched by grace, impervious to the gradual winding down of all things, but who for the past month has been confined to his sickbed, stricken with the final stages of an irreversible disease, his withered limbs cruelly mimicking the degeneration of a mind once considered legendary in the school's storied history.

"We don't expect him to see the first rains of spring."

"And yet he continues to defy the odds."

"A most unusual case."

"Such suffering."

"If God would only call him home."

"Perhaps new measures should be considered?"

"Under certain circumstances, gentlemen, the tomb can be a most inviting place."

Their thoughts teeter dangerously close to perdition, their proposals and conjectures taking on frightful forms, and a few of the men breathe a sigh of relief when Tom Wentworth appears at the threshold and raps gently on the door.

"Please," says the principal, "come in."

The boy stands at attention in the center of the room, his head bowed, his hands clasped together behind his back like some captive New World heathen brought before a tribunal of inquisitors. The priests take long, contemplative puffs on their cigarettes, cautious sips of their artificially sweetened coffee.

The principal indicates the empty chair. "Take a seat."

Tom obeys, but reluctantly, as if afraid the chair might be covered in a bed of red-hot nails.

"I assume you know why we have called you here today?"

"No, sir."

Tom crosses his legs, uncrosses them, squirms, stares at

the tips of his shoes. A nervous boy, powerless and without recourse. This is as it should be. Part of the natural order.

"Then let me remind you," says the principal, leaning forward. "You didn't pass your science exam last term, and in order to graduate with the rest of your class, you will need to do some kind of . . . additional work."

Though entirely capable of making stern pronouncements, the principal can also address his charges in an oddly solicitous manner, and this is the way he speaks to Tom now, his elocution flawless as ever, the greatest of orators—golden-mouthed, honey-tongued, as is frequently noted by the multitudes of mothers, who along with their loyal husbands and dutiful sons, listen to him each Sunday morning and become so enraptured by the powerful thrust of his arguments, the vatic amplitude of his sermons, the exhilarating descriptions of how they will burn in the lake of fire for all eternity, that they shudder and sigh and then rush to his confessional after Mass, eager to reveal every scandalous detail of their private lives.

"This matter requires a quick resolution," the principal continues. Blue cigarette smoke spills from his lips, looping and coiling into helixes of meaning. "We know you're clever, very bright indeed, and we want you to succeed, want you to distinguish yourself in some important way. So this is our proposal to you." He shifts his eyes toward his colleagues. "We'd like you to visit a . . . *tutor* who, after a sufficient amount of time, will . . ." again, a slight shift of his eyes ". . . *test* your ability to analyze and interpret the hypotheses of the doctors of the Church."

Tom flinches. "Doctors, sir?"

"Well, yes. Anselm, Aquinas, Augustine. Start with the A's."

The priests offer Tom their jack-o-lantern grins and in faint, parched whistles give him their consent—"Trenchant advice, a most excellent idea, very sensible, quite expedient"— even though a number of them have serious misgivings, believe Tom too incompetent to serve his dark purpose. Privately they wonder why the principal doesn't ask the boy to clean out his locker and leave the premises once and for all or send him to a remote outpost in the mountains to do missionary work. The principal, perhaps, is more sympathetic to the boy's plight.

"We have given your situation a great deal of thought," he continues, "and we are all confident—aren't we, gentlemen?— that you will fulfill your obligation."

No one says a word, and the silence is so ponderous that it seems to change the shape of things, makes the tables and chairs buckle under its immense weight. But then there is a single, drawn-out, high-pitched squeak like the sustained, wavering note of a toy trumpet, and Tom's grim invigilators suddenly blush like schoolboys, clear their throats, brush lint from their lapels, pretend to notice something interesting outside. The principal waves his hand, though whether to dismiss his charge or to disperse the foul gases seeping silently into the room is unclear.

Tom stands up and thanks the priests for their time, but he remains skeptical of these men and their intentions, and he worries that despite their debilitating age, they might spring from their chairs with miraculous agility and pelt him with stones. Never daring to turn his back to them, he moves toward the door. He is careful not to hurry or to make any unusual gestures, but at the last possible moment, when he is certain the old men are no longer watching him, Tom shoots a hand toward an ashtray and slips a pack of matches into his pocket. Only then does he turn to go.

"Wentworth!"

Tom pauses in the doorway, and for the first time since entering the office, he makes direct eye contact with the principal, gives him the slightest hint of a smile, a puzzling sort of grin, greased at the corners, his lips sliding from humility to treachery. The principal dabs his forehead with a handkerchief, takes a vigorous drag on a cigarette that, over the course of the meeting, has become a flimsy stick of ash hanging from his lower lip.

"You hover on the edge of a precipice, young man," he warns.

"I understand," says Tom. "Thank you for giving me this opportunity. You won't be disappointed. I promise."

II

Eighteen, everyone will surely agree, is a difficult age, and some of the boys, the more reckless among them, gather in the alley before classes begin to gulp vodka and orange juice, wincing like small children forced to swallow bitter and gelatinous medicine, but Tom doesn't join them; he isn't a troublemaker, not in the usual sense of the word. He never comes to class drunk or high like so many of his classmates, though he once tried marijuana at the homecoming dance, only to find that it gave him an inexplicable urge to eat an entire bowl of stale pretzels with machine-like precision while the other kids looked on and laughed. He never smirks at his teachers in a way that suggests he is somehow superior to them, though in truth some do suffer from low morale and feel trapped in the intellectual purgatory of a high school classroom, doomed to repeat the same insipid lesson plans over and over again.

By most accounts, Tom is docile, timid, pathetic even. He sits alone in a far corner of the cafeteria, where he sips hot chocolate (the Jesuits forbid the sale of coffee) and plays a game of solitaire with a deck of worn and spindled cards. He practices sleight of hand, too, palming and levitating and crimping cards, hobbies that seem innocent enough, so long as he doesn't encourage the other boys to gamble. Too many have a fondness for poker and blackjack. The priests, had they bothered to look a little more closely, would have been shocked by the lewd images on the back of the cards, naked women contorting their bodies into improbable tantric positions. But no one bothers to check. No one wants to get that close to him.

Tom always looks a mess, his shirts stained with the remnants of a hasty lunch—a smattering of pizza sauce, a bright slash of mustard, a dark dollop of chili—and when he slinks through the hallways between classes, he seems almost to encourage the taunts of his fellow students, the callous ones, the trust fund kids. They jeer at his incredible bell-bottom pants rescued from the forgotten racks in resale shops, his knitted ties unearthed from moldering cardboard boxes at garage sales, his wool scarves, fedoras, and cowboy boots, a schizophrenic collection of old and new, a hodgepodge of different decades, regions, sensibilities. "He could pass for a bohemian," his teachers quip, "if he wasn't so damn crazy."

Maybe an understanding and patient woman could have been of some assistance here, a fussy schoolmarm to demand that he brush his teeth, comb his wild mop of hair, and wear a pair of matching socks, but there are no women in his life, no doddering old aunts or devoted girlfriends. His mother is no longer in the picture. She slipped away in the middle of the night three years ago. Bipolar, they say. An abuser of drugs and alcohol, if the rumors are true. There have been sightings—a ragged figure wandering the streets during the day and sleeping in the park at night—but Tom's father seems almost relieved that she is gone and can embarrass the family no further. He is a longtime faculty member, a science teacher who earns a very modest salary, barely a living wage, if the priests wish to be honest about it.

Because of their difficult financial situation, Tom is compelled to take a job as a janitorial assistant at the nursing home down the street. This puts a little money in his pocket, but rather than spend his checks on new clothes and school supplies, he resorts to rummaging through garbage cans after class, looking for pencils worn down to chewed, yellow stubs and tearing out blank pages from notebooks used by his classmates to draw cruel caricatures of their teachers.

The Jesuits understand the many hardships Tom faces—how can they not; they've taken vows of poverty—so if they pity him, it isn't because of the missing buttons on his winter coat or the dangling threads on the cuffs of his shirts; rather, it's because of a shocking incident that occurred several months ago that left them wondering if their rigorous curriculum and strict code of conduct played more than superficial roles in what the principal calls the boy's "spiritual crisis."

Initially, his father wanted to remove him from school altogether, admit him to a psychiatric ward, let a team of doctors that specialize in emotional disorders poke and prod at their young patient, draw blood, take urine and stool samples, scribble clinical jargon on his chart, pump him full of mood-altering drugs—modern science has so many curious treatments these days—but the Jesuits frowned upon this idea. Physicians tend to be materialists, no better than mechanics tinkering with the engine of a car. The priests, on the other hand, understand that the body is merely a vehicle for conveying a soul, and they have long considered themselves experts in the cure of any soul that is damaged, diseased, broken, benightmared.

The incident in question took place during biology class on a blustery Saint Patrick's Day last March. The instructor, Father Loomis, should have responded more quickly, but he was an elderly fellow whose eyesight and hearing, not to mention lucidity, had been in steep decline for some months. That he looked ridiculous probably didn't help matters. Later, when the other priests questioned him about the episode, he tugged at the wheel of flesh around his throat and cried, "Idlers! Those boys are idlers, every one of them!"

A portly man, famed for his ability to guzzle tremendous amounts of ale from the local brewery, Father Loomis resembled an ancient temple, something that didn't need to be bathed and powdered and dressed each morning so much as scaled at the appropriate solstice or equinox and upon which propitiations had to be made to a pantheon of temperamental gods. Students never tired of ridiculing him. They made vulgar and obnoxious sounds, pretended to fart and wheeze and gag when he waddled his hamburger-and-beer-bloated body into the biology lab. A man didn't reside within that body, they claimed, but an overactive mutant gene about to burn out like an old fuse. He was an expanding star, a red giant exhausting the last of its hydrogen. He was a tremendous boulder rolling down a slope that led to the third circle of hell, a cold realm of torrential rain reserved for unrepentant gluttons. Unfortunately, heaven was too steep an ascent and Father Loomis little more than a corpulent Sisyphus burdened by his big ball of flesh.

"Now then!" he said, rapping a yardstick against his chair. "Today we will be doing dissection." He hummed, whistled, quoted with a chuckle, "Faith is a fine invention when gentlemen can *see*, but microscopes are prudent in an emergency." He unlocked a cabinet and then placed the glass jars in neat rows at the edge of his desk. "Before making your first incision, you must . . . First, you must . . . Gentleman, your animal. Anesthetize it. Remember. Always remember. They are created creatures . . ."

He seemed suddenly confused, and maybe in his confusion, he thought he was standing before the church altar, struggling to transform the bread into the body of Christ. After reciting the necessary formula—*"Hoc est enim corpus meum"*—he raised each consecrated frog by his forefinger and thumb and distributed them to his pupils like hosts on a day of holy obligation.

At the front of the line stood Tom Wentworth, who accepted his frog in an almost reverential manner, perhaps expecting, and even hoping for, a sense of peace and tranquility to invade his soul, to cleanse his troubled mind. Indeed, a great and disturbing calm fell over him, almost as though some ultimate Truth, awful in its lack of humanity and complete absence of purpose, had stalked into the room. He sat perfectly upright on his stool, muttering words without sense or meaning. The other boys watched his lips move, his eyelids flutter. They prodded him with their rulers and slapped the back of his head.

"Hey, man. What the hell. You flippin' out, or what? You *on* something? You gobble a few pills? Whatever it is, let us have some."

Oblivious to their taunts, Tom turned his attention to the work at hand, but rather than smother his frog with a chloroform-soaked cotton ball, he reached into his backpack and grabbed his geometry compass, the one he used in geometry class to draw concentric circles and to make arcs along a plane like a carpenter's apprentice. With the sharp point glimmering under the fluorescent lights, he stabbed the back and legs and the soft, pliant skull of his thrashing frog, never flinching at the sharp pop of the spleen and the long, sad wheeze of the evacuating rectum. From the sounds alone he could identify each organ.

"Liver! Lung! Ovary!"

After decapitating the frog, Tom raised the dripping point of his geometry compass high above his head and, running around the lab, stabbed the other frogs, methodically gouging out eyeballs and genitals, severing legs, snapping bones sickening in their elasticity. His classmates recoiled from the viscous, milky fluid that meandered across the surface of the countertops and trickled to the floor. Nobody tried to stop him. They were afraid he might turn the weapon on them, or even on himself; self-mutilation wasn't beyond the realm of possibility. Best to wait for Father Loomis to take charge, to *do something*, but the old man was in a daze, his finger buried deep in the back of his jaw, trying to dislodge a hunk of sausage, a soggy lump of toast. Before coming to class, he always ate a hearty breakfast and almost never flossed.

If Coach Kaliher hadn't been passing through the halls and wrestled Tom to the ground, things may have gotten completely out of control. By some miracle no one was hurt, though in the turbulent confusion, Coach Kaliher was forced to take some extraordinary measures. He put the boy in a stranglehold, pounded his head on the floor, and he may or may not have called the boy a "fucking psycho"; accounts vary on this last point, but given the circumstances, it was certainly an understandable reaction.

Tom writhed and squirmed. He kicked over a chair and managed to shatter a glass jar. He gasped and spat and sputtered vicious threats. His face went pale, then turned eggplant purple. His smashed nose spurted blood. Meanwhile, his classmates, happy for any opportunity to make mischief, formed a circle around Tom and did a spirited Irish jig in his honor, their mirthless laughter ringing through the hallways.

III

Now, with thirty minutes to kill before his appointment with the tutor, Tom Wentworth takes a leisurely stroll through the neighborhood, passing abandoned factories and warehouses, ungainly edifices of a dead industrial age transformed by the shifting shadows and lacerating winds into sculptures of strange shape and contour—giant locusts and ancient armored lizards hunkered down in the drifting, yellow leaves and swirling coal fire soot. Outside the creaking iron gates of the public park, Tom pauses to observe the homeless women who have come here to stake out their benches before sunset. In filthy trench coats that exaggerate the slump of their shoulders, they look like a nightmare version of the parish ladies who visit the school chapel on Sunday mornings, wrapped in red velvet and white ermine. Through the metallic autumn light, they move as though straining under the weight of chainmail, inadequate protection against the terrible things that will come for them during the darkest hours—the long-tailed rats that scurry across heaps of broken brick to nest beside their bundled newspapers, and the elusive "madman" who selects his prey with great deliberation and takes his sweet time before carrying out his despicable deeds.

Tom tries not to think of this scene in terms of its goodness or badness. He enjoys wandering the streets without the burden of having to measure the value of things. The Jesuits try to place a value on the whole of creation. They use words like *assessment*, *appraisal,* and *analysis*. Humanity has been placed upon this earth, they believe, to quantify the cosmos—physically, psychologically, spiritually, morally—and by adhering to the correct methods and utilizing the proper instruments, the priests, never short on ambition, hope to perceive the very mind of God. Tom takes this as a sign that the Jesuits have yet to escape the seductive spell of modernity altogether. Like scientists, they insist upon independent observation, because even men with an unreasonable belief in the supernatural yearn for evidence and incontrovertible proof.

At four o'clock, Tom ambles over to the rectory at 1545 Dickinson, the Ancient Homestead, as the students call it. He knocks three times and waits for Ms. Higginson, the housekeeper, to open the great, paneled door. The peephole darkens and a magnified eyeball regards him with suspicion. A bolt turns, a chain rattles and unfastens. The residents have gotten into the habit of locking their doors during the day. Their precaution has turned to paranoia.

Ms. Higginson thrusts her nose through a narrow opening. "Wentworth?"

Tom takes a step back. "Yes, I'm—"

"You're five minutes late!"

Her voice lashes him like an old bicycle chain. Small particles of rust and grit burst from her lips and float on the wind. She is a tall woman—broad-shouldered, solid, severe, with a complexion as gray as the afternoon sky, an indoor face unaccustomed to sunshine and fresh air. She looks like one of those sepia-toned photographs from his history textbook of nineteenth-century washerwomen, their sleeves rolled up past their elbows to show off their well-defined triceps.

She sneers with disapproval but waves him inside. "This way, this way!"

Tom stumbles over the sill and almost falls to his knees. Ms. Higginson clicks her teeth. How many oafish boys has she led into this house without the courtesy of saying, "Please watch your step," just for the small pleasure of seeing them trip and turn red with embarrassment?

She leads him through a maze of corridors, her heels going *clippity-clop* against the hardwood floors like the shoes on a grizzled packhorse. Trying to suppress a smile, Tom recalls the lurid tales he's heard about Ms. Higginson: she has insatiable urges, it is said, and has seduced the burly maintenance man, who is often seen coming and going at odd hours, his clothes disheveled, his face distraught; she also serves as a kind of madam for the priests and on the weekends procures women of every stripe for them—short, fat, lean, shaved, bristly, bushy. It's well-known that the Jesuits have their fetishes.

"Now then," she says, "what is it you're supposed to study?"

"Study?"

She sighs. "Really, Wentworth, must I repeat the question?"

Tom stammers. "Augustine? No, Aquinas."

Ms. Higginson rolls her eyes. "Oh, the Jesuits do get strange ideas."

The interior of the rectory reminds Tom of the nursing home where on the weekends he mops the piss-splattered floors, wipes off trays smeared with pureed vegetables, tosses big bags of medical waste into the incinerator, and, since there seems to be no one else who can be bothered with such a menial task, listens to the elderly residents as they struggle to put the ruined battlefield of their memories in some kind of sensible order. Despite the onerous nature of these chores, Tom rather enjoys the job. Because there is an almost complete absence of supervision, he can come and go as he pleases, and this in turn has made him a more dedicated worker. Rarely does he show up to the nursing home empty-handed. Each day he brings the residents small gifts scavenged from the garbage heaped on the curb—charms and bracelets and plastic trinkets—things meant to distract them while he removes the lethal bottle from his backpack. When they see the skull and crossbones on the label, they gasp and whimper like children. As a joke, he twists the cap off and says, "Open wide . . ." The chemical stings their eyes, irritates their skin, smells sharp and oily like the formaldehyde that will be used to disinfect and embalm their decaying remains.

Ms. Higginson snaps her fingers.

"Stop daydreaming!"

They continue walking, and she leads him into a spacious library. Except for the firelight coming from the hearth, the room is quite dark. Long shadows leap across the bookshelves and oak paneling.

"Wait here," she says. "I'll be back in a moment."

She disappears into the vast curling gloom of the house, and for a few glorious moments, Tom is left alone to savor the silence and to feel the pleasant warmth of the fire. He marvels at the number of books, and wonders if the priests ever bother to read these century-old variorums and antiquated encyclopedias or if the books are just meant for show. One volume in particular catches his eye, and from its fragile cover, he parts a sea of dust. In the cracked leather binding, he sees the faces of saints and sinners, the anguished cries of apostates, the acrimonious scowls of heresiarchs. Even the title strikes him as slightly monstrous: *Black Mass and Black Death: Gentile da Foligno in the Time of the Bubonic Plague*. The pages are stiff and brittle, like bloodless autumn leaves, and as he flips through them, they crackle quietly like kindling—combustible and easily ignited.

He scans the small print from right to left, a little game he enjoys playing. From what he can tell, there lived in fourteenth century Italy an eccentric but well-intentioned priest who married off some affluent schoolboys to a group of prostitutes. This, the priest reasoned, was the only way to protect the otherwise defenseless women from certain exposure to the deadly disease. Tom closes his eyes and takes a moment to contemplate the tale. Surely anyone who would commit such a wicked act should be condemned . . . but condemned to what? He dreams of the appropriate punishment, a thousand eternal torments, but in the midst of this sublime meditation, he hears a voice, odd infantile gurgling, vulnerable as the pages of the book he is holding.

"Oh God help me please oh please God help me help."

Tom spins around and peers into the darkness. At first he

can't see anything too clearly, but then, gradually, as his eyes adjust to the gloom, an awful vision begins to emerge. The priests have assured him that the things he sometimes sees are not always real, but this vision persists and will not vanish from the shadowlands of his mind. Somehow it is made even more terrible by the sounds of the settling house, the creaks and groans of the joints and floorboards. Using the book as a kind of shield, he approaches the misshapen wretch. Concealed under a thin sheet like a circus freak behind the curtain of an arched proscenium, the gibbering, drooling, cadaverous creature, its desiccated flesh pale blue, vaguely aquatic, almost translucent, squirms in a hospital bed and claws at the air with nails so jagged and yellow that they seem capable of infecting anyone foolish enough to get too close.

"For heaven's sake! Still dawdling?"

Ms. Higginson stomps back into the library, this time carrying a bowl of steaming soup. She kicks each wheel of the hospital bed with the toe of her shoe and checks the guardrails to make sure they are secure. Then she places the bowl on the dining tray, and without ceremony, without even saying grace, she shoves a spoon toward the creature's mouth, waiting for its purple tongue to slither from its toothless black lair to lap up the broth and bobbing bits of congealed chicken fat.

"Would you like a reading lamp, Wentworth?"

The thing slurps and pants and coughs, leaving dark droplets on Ms. Higginson's blouse. She doesn't seem to notice. With the cold precision of a machine she dips the spoon back into the bowl and dangles it above the creature's twisted lips. "As you can see, we keep it dark in here. Father has become sensitive to the light. You do know Father Loomis, don't you?"

Tom utters a faint "Yes?"

When she notices the look of dismay in his eyes, she says, "Ah, you probably recall how heavyset he used to be. At first, it was inconvenient to move him up and down the stairs, so we decided to put his bed in the library. Of course now that he's lost so much weight, we can lift him more easily. But he seems to enjoy being in the presence of books. He's like one of those antique volumes." She leans over the rail and shouts into the old man's ear. "Isn't that right, Father? You like it here, don't you?"

With great effort, the old man manages to lift his head from the pillow and grabs Ms. Higginson by the wrist. He gurgles and wheezes and marks the bottom of the hour with his ghastly refrain: "Oh God help me please oh please God help me help."

She pushes him back down with both hands. "Oh, I do think this arrangement will work quite well. Don't you agree, Wentworth?"

"Arrangement?" Tom whispers.

She wipes the old man's chin and dabs the corners of his mouth. "The Jesuits didn't explain things to you? How typical."

"They told me—"

"Never mind any of that. We're aware that you've had a great deal of experience at the nursing home, and we believe you can be of some use to us here. You are to spend some time with Father Loomis, reading to him a little each day. A simple enough task. Even for someone like you." She points to the book in Tom's hand. "I see you've found a copy of *The Black Death*. One of Father's better efforts, I must say. We'll take that as a sign. He wrote it many years ago as a young seminarian. It's out of print now. A pity. He was such a great scholar. Studied the history of disease. He could have taught graduate classes in epidemiology at a Jesuit university if he wished, but he preferred to stay here and cultivate young minds." She shakes her head in mild disbelief. "Well, you may as well get started."

She picks up the bowl, straightens her long twill skirt, and stands to leave.

"You mean, you're not staying?"

She laughs. "I have other things to do, Wentworth. This rectory is falling apart. The boiler is on the fritz again. I have a man coming to fix it. That fire won't burn forever, you know." On her way out, she pauses in the doorway. "Father Loomis has his good days and his bad. On good days he's been known to rise from his bed. Like Lazarus. The important thing is to make sure he doesn't wander off."

Tom watches her leave. She is probably standing in the hallway, waiting for him to call her name, but she is a fool to believe he is just another diffident schoolboy. In fact, Tom Wentworth finds this whole situation rather amusing.

He leans over the bed and says, "Good afternoon, Father. Do you remember me? No? I didn't think so. Here, maybe this will help you to remember . . ."

From his bag he retrieves his deck of pornographic playing cards and holds them up to the old man's face. In order to describe the alien things pictured there he uses the words "snatch" and "twat" and "box," speaking them loud and clear. "Sinful, isn't it, Father?" says Tom. He places each card beside the pillow and then fans them out around the old man's head.

Beneath the sheets, Father Loomis begins to convulse. He rasps and groans and pleads clemency from a tyrannical and pitiless judge. Gone is the fat, cantankerous science teacher.

What remains is a jumble of calcified bones that, through some kind of ancient and forbidden magic, have been reanimated, and no medicine in the world can quell their macabre clattering or silence the old man's mournful and inexhaustible petition to heaven.

"OhGodhelpmepleaseohpleaseGodhelpmehelp . . ."

IV

Though he gives the matter some thought, Tom elects not to go home right away. Instead, he stops at the corner store.

Behind the counter, watching him with a weary expression, stands the Tanzanian shop owner, ready as always to reach beneath the cash register with the dexterity of a gunslinger. Heavy drops of sweat cascade over his perpetual five o-clock shadow and sink into a deep crevasse of flesh at the base of his neck. His shop has been robbed many times, but during the last incident, the owner managed to shoot and mortally wound the thief, a teenager from the projects along the river. The boy, drenched in blood and surrounded by shards of glass that sparkled under the streetlights, shielded his face with his hands and begged for his life. The residents of the neighborhood now regard the owner as a hero. "The police are of no use to me," he tells his customers. "I am not a man of the book. I am a man of the gun."

Not wishing to test his patience, Tom finds the latest edition of his favorite comic book buried behind the porno magazines on a rack near the front counter. He flips through the pages and briefly studies the vivid images. In some ruined city, not unlike the one in which Tom lives, dozens of terrified citizens run screaming through the devastated streets, their clothes set ablaze by a pack of chortling, green mutants, slimy-skinned humanoids, half-man, half-frog, with giant webbed feet and sharply defined buttocks. The monsters leap effortlessly across the cratered landscape to burn the remaining survivors with torches dipped in tar and oil. Inspired by these gruesome drawings, Tom puts the comic under his arm and then selects a bottle of lighter fluid from the bottom shelf. He brings these items to the register and produces several bills from his wallet.

The owner scratches his stomach and coughs. "This will be all, young man?"

"Yes, sir."

"You will be needing a bag?"

"If it's no trouble."

The owner smirks, lets his eyes linger for a moment on the boy's face. "It's no trouble." He places the items in a paper bag and gives Tom his change. "Please, come again."

After leaving the store, Tom walks three blocks to the small public park and slips past the iron gates. Stealthy as a sewer rat, he creeps toward the circle of benches and slides beside one of the shivering women whose oily hair is buried beneath a bundle of newspapers and stinking rags. The arctic wind scrubs the air clean but cannot disguise the malodorous tentacles of piss and madness that waft toward him. He leans in close, hoping to sniff something more elemental, things barely remembered—sour milk, perfume, booze, painkillers crushed into a fine powder.

A police cruiser rolls by. He can't stay here for long without arousing suspicion. Quickly, he stuffs more newspapers under the woman's shoulders, her back, her thighs, then he removes the bottle of lighter fluid from the bag, tears off the cellophane wrapper along the perforated edge, and, with an expert flick of his thumb, pops opens the red cap. He squeezes the sides of the bottle, sending a perfect parabola of fluid arcing through the artificial light. He searches his pockets but finds only lint and dirty tissues.

The woman struggles to come awake. She touches her damp hair with her small hands and chewed cuticles.

"What time is it?" she asks.

"It's late," he tells her.

She raises her head. "Damn, I have to get back."

"Get back where?"

"To Zanzibar."

"Zanzibar? How exotic."

"There's a party. Important job."

"You still have time," he assures her. "Go back to sleep."

"Maybe you're looking for a little fun, a nice gentleman like you."

"No, not tonight, thank you."

"Such a fine-looking young man. You got something there to drink? I'm so dry."

He gives her the bottle of lighter fluid and continues to search his pockets until he finally finds the book of matches he stole from the principal's office earlier that afternoon. He waits for the wind to die down. Five seconds, ten seconds. He is patient. Somewhere nearby, dogs are barking, getting closer, hunting their quarry. Suddenly there is a small break in the clouds. A tight pool of pale moonlight fills the park. The wind melts away. Everything is eerily still. Tom lifts the matchbook cover, feels the stiff paper sticks, the phosphorus tips. He strikes a match, holds it to the newspapers and to the loose threads dangling from the hem of the woman's purple dress. The advancing blue flames give a quick whoosh. Sparks soar heavenward. Fire licks the sky. A burnt offering. The woman flails her arms, rolls into a pile of dry leaves, but unlike so many of his other victims she does not scream.

Tom checks his watch. Though he would like to stay and enjoy the fire, he really must be heading home. It's his eighteenth birthday, and by now his father must be wondering about him. Guests will be waiting in the dark, whispering, giggling, eagerly anticipating that magical moment when they can turn on the lights and shout, "Surprise!" Everyone is sure to be there, everyone except, of course, his mother.

He puts the comic book in his coat pocket, and as he leaves the park he glimpses the Gothic tower of the Jesuit school above the rooftops. The priests have always said that a young man with one set of ideas might, with age and wisdom, grow into an altogether different kind of man with an entirely new set of beliefs. Maybe so, but Tom suspects that the universe and the people who inhabit it are essentially static and hostile to change, that all things are headed toward one ineluctable destiny. Eternal stasis can be achieved only if there is good *and* evil. The powers and potentialities of darkness are not to be denied or suppressed. They, too, are essential parts of this cosmic equation. Some people are Creators, others great Defaulters and Destroyers, not unlike the Ancient of Days, who from the skies above a fated empire once railed, "I will smite your whole territory with frogs, which will come up and go into your house and into your bedroom and into your bed and into the houses of your servants and into your ovens and into your kneading bowls."

These things Tom knows to be true—he has read about

them in holy books, and as he hurries through the desolate streets and alleys, he thinks of Father Loomis and looks forward to the hour when he can retreat to the sanctuary of his bedroom where, amid the sounds of music and laughter, he can carefully craft a plan for tomorrow's terrible ordeal.

The Spy

I

On the steps of his front porch, resting his head against the top stoop, George Fenner smokes his last cigarette and marvels at the shifting shapes of passing clouds. The early morning rain that came sluicing sideways out of the sky has given way to brief glimpses of rusty sunshine, but in the distance, far out over the lake, an immense wall of dark clouds pushes ever closer to shore, rumbling weirdly with thundersnow. To George the soaring cloud tops look solid and muscular, like figures masterfully crafted from massive sheets of steel, a three-headed hellhound, maybe, bounding toward heaven, eager to taste the tender flesh of angels' wings. The vision seems all the more real thanks to the mangy dogs that trot up and down the narrow brick lane in front of his house, lifting their hind legs to mark their territory, shitting on the sidewalk, pillaging trash cans, competing for nonexistent scraps of food. George feels no pity for them. Like every creature condemned to live among these streets, the dogs must learn to accept suffering. Winter is almost here, spring a million years off. Soon there will be no escape from the punishing cold and constant hunger unless, of course, death whisks them all away to an even colder grave.

The change of weather doesn't seem to trouble Billy. In a red cape and blue tights, the boy runs back and forth across a muddy patch of lawn, chasing after the grackles that haunt the rotten windowsills and mossy roof peak of the vacant house next door. At his approach the birds flutter away, easily evading his desperate lunges. A few even make a game of it. From the low branches of a stately maple at the center of the yard, the birds hop up and down and screech at the ungainly biped that comes stumbling through a swath of dead yellow grass. Billy stops to study the birds, his eyes unblinking and inscrutable as a cat's. He bobs his head as they do, makes little chirping sounds, tries to find a way to ingratiate himself with them, but his efforts only make the birds squawk all the louder. They run nimbly along the limbs of the tree and kick acorns on his head. With a grunt of exasperation the boy adjusts his Halloween costume, yanking the tights from the crack of his ass, and suddenly charges, his arms pin-wheeling, his shiny black boots slipping sideways in the muck.

Sensing disaster, George sits up and shouts, "You goddamn birdbrain, watch where you're going!"

But the warning comes too late. The boy collides with a crooked fencepost, and for a long time he lies on the ground, his face buried deep in a pile of moldering leaves. He might be unconscious, he might be dead. George checks his watch and waits for a hopeful sign.

It's only four o'clock. His wife won't be home from the foundry for at least another hour. With a long yawn, he bundles the collar of his jacket around his throat and wonders how he will survive so many days tethered to this wretched madhouse. Trying to find different ways to idle away the dwindling hours of October daylight has become his sole occupation, or perhaps preoccupation, since boredom has become a living thing in his life, a chittering, winged serpent that coils on his chest while he sleeps and waits for him to open his eyes each morning. All day long it hovers over him, and because he has no hobbies, no skills, no friends to visit, he cannot defend himself against it or silence the sound of its flapping wings.

Now he opens the plastic bag at his feet and tosses a handful of candy near the boy's inert body. The birds ruffle their iridescent feathers but dare not swoop down to investigate. After a few minutes Billy lifts his head and from his bruised face peels away a mask of wet leaves. Had another child been injured—a *normal* child, thinks George—there would have been a high-pitched scream, inconsolable wailing and blubbering, but from his son there comes only a strangled, drawn-out hiss, the sound a vampire makes after it has been cornered in a crypt, its forehead seared by a crucifix, its glassy, black eyes maced with holy water. In his four years of life Billy has never uttered a word, not a single one, and seldom moves his lips with make-believe speech.

Sometimes George actually pities the boy. There are even moments when he wonders if he is personally responsible for Billy's mysterious affliction, if he damaged the child during one of those infamous lost weekends—dropped him, shook him, put whiskey in his bottle instead of milk, vodka instead of formula. Sobriety should help George remember these things, so say his fellow alcoholics during the weekly AA meetings in the smoky church basement, but the past will not give up its secrets so easily, and for that he is grateful.

His wife, however, is not the type to forgive and forget

and is only too happy to remind him of the terrible things he has done. A deeply religious woman, she believes in the redemptive power of shame and spends long hours recounting, often in meticulous detail, his innumerable failures as a father and husband. Without asking his permission, she goes to the rectory, where she consults the Jesuits about their son, but the priests only offer their usual crackpot diagnoses, use the cryptic words "solipsism syndrome," and suggest that Billy is merely speech delayed, nothing more. "Prayer will solve the problem, sure enough," the priests tell her. They lounge in an enormous parlor, shielded from reality by ornate tapestries and heavy brocade curtains, as Ms. Higginson, their surly housekeeper, serves tea, pours the cream, counts out the lumps of sugar, attends to their every need, all the while listening to the conversation with special interest.

George does not approve of these clandestine meetings, and he isn't particularly interested in the Jesuits' armchair psychology. He believes the boy is disturbed, plain and simple, and he isn't afraid to say so. The neighborhood has a tendency to breed monsters. Newspapers tell grisly tales of murder, incest, rape, a veritable Decameron of horrors not to be believed. The people here are diseased, their brains warped from breathing the poisoned air and drinking the tainted water.

"I should have a say in these matters," he told his wife that morning at breakfast. "I'm still the head of this household, and I believe the boy needs to see a proper physician."

"Head of the household!" His wife laughed bitterly. "Well, aren't you old-fashioned?" She crushed out her cigarette in an egg yolk, then laced up her steel-toed boots. "We can't afford a doctor. We lost our medical insurance when you were fired, remember?"

"Laid off, you mean."

"Right, laid off. Sorry."

Trying to ignore his wife's sarcasm, George focused on his plate, sopped up a pool of bacon grease with a triangle of burnt toast, and crammed the whole thing into his mouth. "Those priests are no better than witch doctors!" He had a bad habit of talking with his mouth full and sprayed his words across the table. "Mortal men claiming to speak for God. They can't even look you in the eye and admit that the boy is daft, that he isn't right in the head. *Look* at him. You'd think he was reared in the wild."

Billy Fenner tugged violently on a scrap of overcooked sausage and slobbered down his chin but otherwise seemed to watch the scene with perfect indifference.

His wife tousled the boy's hair. "He's fine. He knows when to keep his mouth shut. It's a sign of intelligence. He's a prodigy."

"Oh, sure, a real fucking genius!"

George chuckled, busy mopping up more grease with a fresh piece of toast, but he should have known what was coming; marriage had conditioned him to be aware of the dangers, but he didn't realize what was happening until he heard the crash of dishes and felt the fork pressed firmly against his neck, the dull prongs dripping with egg yolk and puncturing his flesh.

"Billy is a gifted boy," she hissed, pushing the fork ever closer to his carotid artery. "He's smart. He knows a lot more than you give him credit for. Do you know what *I* think? *I* think with just a little more encouragement from his father, Billy can accomplish some extraordinary things."

Billy gnawed at a leathery strip of bacon with great determination.

George nodded and, through clenched teeth, whispered, "Yes, dear, yes, you're absolutely right . . ."

His wife seemed to be mulling over her options, contemplating the benefits and drawbacks of murder. Her eyes twitched with something primordial, barely mammalian, as if one of the gray moles nesting in the tangled weeds around the front porch had scurried into the bedroom late at night and tunneled deep inside her brain, gobbling up every last morsel of her compassion and sanity.

The clock began to chime.

"Dammit, I'm going to be late for work." She threw the fork down on the table and then hurried to the closet to get her lunchbox and welding hood.

It took a few minutes before George realized he was bleeding. With a paper napkin, he gently dabbed at the thin trails of blood trickling down his neck and pooling in the hollow around his collarbone. He trembled at how very close he'd come to confessing everything, every terrible detail of the past few months. From now on, he would have to proceed with caution. He had no desire to be blinded or castrated. There were women like that, women who were capable of maiming a man; he'd known a few in his time and had the scars to prove it. Concealing the truth from his wife had suddenly become a matter of life and death. The risk was especially dangerous since it involved their son. Still, he had no choice but to carry on. The alternative was to remain completely dependent on her. She held the purse strings and seemed more determined than ever to turn his existence into a grueling spiritual pilgrimage to the impossibly distant shrine of sobriety.

Before leaving the house, she kissed Billy on the cheek. "I'll see you tonight for trick-or-treat." Then without acknowledging her husband, she stormed out of the house and marched down the street to catch the bus.

II

The phone starts ringing (another creditor, more likely than not, calling to harass him), but George considers any phone call a welcome distraction. Brushing cigarette ashes from his coat, he stands up and shouts to his son, "Hey, Superman, don't fly off anywhere!"

He goes inside the house and picks up the phone.

"Hello."

"That you, Fenner?"

He pauses a moment before responding. "Ms. Higginson. How nice to hear from you. It's been a while."

"You sound a little uneasy, Fenner. Something wrong?"

"That depends."

"On what?"

"My wife. She's not over there at the rectory, talking to those priests, is she?"

"Haven't seen her since last week."

"Well, then, everything is just fine."

"Not quite everything."

"What could possibly be wrong?"

"Don't be dense, Fenner. You know."

"Afraid I don't, Ms. Higginson."

There is a long pause before she finally says, "Boiler is on the fritz again."

"Ah, so that's it."

"How soon can you be here?"

"Could it wait till tomorrow? I'm in charge of my boy today."

"Poor child. He's probably running wild in the streets."

"Everything's under control. Billy is always safe when his daddy is around."

"Well, bring him with you. If he's still in one piece."

"I'm not sure that's such a good idea. It's Halloween. My wife wants us all to go trick-or-treating. It'll be getting dark in another hour."

"I'll gladly call another repairman, if you'd like. Plenty of men looking for work these days."

"Oh, don't do that. Matter of fact, I was thinking of heading out the door anyway. Just finished my last cigarette. Gotta go to the corner store and stock up."

"Better get a move on then. The priests will be back soon."

"Must be a desperate situation, eh, Ms. Higginson? A real emergency."

"I wouldn't go that far, Fenner. The boiler's overheating. That's all. It happens sometimes. You should be grateful."

The line abruptly goes dead.

After hanging up the phone, George struts over to the mirror above the mantle. Using his fingers, he plucks the coarse black hairs sprouting from his nostrils. He regrets not having showered or brushed his teeth that morning, but he never expected to leave the house. Unemployment has turned him into a recluse.

He steps outside and walks over to the garage. The place is a wreck, and in order to reach the makeshift shelves hammered into the back wall he must scale a treacherous deadfall of plywood and particleboard. He has been meaning to build a tree house for Billy but hasn't gotten around to it yet. Under a pile of greasy rags, he finds the adjustable wrench, pliers, channel locks, a chisel, tools so old and rusted they can no longer serve any practical purpose, but he can't very well show up at the rectory empty-handed. A proper tool set, no matter its condition, makes a man look professional and gives him an air of authority. People passing on the street are more likely to regard him as an honest tradesman, one who has fallen on hard times perhaps, but a tradesman nonetheless, a skilled laborer who is willing to work long hours for a day's wages.

After securing the latches on the toolbox, George goes to the front yard and finds his son racing around the maple tree, the mud-splattered cape billowing up behind him.

"Hey, you, stop monkeying with them birds!" With an impatient huff, George yanks the boy by the arm. "Let's go. We have a job."

Father and son start the five-block journey to the rectory on Dickinson Street. Billy struggles to keep up, his grunts becoming more pronounced with every step. George turns to him and says, "Listen, you're going to do exactly what I tell you, right? If you follow my directions, we should make out like bandits. This is going to be a lot more fun than trick-or-treat. Now here's the plan . . ."

III

Standing behind the elaborate cast-iron gate, Ms. Higginson looks not unlike one of the statues in the overgrown cemetery across the street, an imposing monument of a middle-aged woman carved from an enormous block of gritty sandstone, perfect in her bleak solidity. Broad-shouldered and flinty-eyed, she watches over the rectory like a sentry guarding a house of the dead. She seems so totally impervious to the world and its distractions, so rigid and immovable, that George is surprised a pigeon hasn't fluttered down from one of the corbelled turrets to light on her head and drape her in flowing ribbons of white excrement. Without saying hello or commenting on little Billy's Halloween costume, she opens the gate and directs father and son through the shadowy courtyard and into the house.

"Hurry along," she says.

George winces. The rectory smells of incense, cheap after-shave, chicken broth, formaldehyde. It has been a few weeks since his last visit (for some reason the word "reconnaissance" comes to mind), and as he passes through each of its enormous rooms, he lets his eyes linger over the curious relics promi-nently displayed in cabinets and pedestals—a triptych of mar-tyred saints painted on three wooden panels; a crucified Jesus stretched across a cracked canvas, the savior's bloody fingers struggling to pry loose the nails driven deeply into his shat-tered palms; chalices of silver and gold etched with ancient symbols; an ivory cross; shiny amulets; ridiculous jujus. Mu-seum pieces of inestimable worth.

Upon reaching the end of a long hallway, Ms. Higginson calls to Billy. "Over here, boy!" She opens a door and points. "Wait for your father down there. It shouldn't take him long."

George whistles. "The basement, Ms. Higginson? Seems a bit spooky for a child, don't you think?"

She puts her hands on her hips. "I won't have some ram-bunctious boy wandering around this house."

"Aw, can't he wait in the library?"

"Out of the question. He'll make too much noise."

George shakes his head. "He won't say a word, I promise you that."

"Down he goes, Fenner, or I'll call Malachy McSweeney and ask him to do the job."

"Him!" George shrugs. "Alright, alright. You heard the lady, Billy. No time to waste."

He shoves the toolbox into the boy's hands and pushes him toward the stairs. With a little yap of fear, Billy begins the steep descent. In the darkness, the boiler skirls and screaks like a steel dragon chained to the floor of a steamy dungeon. The galvanized pipes overhead cast ominous shadows across the boy's face. He stands against one of the sooty cinder block walls and with imploring eyes looks up at his father.

Before slamming the door closed, Ms. Higginson hits a light switch and says, "If he knows what's good for him, Fenner, he'll stay right where he is."

"Oh, yes, he's a very meek child."

"Alright then."

She leads George into the kitchen, where the table has been set for dinner, the white tablecloth and napkins neatly pressed, the silverware polished, the fine bone china dried by hand to avoid spots and streaks. George marvels at this fancy presentation, a still life that could easily grace the cover of a magazine, and wonders what's on the menu tonight. A big pot of chicken soup simmers on the stovetop, but George knows that for an appetizer the priests always eat their God, served in the form of a small, white wafer of unleavened bread. It is forbidden to chew him, but chew him they do. This causes God to become wedged between their tobacco-stained teeth and cemented to the roofs of their mouths. With palsied fingers, with toothpicks, with dental floss, the priests try to loosen their delicious deity, but this only complicates matters and creates a particularly thorny theological question. As God hangs wetly from the floss in small beads, almost like some culinary rosary, the priests wonder if they should consume the remnants before discarding it. Surely it's an abomination, a sacrilege of the highest order to throw God into a garbage can or to dispose of Him in a toilet bowl. Since they aren't in the habit of reading every papal encyclical, the priests aren't sure what the Church teaches on this matter. Even for staunch defenders of the faith, canon law can be a most troublesome thing.

Well, no one can follow *all* of the rules *all* of the time, as George Fenner can attest. When he spots the bottle of red wine at the center of the table, for instance, he claps his hands and then reaches for one of the crystal glasses.

"Don't!" Ms. Higginson says.

"Why shouldn't I?"

"The priests mark the bottle."

George laughs. "Those tight-sphinctered devils, they get plenty of this stuff every Sunday, I promise you that. Blood of Christ, my foot."

"I thought you gave up the booze."

"Let's just say there are occasions, Ms. Higginson, when I feel justified in taking a sip or two. It gives a man strength."

"Is that what you tell your fellow drunks at the weekly AA meeting?"

"Everyone cheats now and then. Maybe you should have a little for yourself. Might help you to relax. It can hardly be paradise, working here for these curmudgeons."

"They're good men, Fenner. They do a lot for this community."

"You're starting to sound like my old lady. She has this crazy notion that the Jesuits are miracle workers who can cure our son. Laying of the hands and all that."

Ms. Higginson huffs. "Is that what you think? That your wife comes here to consult the priests about your boy?"

"What other reason can she possibly have?"

"She comes here to give me the evil eye."

"What's that supposed to mean?"

"She's no fool, Fenner. She knows what we've been up to, you and I."

"Like hell she does."

"Women can sniff out treachery. She's toying with me, waiting for me to break down and confess my sins in front of the priests."

George takes a step forward and whispers in her ear, "But you won't confess, will you, Ms. Higginson?"

She uncrosses her arms and shoves him against the table. With her calloused housekeeper's hands, she unbuttons his flannel shirt and pulls it from his back. He smiles, kisses her neck, lifts up her heavy wool skirt. Physical intimacy transforms her from a cold statue into a scratching, writhing hellcat. She pants and whimpers and grinds her powerful hips against his gyrating pelvis, but before things can really get started she digs her nails into his shoulders and gasps, "Dear God in heaven!"

"What's wrong?" asks George.

"Your little boy . . ."

"Ha, he doesn't mind."

"But he's *watching* us."

George turns.

Standing in the doorway, clinging to his red cape and sucking his thumb, is little Billy Fenner. He gazes with indifference at his father's grizzly buttocks and Ms. Higginson's muscular, white thighs.

"Get outta here, you!" George grabs his flannel shirt from the floor and lobs it at the boy's head. "Back into the basement!"

With a loud bellow and croak, the child scampers down the gloomy corridor.

Ms. Higginson says, "Maybe we should stop."

But George pushes her down so she is sprawled across the kitchen table like a ritual sacrifice, and in no time at all the two of them fall into a mutually satisfying rhythm. At the Jesuit school, the chapel bells begin to chime. Soon the priests will say grace and break bread at this very table. It's an image that gives George Fenner such a perverse sense of pleasure that he nearly climaxes prematurely.

IV

Thirty minutes later, father and son hurry back home through streets teeming with groups of neighborhood children in their Halloween costumes.

When they are no longer within sight of the rectory, Billy nudges his father and places a small rectangular object in his hand.

George pats the boy's head. "Ah, the cat burglar strikes again."

After several weeks of training, Billy has become a true master of deception, conveying to one and all an air of dim-witted innocence. If he puts his mind to it, he can creep through any house virtually undetected, and over the past few months he has managed to pilfer numerous odds and ends from the homes of relatives and acquaintances. Occasionally his work yields big dividends—prescription pills, bags of marijuana, a collection of rare coins, watches, credit cards, a book of blank checks. The Tanzanian shopkeeper pays handsomely for the looted goods, tens and twenties are the standard rate of exchange, and he never asks questions. With the proceeds from these sales, George is able to maintain some semblance of a social life, sneaking a few pints at the local brewery while his wife works at the foundry.

But now, after a string of successes, disaster suddenly strikes.

"What the hell is *this*!" George cries. "No cash? No booze. No pills?"

Rather than find anything of real value, Billy has engaged in a sort of spiritual espionage. While having no monetary value, the boy's startling discovery does prove one thing: that the old men, stooped and bent with the unyielding cynicism they harbor for their fallen parishioners, are no better or worse than anyone else—they have their weaknesses, their secrets, their forbidden pleasures. George considers turning around and confronting them, just for the small pleasure of watching the priests choke on their guilt and indignation. "What sorts of disgusting things go on here?" he wants to ask them as they sit down to dinner. "You monsters, you're to blame for my boy's troubles. It's you who have traumatized him. I've known it all along, and now I have proof!" At this point, George would step forward and hold up the deck of pornographic playing cards for all to see.

Billy lifts his head and growls at his father.

George stops, glances back at the rectory, pinches his chin. "I dunno. We should probably get home. It's getting pretty late. And your mother isn't a very patient woman."

He flips through the cards one last time and then tosses them to the ground. Billy lets outs a high-pitched squeak and chases after them, an orgy of big-titted, suntanned harlots engaged in carnal acts with mustached kings, leering jacks, and a cross-eyed joker, his erect penis painted in motley and adorned in cap and bells.

When they finally get home, they see a figure sitting on the front steps. George's wife yanks the bandanna off her head, releasing a shower of graphite dust, and then crushes out her cigarette with the heel of a steel-toed boot. She immediately lights another and exhales an iron spike of smoke.

George smoothes back his hair, searches his pockets for a stick of chewing gum. He can still taste Ms. Higginson on his lips. For the first time in months he looks at his wife with a tinge of remorse, with something that might even be described as old-fashioned Catholic guilt. She's a scarecrow of her former self, shockingly thin, with dark circles of exhaustion under her eyes. She struggles every day to provide for the three of them, but somehow George suppresses this knowledge and has learned to live with his immaturity, his irresponsibility, his selfish pursuit of women and drink. The trick, he finds, is to turn his sins into virtues.

"No overtime tonight?" he says with a timid wave of his hand. He tries not to blink, not to turn away from his wife's lethal stare. "Ah, you bought some cigarettes, I see."

"Where the hell have you been?"

He grins. "Glad you asked. I was doing a good deed. For the Jesuits. The boiler sprung a leak. Over at the rectory."

"The boiler?"

"Yes."

"At the rectory?"

"That's right."

"Is this true?"

"Is *what* true?"

His wife glares at him. "I wasn't speaking to *you*. I was speaking to Billy. Well? Was your father fixing the boiler?"

George laughs. "You know damn well the boy doesn't talk. It's your fault, if you ask me. You treat him like an infant."

"He may not talk," she says calmly, "but he tells me things, all sorts of things. Everything worth knowing, anyway. I've trained him, you see, trained him well. Didn't I, Billy?"

George feels a small but noticeable change in the air. His smile fades, his stomach tightens. He wants to hurry down the street to the brewery, but since he is flat broke, he can only stand before his wife like the accused before a jury, helpless to defend himself against the trumped-up charges. With mounting horror, he watches Billy approach his mother. He looks like a toy soldier on the march, chin held high, shoulders back. A terrifying vision of precocity, a diabolical scourge. Suddenly the boy whirls on his heels, points an accusatory finger at his father, and, flashing a malevolent grin, holds up the deck of playing cards.

Uncreated Creatures

I

Three years after his wife abandoned him (left in the early morning hours just before dawn, slid from under the sheets without letting the bedsprings creak, put the car in neutral, pushed it down the driveway and into the street before starting it), Devin Wentworth finally musters the willpower to attend a colleague's party. Someone has just published a book or received a grant or had a marriage annulled—rarely is there a point to these kinds of things, any excuse to get drunk before the start of a new semester will do—and though he is a little uneasy about leaving the comfortable clutter of his books and the logic of his coffee-stained papers with their indecipherable marginalia, he is glad for the opportunity to socialize with old friends and to politely laugh at the same banal jokes they have been telling for years.

With a pensive grin, he enters the crowded house at the corner of Breyner and Andersen, but before he can say hello to the other guests or thank the host for inviting him, he is ambushed by a small, sprightly woman with short, boyish hair who takes him by the arm, leads him over to the makeshift bar in the dining room and selects, from the dizzying assortment of booze, a bottle of "homemade medicinal tea."

"You have to try some of this," she says, firing up a cigarette, "if only for the miraculous health benefits."

He declines her offer, fixes himself a Scotch and water, and as he waits for the liquor to take effect, he stands against a wall like a cornered animal and lets the woman do all of the talking. She proves to be exceptionally erudite, and for the next thirty minutes, without pausing to allow anyone to formally introduce them, she tells Devin that she is outlining a novel and demands a quick tutorial on the "ins and outs of monkey sex from a guy who knows his stuff."

"The plot concerns a certain high school athlete," she explains, "but that's all I'm willing to divulge. I never discuss any of my current projects. I'm superstitious that way. Most writers are. That probably sounds ridiculous to you, a man of science."

"Not at all," he says. "In fact—"

"Listen. I absolutely *must* know the specifics about Bonobo chimps and their sex rituals. Surely our nearest relatives engage in . . . unusual sexual practices. Apes doing it doggy style. I've asked around, and everyone tells me that this is your area of expertise. Maybe you can recommend some recent books on the subject? A kind of *Kama Sutra* for concupiscent primates?"

Devin answers with an uneasy laugh and plays with the buttons of his sport coat. A bookish man, awkward, poorly dressed, horribly out of practice when it comes to engaging members of the opposite sex in casual conversation, he is not exactly sure how to respond to this outlandish woman. He feels trapped, cornered. There is a constriction in his chest, a painful throbbing behind his eyes. With a handkerchief that may or may not be clean (he's not sure how long it's been in the pocket of his sport coat), he dabs at the beads of sweat that have formed on his brow, and to calm his nerves, he gulps down his cocktail. Above the clink of ice cubes, he catches the woman saying something about the Whittlesey Indians and their belief in a malevolent spirit who presides over creation and drives all of humanity to the brink of madness with loneliness and pointless suffering.

"Oh, how insensitive of me," she says, raising a hand to her mouth, "to speak of suffering." Like the other guests at the party, she knows all about his failed marriage, his schizophrenic wife. "I'm such a *farshikkert chaleria*. But I've never been one to shirk from the truth, no matter how embarrassing it might be. I've personally outed many people. And not just closeted homosexuals. Atheists, too. It's all for the best, don't you think? Cathartic. Let the cat out of the bag, I always say. Secrets are nasty things, bad for the soul. They're the ruin of so many men I know. People are going to talk anyway. Sooner or later word gets around."

Though he is not sure he agrees with this view, Devin indulges her with a smile, the way a man sometimes will when he knows he is dealing with a beguiling and slightly dangerous personality. Her eyes are crafty and unwavering, the color of the Mediterranean Sea as viewed from high on a hillside in the sunny Algarve, blue-green, silvery-teal, eyes made a little bleary by her medicinal tea. Devin isn't sure why he thinks of the Mediterranean, of Portugal; he's never been overseas. In fact, his travels have never taken him far beyond the great lake of his hometown, a body of water that for half the year is a frozen waste that shimmers like an enormous piece of sheet metal in the feeble gray light of winter. As he ponders this mystery, the woman says something that so bewilders him that he momentarily abandons his cherished principles of logic and embraces the romantic notion of kismet.

"As you can probably tell, I'm a passionate person. Until the auto-da-fé, my ancestors were sojourners in Portugal, and the Portuguese are a very passionate people—politically, theologically, sexually. I seem to have inherited a rapacious appetite for all things Portuguese. Their writing has a noticeable effect on my intellect . . . and libido."

By nature and training, Devin is a devout skeptic and has learned to doubt his own intuition, but after carefully assessing the situation he arrives at a startling conclusion: this woman is flirting with him. When was the last time that happened? College? Graduate school? Primatology seems to be the last thing on her mind. It's a matter of simple deduction. He observes the way she moistens her lips, plays with the ends of her hair, lets her blouse sink lower and lower to reveal her surprisingly ample cleavage.

With a haughty smile, she touches his hand and, leaning in close so that her breath makes his flesh tingle, she tells him how the work of Luís Vaz de Camões inspired Elizabeth Barrett Browning to write *Sonnets from the Portuguese*. "Allow me to give you a little recitation," she whispers. "'How do I love thee? Let me count the ways . . .'"

II

As the party winds down and only the seriously inebriated remain, Devin is given some sobering information.

"Ah, yes, that's our newest faculty member," says the principal. "Batya Pinter."

The old man stumbles along the foyer to the front door, the last of the Jesuits to leave the party and one of the few in attendance who doesn't attempt to disguise his penchant for whiskey with hypocritical proclamations about the wickedness of drink, the lure of the bottle. "From the way you two were yammering away, I assumed you already knew each other. She'll be teaching English and editing the literary magazine. She boasts a number of important connections in the world of letters. That's why we hired her. She's actually interviewed dozens of luminaries—José Saramago, António Lobo Antunes, even the legendary Ricardo Reis. Last month she translated and published a posthumous collection of poems by Fernando Pessoa. She's quite brilliant. But I'm afraid she's also . . ."

The principal coughs into a fist and glances over his shoulder to make sure no one is within earshot.

"This information is strictly confidential, you understand, but since your son may come into contact with this woman, I feel you have the right to know." He tries to enunciate his words, but the consonants are slurred, the syllables protracted and a bit garbled. "Some of us think Pinter is a sexual omnivore, bedding men and women as the mood strikes her, and that she may be guilty of, how should I put this delicately, *debauching* a few of our students, those giggling pimply-faced boys with grand ambitions of becoming the next Nabokov. Of course we can't *prove* these allegations, not in the legal sense of the word, but we do have circumstantial evidence. She keeps strange hours, locks herself in her office late at night, requests certain students stay after school for reasons that are never made clear . . ."

Devin shakes his head and dismisses these allegations as the drunken maunderings of paranoid cleric. He has never taken seriously the rumors circulating around the school. The Jesuits are terrible gossips, worse than any cloister of women.

"I couldn't help but notice," says the principal, "that Pinter has taken a sudden *liking* to you. In fact, she seems overly friendly, if I may say so. A most interesting development. Yes, quite intriguing." He places his hands on Devin's shoulders. His breath smells of liquor and cigarettes. "Allow me to ask a small favor of you, Wentworth. Keep an eye on her. Get to *know* her better. Oh, I don't expect you to *spy* on the woman, not exactly. Just find out if things are . . . kosher, if you get my meaning."

Devin nods. He has always been a most ingratiating fellow.

The principal pats his back. "Ah, you're a gentleman and a scholar!" He steps outside and totters along the sidewalk. "I know I can trust you to fulfill your mission."

Devin offers a quick salute and then turns to the mirror in the foyer to check his reflection. He is as unassuming as a character in a Graham Greene novel—a bit ruffled perhaps but still presentable, guilt-ridden of course, that goes without saying, and maybe just a little desperate, but also poised, classy, determined. He lowers his head, pinches his chin, cocks an eyebrow. The scotch gives him a sudden surge of confidence, makes him brash, Bond-like. He struts boldly over to Batya, puts an arm around her waist, and suggests she accompany him back to his house a few blocks away in what the students call the Faculty Ghetto.

"We can ransack my shelves," he tells her, "for books about the autoerotic behavior of Bonobo chimps. I'm sure we'll find something that will . . . *satisfy* you."

She drops her cigarette into her cup of tea. "Let me get my coat."

As they walk along the midnight streets, they listen to the familiar wail of police sirens, the flapping of newspapers in the trees, the loud splatter of urine from a bag lady squatting in an alley. Batya leans against Devin for support; she is very drunk indeed ("What kind of tea *was* that?" he asks her), but once inside his house, she lunges at him with animal ferocity, something Devin actually knows a little about and is able to assess the following morning by the severity of the scratches on his back and the number of bite marks on his shoulders and neck.

That night if he lasts longer than his usual four minutes, it's only because he, too, is cross-eyed drunk and keeps yowling with pain and pleasure whenever Batya, nimble as a gymnast, bends and slides and twists her glistening body over the bed. She slaps his ass, tugs his hair, wraps her legs around his neck and, in a style that can be described only as dictatorial, shouts filthy words in an ancient tongue, demanding that he make her scream with his *langer lucksh*, that he abuse her with his *batampte shmeckle*.

She yearns for abuse, wants to be dominated, victimized, but it's all a ruse; she is in total control, Devin knows this perfectly well, and he tries to oblige her until the final moment, the *supreme* moment, when she groans between clenched teeth, "I love thee to the depth and breadth and height my soul can reach!"

III

To his credit, Devin has never brought a woman back home for the purposes of copulation (in fact, Batya is the first woman he has taken to bed since his wife left him), but this does not excuse the lurid and passionate caterwauling that keeps his son Tom up half the night. At first, Devin isn't too terribly concerned about his naughty behavior. Surely by now Tom must understand that his father, like all men, has certain needs. Besides, teenagers these days are pretty savvy about the ways of the world. Nearly half the students in this year's graduating class come from broken homes and have witnessed scandals of every sort, things unmentionable, unpardonable, excommunicable. In any case, this encounter with Batya was merely a moment of weakness on Devin's part, nothing more.

"Sometimes a man's weakness can be his best asset," Batya tells him the next morning as she gathers her clothes from the floor. "Sin opens a door to a world of possibilities. Virtue only slams it shut."

To his surprise, she says she wants to see him again, and in the days that follow, Batya liberates him from the pitiable consolation of masturbation and converts him to a whole new world of hedonistic pleasure. Suddenly his lonely nights are filled with delights and enchantments of every sort. The sex is raw, filthy, probably illegal in several states, and Devin, who resigned himself long ago to a life of celibacy, nearly weeps at this incredible stroke of good fortune.

Still, he has a sense of decency and wants to protect Tom's innocence, so he takes Batya to a decrepit flophouse down the street, the Zanzibar Towers & Gardens, where the landlady rents rooms by the hour. The seediness of the room adds an extra element of eroticism to their coupling, but the novelty quickly wears off. Domesticity is a force to be reckoned with, it tends to burn its heretics at the stake of public opinion, and while Batya is, in many respects, the most modern of women, she is also the product of an orthodox upbringing and cannot dispense with tradition altogether.

"Technically speaking, you're still a married man," she reminds him as they lie in bed. She puts an ashtray on his chest and taps hot embers from the tip of her cigarette. "You never divorced your wife. And here we are running off to some roach-infested room. What, you don't think people will talk? The Jesuits? Your students? Your son?"

He doesn't like the tone of her voice, the sudden seriousness of it, and rather than answer her right away, he takes a moment to study the cracks in the ceiling. He looks for patterns, tries to find the point where the fractures begin.

Batya sighs. "You realize what the real problem is, don't you? After your wife flew the coop, you never sat down with Tom to discuss his feelings."

"Fathers and sons don't talk about those kinds of things. We internalize our despair, our rage, our angst. It's perfectly natural. It's inherent in the genes. It has something to do with evolutionary conflicts, group selection. Complicated stuff. Technical."

"Dear God, listen to this man!" Batya says in exasperation. "Your son needs you, and all you ever do is talk monkey business."

The truth is, Devin no longer understands his son. While most boys his age try out for the football team or write for the school newspaper or pilfer a few beers from the fridge to share with their buddies around a bonfire, Tom spends much of his time alone in the spartan cell of his bedroom, poring over his books of eschatology like some lunatic monk. What he does in there Devin cannot say, but sleep doesn't seem to be part of the equation. Admittedly, Devin has pressed an ear against the door but has been reluctant to trespass on his son's privacy. He is afraid of what he might find inside.

After one wonderful month of bestial rutting, Devin and

Batya return to the relative respectability of home and hearth, where their relationship becomes quite tame, conventional, uninspired. Though he has never been particularly susceptible to paranoia, Devin finds himself sitting quietly at the edge of the bed, having hardly broken a sweat during their brief roll in the hay, obsessing about the inadequacy of his cocksmanship. He counts the reasons why an attractive woman like Batya would remain faithful to him, her fumbling and incompetent middle-aged lover.

He is no sexual dynamo, he is willing to admit as much, but he believes that all men are inept lovers to some degree, clumsy and insensitive. On this point most women will surely concur. Among great apes, the sex act is not the stuff of sonnets and flower gardens. Male chimpanzees climax with quickness and ease; they seem to understand the brute necessity for reproduction and the importance of passing on their genes. Human males aren't so different. On average (and in this regard Devin is quite average), a man has an orgasm in less than five minutes, a disheartening statistic for any woman hoping to fulfill some erotic fantasy, the details of which may have been carefully worked out weeks, even months, in advance. It is perhaps for this reason that most women in a committed relationship never bother with infidelity.

And yet there is a paradox here. Unlike men who tend to be visual creatures, always sizing up height and weight and firmness of tit, women are much more discriminating, selecting mates who will make for excellent long-term partners; they look for certain qualities in a man: stability, intelligence, sanity—a tall order to fill, no doubt. Chances are Batya will find someone or something—man, woman, vibrator—that can pleasure her physically rather than emotionally and spiritually.

IV

On a Sunday morning in October, as he reads the newspaper, alternately shaking his head at the puerile arguments on the op-ed page and sipping a cup of instant coffee, Devin hears the sound of bare feet slapping against the linoleum floor and looks up to see his son trudging toward the refrigerator. A skinny, hairy, greasy mess of a boy, Tom resembles an obdurate Iron Age patriarch—angular, gaunt, hunched over, staring into space with eyes that are bloodshot and crazed, as if trying to calculate the distance between the present moment and the final one, the great mystery of death, so that the reality all around him is almost nonexistent.

"Good morning," Devin says.

Tom mumbles something terse. He drinks straight from the carton of milk. He smacks his lips and wipes his mouth with the back of his hand. After emitting a low, gurgling belch, he scratches his face and stands beside his father's chair.

With some reluctance, Devin folds the newspaper and places it on the kitchen table, hoping Tom will take the hint and decide to leave him alone. Batya is right, of course. He should probably speak to the boy, ask what's on his mind, but dealing with teen angst used to be his wife's forte, not his, and he doesn't especially want to hear about his son's personal problems. It's much too early in the day for that sort of thing.

Tom glances at the pack of cigarettes on the kitchen counter. "Is Batya still here?"

"No, she left early this morning to conduct more research on her novel."

Though he has never been permitted to read a single page of her book or invited to spend the night at her house in the country, Devin is thrilled to be involved with a creative type, a real bohemian, someone the Jesuits claim to respect and admire but secretly abhor and distrust. After leading an uneventful life, Devin has become a kind of double agent, a man of high adventure who obtains precious bits of information through subterfuge and seduction.

Tom crosses his arms. "Too bad. I was hoping she'd still be here."

"Why is that?"

"Because I'm going to Mass."

"Going where?"

"To church, Dad. It starts in . . ." he glances at the clock " . . . less than an hour. I wanted to know if Batya cared to join me."

"Did she express an interest?"

He shrugs his shoulders. "Sort of. I'd ask you to come along, but I know how *you* feel about these kinds of things."

"What kinds of things?"

"Religion. The hereafter. God."

In this house, the topic of religion is taboo. Devin's agnosticism must always be kept secret. Aside from the occasional wedding and funeral, he does not attend church services and tries to avoid them whenever possible. He can't comprehend why so many otherwise perfectly rational people take solace in this nonsense, and it is only by consulting the dusty tomes written by his colleagues that he can distinguish between the warring factions of Christian denominations that flourish and spread like a green muck in the steaming malarial swamps of the American spiritual landscape. As much as he detests ritual, Devin hates scripture even more. The cloying and calcified style of biblical prose fills his mouth like the dust and grit of the Sinai itself, although he has, out of curiosity, skimmed a few passages from the Old Testament. He read about King Saul, who, despite passing laws prohibiting his subjects from calling upon witches and mediums, traveled incognito to the desert oasis of Endor to consult a necromancer from whom he hoped to receive the guidance of the dead. From this story, Devin has devised a simple axiom upon which he can base all arguments about religious thinking: *The level of devotion among the faithful is in direct proportion to their hypocrisy.*

Now he pushes his chair away from the table and says, "Tom, let me ask you something. What kinds of things have the priests been teaching you lately?"

With an impudent smile, the boy answers, "Don't worry, Dad. They haven't been brainwashing me, if that's what you want to know."

In fact, it *is* what he wants to know. He sends Tom to the Jesuit school not for the tiresome tautologies of the elderly clergyman, but for the rigorous curriculum, the militaristic discipline, and, since Devin is a faculty member, the free tuition.

"Indoctrination, Tom, that's what I'm worried about. Disinformation. Manipulation."

"I'd just like to go to church, Dad. The Jesuits have nothing to do with it. I'm leaving in ten minutes."

Devin stirs his coffee and watches the cream spiral slowly into an infinitesimal galaxy. By adding another drop of cream, he transforms the Milky Way into a rapidly expanding Crab Nebula. For a long time, he stares into his mug, contemplating the far-flung stars, and after some consideration, he agrees to accompany his son to Mass. He wants to see what the boy is up to, surely he is up to *something*, all seventeen-year-old boys more or less are, but he is also curious to find out what the priests are up to. Over the years, Devin has become better acquainted with these men, with their values, their ethics, their politics, and though they profess to be well-meaning, they are always a little too eager to take advantage of a boy who is susceptible to the Jesuitical arts of rhetoric and persuasion.

V

Intentionally designed to look out of place among the warehouses and factories of this industrial city in terminal decline, the little Romanesque chapel, built of flint and rubble masonry, is exactly the kind of structure an American traveler hopes to encounter while passing through an isolated Irish hamlet, and indeed the place seems to echo with the ghostly voices of peasants ground to dust by the rigid doctrines of a dying priestdom. The curious carvings on its archways seem so ancient and faded from wind and rain that they might predate Christianity, the work of recalcitrant pagans, barbarian invaders, heavy-browed Neanderthals. The enormous frescos that dominate the apse depict vengeful angels and valiant missionaries, legendary figures meant to instill the requisite awe and humility in the parishioners.

Today the chapel is filled nearly to capacity. Devin and Tom manage to squeeze into a back pew near the heavy wooden doors. *A dungeon door*, thinks Devin, and as he mentally prepares himself for an excruciatingly boring ceremony, he looks around and is surprised to see so many of his rambunctious pupils sitting in silence, their hands resting on their knees. If only they would behave this way in the classroom. Eager to record their unusual behavior, Devin reaches for the pencil and scratch pad he keeps handy in his coat pocket (no self-respecting scientist would leave home without these essential tools), but before he can jot down his observations, the pipe organ blares an alarming chord. The congregants jump to their feet, open their hymnals, and lift their voices high.

The principal emerges from a cloud of incense and marches down the aisle to the tabernacle. When the lugubrious singing finally ends, the priest raises his arms and recites the opening prayer. The ceremony goes slowly, and Devin is forced to suppress his yawns as he listens to the introductory rites, the act of penitence, the Kyrie, a reading from the Gospel of Mark. It isn't until the homily that he becomes fully aware of the boom and thunder of the principal's baritone as it sweeps back and forth across the chapel, an impressive instrument that startles Devin out of a daydream about Batya's tight abdominal muscles.

"Whenever we encounter evil in the world," says the principal, "we must turn the other cheek. The Lord instructs us to do so. He asks us to tolerate and understand our ideological foes, demands that we refrain from casting judgment on our enemies. There is evidence for this in the scripture, certainly there is, but Christ also provides another kind of teaching, one that we must carefully consider in our own day and age.

"Today's reading from the Gospel of Mark deals with a man from Gadarenes who was possessed by a legion of demons. Shunned by everyone in his village, the man lived alone among the tombs near the sea. Upon encountering this poor fellow, Jesus quickly assessed the gravity of the situation and took action. Jesus did not ask permission to cast the demons into a herd of swine, nor did He ponder the ethics of slaughtering those innocent animals.

"This may seem like a distant episode until you realize that a legion of devils dwells in the minds and bodies of so many people today. Look no further than the high school classrooms where some teachers have fallen prey to the insidious cult of secular humanism and the fanciful theory of natural selection. But I ask you: what is so natural about natural selection?

"Science tells us that nature isn't a *thing* but a *process* of infinite change, turmoil, boundless confusion. Nature abhors order, and as a result, the universe is in a continuous state of flux. Nothing is permanent. There is no ground of being, no definitive order to the cosmos, no guiding hand. There is no grace, no wholeness, no divinity, no fixed intent. Science goes even further and makes the wild and unsubstantiated claim that human beings are not separate from nature but are merely the end result of random processes. Indeed, we *are* the process, we *are* nature. Surely this accounts for the insidious belief that humans have evolved from clever chimpanzees with a penchant for sodomy.

"Why, no less a genius than Pierre Teilhard de Chardin satirized these dangerous ideas with his paleontological hoax Piltdown Man. He understood that we are fundamentally different than the beasts of the field, that we are more than ashes and dust with a primal urge. God created us in His image. He gave us the breath of life. But scientists, by rejecting God and the concept of original sin, gamble with the fate of their eternal souls and with the souls of their students. They commit the most egregious crimes upon their charges, turning them into materialists, religious skeptics, freethinkers.

"And so we return to the man from Gadarenes, and we must ask ourselves an obvious question: do such demons lurk within the hallowed halls of our own institution, *can* they dwell among us, unnoticed, unseen, untouched? Have some of our teachers been infected with a sickness that is rapidly spreading through the entire society? Have they infiltrated our community through treachery and deceit?"

Devin's heart begins to race. He desperately wants to look around the chapel to see if anyone is whispering and pointing in his direction, but he manages to keep his eyes focused on the principal. Someone has ratted him out, he's sure of it. Someone has told the principal that he is an apostate, an unbeliever, a trespasser. But who could it be? Who would double-cross him? Batya? Tom? One of his students? And if so, why? What's the motive? Then again, perhaps a motive doesn't matter all that much. In this world, there is no shortage of insidious plots, and behind each one there is a Judas willing to make a moral compromise for a short-term gain.

The principal grips the sides of the pulpit and cranes his neck past the microphone until his head seems to hover above his flock, and this time when he speaks, he sounds not like a man of learning but a crazed apothecary hawking his worthless elixirs to a hostile mob on the verge of tarring and feathering him unless he can produce some tangible results.

"The faculty members of this school are committed to the core values and teachings of the Church, I am convinced of this. But let me be clear. Should I find an impostor among us, I will not hesitate. Like Jesus I will fight the devil tooth and nail. I will banish him from this holy place. And believe me, believe me all of you, I will win the battle.

"But victory in one battle does not mean victory in war. And that is why I've come before you today. Students must take part in the struggle, too. It is up to you to keep your eyes and ears open and to spread the gospel by traveling to those places where the divine Logos has been distorted by this new religion called science. Missionary work, gentlemen, mission-

ary work is required of you. Because a day of reckoning is
coming, yes, it most surely is. For God is blind with purpose!"

VI

For the rest of the day, Devin tries to unravel the meaning of
this homily.

The need to personify evil is deeply ingrained in the
imaginations of today's congregants, but because modernity
has forced them to abandon the old mythological symbols—
Beelzebub sharpening his pitchfork and setting aside time
in his busy schedule to pose for another Hieronymus Bosch
triptych—they demand the Church provide them with a new
and improved devil, one so clever and insidious that he might
even be sitting beside them in the pew. Gone are those innocuous hymns of love and praise that once filled the chapel. In
their place are the words of an ancient deity who speaks from
out of a pillar of fire and cloud and who takes great delight
in wreaking havoc on the minds of credulous churchgoers,
drowning them like a heathen army in a sea of absurdities.

On Monday morning, certain that he will find a pink slip
pinned to his office door, Devin takes the unprecedented step
of altering the content of his lectures and gives them a more
faith-based tenor. After a brief talk on "primate spirituality," he
shows his students a documentary on how chimpanzees display
grief at the passing of a loved one. He draws their attention to
the look of sorrow and bewilderment in the eyes of these creatures and how they seem to kneel before the dead. "It's almost as
though they're *praying*." Convinced that his classroom is bugged
and has probably been under surveillance for several weeks,
Devin takes care to speak the words with great conviction.

At noon he joins Batya in the faculty lunchroom. Since he

doesn't have much of an appetite, he spends his time trying to read the faces of his colleagues. He observes their body language and makes a mental note of those who avoid eye contact with him. Which of them is the professional character assassin? It's impossible to say. They all wear masks of total indifference, including Batya, who tosses his name into a hat for the "monthly drawing." Everyone is eager for another night of reckless drinking, and as the seasons wheel around, each faculty member takes a turn hosting a party—the obligatory Christmas celebration, the Saint Patrick's Day bash, the Memorial Day cookout—and now, as luck would have it, Devin is picked to host this year's Halloween masquerade.

Sensing his trepidation, Batya strokes his knee under the table and says, "Just remember, if it hadn't been for the party at the beginning of the semester we never would have gotten involved."

Devin gives his grudging consent because, he must admit, without Batya his social life would be very pitiful indeed.

He has plenty of time to berate himself afterward. On the day of the party, Batya is nowhere to be found, and Devin, a chronic procrastinator who has never hosted a formal gathering of any kind, is soon overwhelmed by the sheer volume of refuse in his house—old phone books stacked in corners, yellowed newspapers bundled beside the backdoor, piles of dead flies that have collected on windowsills and have turned into brittle, black shells. He vacuums the rugs, sweeps the hardwood floors, wipes the walls, brushes cobwebs from the ceiling. He can't remember the last time he changed the sheets on his bed, a thought that troubles him greatly. What kind of woman would tolerate a man who lives in such spectacular squalor?

He considers asking his son for help but decides he doesn't want to be left alone with the boy for an extended period of time, especially not today. It's Tom's eighteenth birthday, an important milestone, but Devin has never been the sentimental sort; he doesn't believe in cake and candles and bright balloons. Small children celebrate birthdays, not grown men. But before he resumes scrubbing the toilets and sinks, Devin slinks along the hallway and slips an envelope with a ten-dollar bill under his son's bedroom door.

VII

With the approach of evening, several figures in black cloaks and Venetian masks knock on the door. Despite their obvious dismay at the deplorable conditions inside, Devin's guests compliment him on the loveliness of his home and waste no time lining up at the folding table to load their paper plates with raw vegetables, spinach dip, and precooked cocktail sausages wrapped in bacon. By eight o'clock, thirty people jostle for space inside the tiny house, and at some point, Devin is not sure when, he's far too busy opening cases of beer and mixing martinis, he smells cigarette smoke and hears shrill laughter.

From the way her eyes are spinning, it's clear that Batya has already had quite a lot to drink. More of that damn medicinal tea, no doubt. She turns on the stereo and twists the dial until the house resounds with a trio of classical guitarists strumming a rhapsodic fado. Satisfied with the volume and the mournfulness of the tune, Batya walks into the living room and holds court near the fireplace. She has a way of attracting an audience, and before long a small group of men is listening intently to one of her stories, whether make-believe or true who can say?

"When I was a child of six or seven," she tells them, "my aunt presented me with the gift of a doll. She felt sorry for me, I suppose—her skinny, oddball niece. I had few friends and avoided the company of children my own age. I spent bright summer afternoons in my bedroom, reading books and acting out plays. After she gave me the doll, she told me to take good care of it. I murmured a quick thank you—my parents raised me to be polite—and then I rushed up to my room. I was so excited I almost tripped over my own feet."

Batya went on to describe how, using a pair of scissors and a coat hanger, she methodically dissected the doll, taking it apart not in some haphazard fashion, cruelly and stupidly as a boy would, no, but with genuine curiosity, piece by piece, thread by thread, to see how it had been manufactured. She became so engrossed in these labors that she failed to notice her doddering aunt standing in the doorway. She was a snoop, didn't believe in knocking, and when she saw the neat pile of arms and legs on the floor and the coat hanger in Batya's hand, she cried out in horror.

"I must have looked like some back alley abortionist."

The men do spit-takes and laugh so hard that they nearly choke on their cocktail weenies. Laughing loudest of all, however, is Tom, who stands apart from the others. In the flickering firelight, he looks deranged, menacing, completely unhinged.

"I didn't see you come in," says Devin.

"Jews are condemned to burn for all eternity!" the boy shouts. "Doomed to the agonies of hellfire, every last one. Moses Maimonides and Karl Marx and Saul Bellow."

Devin doesn't know what to do; he isn't very effective at diffusing confrontation and could use some help, but when he turns to Batya for support, he sees in her eyes something that alarms him, a look he recognizes from their first night together, the night when she initiated their affair and coaxed him from his clothes, but only now does he begin to understand that she possesses an extraordinary gift. Where another woman might simply see an emotionally distraught male, Batya envisions someone with enormous potential, a sad prattling homunculus, a half-formed and imperfect creature that, with patience and care, she can mold to her stringent specifications. Far from being angry with Tom, Batya in fact seems oddly moved by the boy's hateful outburst and has an irresistible urge to mentor him as she has reputedly mentored so many boys before, the wayward athletes and those docile, delusional scribes who toil away on the school's literary magazine long into the evening hours like children in a sweatshop, gangly and bespectacled copy editors who leaf through insurmountable piles of manuscripts and smirk at Devin, the ridiculous cuckold with the thinning hair and noticeable paunch, who occasionally shows up at the office to invite the revered editor to dinner.

Devin is about to object to his son's words when Batya sets her drink down on the coffee table.

"So, Jews are going to burn, are they? You forgot to mention George Gershwin and Groucho Marx and Woody Allen."

This generates more laughter from the guests.

"I'm simply giving you the facts," Tom tells her, "and the fact is you'll burn, you'll *burn*."

"My dear boy," says Batya in a calm tone, "you're not being reasonable."

"It's not me, it's God. And you can't *reason* with God. He does what He pleases. He makes the rules and enforces them. And *He* says that unbelievers will burn!"

Tom marches closer to the fireplace. In his hand he holds several copies of the literary magazine, the ones Batya has personalized for Devin with salacious notes and crude drawings. She is particularly adept at sketching phalluses, proudly erect, and beautiful women who caress them with their hands and loving lips. One by one Tom tosses the magazines into the fire. The pages shrivel, curl, and blacken. Devin gazes into the fire and is startled to find that the ashes of the journal look no different than the ashes of the newspaper he used earlier to kindle the flames. In some strange way, he feels like he has been duped, that despite what the experts say, genius and mediocrity meet the same fate and in the end are indistinguishable from one another.

Batya smirks. "Looks like we're going to have us an old-fashioned book burning, folks!"

With a wavering voice, Devin says, "Tom, I think you should go to your room."

"My *room?*" Now comes a dark, disgusted, incredulous laughter. "Don't worry, Dad. I won't disturb you. I'll leave you two alone tonight so you can fuck each other silly. Fuck your brains out!"

The boy storms out of the house, slamming the door behind him.

To Devin's surprise, the guests do not check their watches, make excuses, collect their coats; they keep on drinking just as before. They are used to unruly behavior from obnoxious boys and don't seem in the least bit bothered by Tom's antics.

"I'm so sorry . . ." Devin says.

Batya pats his hand. "Don't worry. Attend to your guests. I'll go check on him. He just needs to talk things over with someone."

Devin is unsure if he should be grateful or suspicious, but he has no time to analyze the situation. The party rages on. His guests demand more beer, more wine, more whiskey. "An old-fashioned Roman saturnalia" is how he might describe the situation, and it isn't until well after midnight, when the last few guests spill from the house, singing a bastardized version of the school's alma mater, that he realizes Tom and Batya are nowhere to be found.

VIII

The next morning, Devin considers calling the police to report the boy missing, but Tom is eighteen now, an adult in the eyes of the law, and the police will simply tell him that a man of eighteen can do whatever he damn well pleases. They will probably suggest he try Tom's classmates to ask if they have seen him, but the idea is absurd since Tom has no friends, no confidantes, no enemies either. Hoping to distract himself from a growing sense of unease, Devin wanders through the house, picking up plastic cups filled with cigarette butts and paper plates smeared with bright orange cheese dip, but after an hour he realizes that there is no sense in delaying the inevitable. He finds the phone under the coffee table and dials Batya's number. It rings three times, four times, and when she doesn't answer he leaves a series of rambling messages that range from anger to despair to outrage. He sits on the couch, waits all afternoon, but she fails to return his calls.

Before nightfall, he makes the journey to her house in the country, a cottage of timber and stone several miles from the closest town, the pastoral writer's retreat that he has been forbidden to visit. He races up the gravel driveway and hammers on the door with his fists until he thinks he might break the damn thing down. Cupping his hands around his eyes, he looks through the front windows. The rooms appear dark, empty, uninviting, but Devin, unwilling to accept defeat, stalks through the neglected flowerbeds thick with weeds and ivy and searches the property until he finds a wooden ladder inside an old tool shed. He props the ladder against the back of the house and climbs to the top window. There he sees a four-poster bed, neatly made, a nightstand crowded with books, an empty glass, a bottle.

Satisfied that she is not home, Devin does something extraordinarily juvenile but also wonderfully gratifying. He climbs down the ladder, gathers a handful of fermenting crab apples that litter the ground and uses them to pelt the house. He smashes a ceramic mug left on an Adirondack chair and shatters a window. Then he unzips his pants and pisses on the hardy mums that grow in big clay pots around the porch.

On Monday morning, he arrives early to school, hoping to confront Batya before the morning bell rings, but he finds a note posted to her office door: "Ms. Pinter will not be in to-day." He walks over to the cafeteria, but Tom is not sitting in his usual spot in the corner, playing solitaire or doodling geometric patterns in his notebook.

Devin tries to stay focused on his work, but as the day wears on, his mind begins to drift. He thinks of all the different people Batya might be with, men and women, boys and girls, fathers and sons; there is never a shortage of willing partners, real or imaginary. During his final lecture, he fervently explains to his pupils how primates experience mental as well as physical pain, that there is no sharp dividing line between human and animal anguish.

"Great apes have been known to combat despair with

dance and mock battles and sport. To call this behavior spiritual or ritualistic is no exaggeration. And that is why we have a responsibility to these creatures. The Hebrew word *v'yirdu* does not mean 'dominion' as it is commonly translated in the first chapter of Genesis. The word actually implies 'rule,' but rule of a very particular kind, rule that is synonymous with stewardship. Like the great biblical kings who ruled over their subjects, Saul and David and Solomon, we are to rule over creation with care and respect and justice. Indeed, we are commanded to do so by the great celestial dictator who rules humanity without mercy. You do see the irony in this, don't you? Of course you do. You're all very perceptive."

The boys whisper and laugh until a familiar voice comes over the public address system.

"Mr. Wentworth, may I please see you in my office?"

For the first time in his long teaching career, Devin begins to understand how his students must feel when the priests reprimand them—it's a combination of resentment, humiliation, and shame, but most of all shame—and when he enters the principal's office, he instinctively focuses on the tips of his shoes, which are old, scuffed, cracked. A pauper's shoes.

"Wentworth," says the principal, leaning back in his chair and lighting a cigarette. A hard rain pelts the windows like thumbtacks. A gust of wind plasters a veil of dead, wet leaves to the glass. "Take a seat. I'm sure you know why I've called you here."

Devin decides not to fight the charges or feign ignorance. Like a groveling sinner, he makes a detailed confession, tells his superior everything that has transpired since the beginning of the semester, how he has been sleeping with Batya and how he believes she has run off with his son.

"That's quite a story, Wentworth." The principal's words are slow and measured. "I must say that I wasn't convinced that you and Pinter were . . . seeing each other outside the classroom. There were, as you may have guessed, rumors floating around, but I never pay any attention to that sort of thing. Gossip is the devil's work, eh? And to be perfectly honest, I didn't think you were capable of . . . committing such a serious infraction. I'll need to give this matter some thought. You are aware, of course, that any kind of romantic entanglement between faculty members is strictly forbidden. It creates the potential for a sexual harassment lawsuit. And we both know how women can be. They see these things differently than we do."

The principal points to the ashtray at the corner of his desk and snaps his fingers.

Devin dutifully pushes it toward him.

"Still, I want to thank you for your honesty, Wentworth. You've obviously been through quite a lot." He crushes out the butt of his cigarette and lights another. "As for your son . . . I think I may be able to help you locate him. I spoke to Tom on Friday afternoon. He seemed troubled, on the edge of a great precipice. I tried to offer him guidance, suggested he spend some time at the rectory. He seemed appreciative. But then, just this morning, I learned that he left town to do missionary work with a group of his classmates. Right now he is in a small town called Gehenna. I only know this, mind you, because his name appears on the list."

The principal slides a piece of paper across the desk to Devin.

"Naturally, I thought he received your permission to go."

"We never discussed it," says Devin. "Is there any way I could call him?"

The principal takes a long drag on his cigarette. "I'm afraid we don't allow missionaries to use any of the conveniences of modern life, telephones and computers and so forth. We want them to have as little contact with the outside world as possible. But I'm only too happy to show you where the boys are. Here is a map . . ."

IX

It takes Devin the rest of the afternoon to drive to that remote corner of the state. Deep in the rounded mountains and misty valleys, he sees few signs of civilization and wonders what life is like for the people who inhabit these impoverished villages with names lost to time—Sheol, Tartarus, Megiddo, Moreh, Tabor, Jezreel. He drives many miles before coming to a crossroads, but this other road—if it can be called a road at all—is just a narrow stretch of mud with the deep markings of combines and tractors. Devin slows down and impulsively decides to make the turn. The grooves and ruts are deep and wide and offer little traction. His rear tires spin. He hits the breaks hard and then pumps the gas. He is pitched and tossed in the front seat, but eventually the car lurches forward.

He passes a simple, white farmhouse and a small, tilled field where wheat or maybe rye once grew. As the sky turns purple with twilight, the road tunnels into a dark wood and skirts the banks of a blackwater river. A colony of rusty ramshackle trailers teeters on the crumbling embankment just above the upper falls as though the inhabitants are simply waiting for the first big rains to sweep them away downstream to a new life. A group of children stands outside in the thistle and cypress spurge. There are six of them in all, a few horribly thin, a few morbidly obese, their skin pale green from the onset of some disease long believed to be eradicated from the earth. In the fading November light, they resemble a lost tribe of gnomes, fabled creatures from the worn and wrinkled pages of a storybook, but a storybook Devin has not read; he was never in the habit of reading to his son, so the children appear all the more sinister to him. He asks for directions. Hooting and whistling, the children scale the frame of a cannibalized pickup truck and point into the distance.

A mile farther down the road, in a steep-sided valley, Devin manages to spot a small fire where the missionaries have set up camp. The boys huddle around the fire, warming their hands, staring intently at the floating embers that cool and fade and turn to ash. They listen to the nocturnal sounds of the marshy woods all around, to the calls of sandpipers and mallards on the river. The place has the feeling of a religious gulag, a rehabilitation camp for nonbelievers, and Devin gets the sense that the principal has sent him here as a kind of punishment.

In the dark it's hard to make out their faces, but Devin can tell right away that Tom is not among them. When he inquires about his son's whereabouts, he notices how the boys look away or cast pitying looks in his direction.

That woman, they tell him, came from the city and ordered Tom to get into her car.

Devin nods. No further explanation is needed. He is about to walk away when he asks, "Who is supervising this trip?"

The boys stare at him for a long time before one of them says, "We thought the Jesuits sent you to be in charge."

They ask if he'd like to join them in their simple meal. The Jesuits, they explain, do not provide funds; missionaries are expected to go from door to door begging for alms in imitation of the saints and prophets, and while it is certainly true that Gehenna is one the poorest towns in the state, the people here are generous and give whatever they can. The boys share a can of beans, a bag of overripe apples, a few ears of corn, some small pieces of gamey meat that they slice into thin strips with bowie knives. Among the cinders are the scattered bones of a large rodent, a rabbit perhaps, or a possum.

After they finish eating, they pass around a bottle of medicinal tea.

"Did *she* leave this with you?" Devin asks when the bottle reaches him.

Yes, they say. A gift.

"But isn't it a sin," he inquires, "to pollute your bodies with this stuff?"

Maybe so, they admit, but the boys do not abide by any rigidly defined dogma, not when they're so far from school. The tea induces visions of a mystical nature, the woman assured them of this, and they are eager to look upon the face of God, no matter how unorthodox the methods. The tea shocks them into a new awareness of the world, aides them in their efforts to escape from the prison of the psyche. The Indians of the Peruvian rain forests have their ayahuasca, the shamans of the American West their peyote, the sub-Saharan Africans their Iboga, the people of Gehenna their white lightning, and the Jesuits their sacramental wine.

Devin has never tried the tea and takes a small, hesitant sip. Its effects are initially quite pleasant—it warms his belly and makes him feel a little light-headed—and during the course of that long night, whenever the bottle comes his way, he takes larger sips. He sits cross-legged by the fire and learns a great deal about these boys, about their beliefs and practices.

Life, they tell him, is a feud between man and the devil; God takes no part in it. That is why there is so much suffering in the world. Suffering is the great answer everyone is seeking, the proverbial meaning of life. Happiness is a temporary thing, impermanent, as illusory as any dream, and suffering is only a prelude to even greater depths of despair. It hints at something far more wretched than the trivial miseries of day-to-day existence.

"What can you possibly know about suffering?" Devin is tempted to ask, but he knows that some of these boys, the unlucky ones, have already seen their fair share of pain—death, divorce, addiction, heartache, disaster heaped upon disaster. Youth offers no immunity from life's tragedies.

At some point, the discussion turns ugly, and the boys begin to argue among themselves; they wrestle near the flames and exchange blows, a clumsy, sweaty two-step accompanied by the clapping of hands and maniacal laughter. Devin can do nothing to stop the chaos. Invisible fingers pin him to the ground, and as the evening wears on, he is beset by many visions. Nightmare creatures, simian in their visage, scuttle out of the cerulean shadows to crouch near the blinding firelight. They—the visions, the boys, the fabular swampland things, he's not sure exactly what—circle around him, inching their way closer and closer. Scabrous, monstrous, scarcely conscious of anything other than their own hunger, they sniff and chortle and prance around the roaring flames. Then they reach out to touch him, to stroke his cheek with their hoary nails. Devin buries his face in the dirt and screams. He screams for the daylight, for mercy, for a reprieve from the unceasing torments of this wretched existence.

X

In the cold, wet, tenebrous morning, an hour before dawn, Devin rises from his makeshift bed near the hissing embers. His head pulses with dark, arterial blood, a pain so excruciating, so unbearable, that he whimpers like a child when he lifts his head. His tongue is swollen from the tea, his eyes sting from the woodsmoke, his brain sloshes around his skull like an evil, black soup. Somehow he manages to get to his feet and staggers away undetected from the camp while the boys are still asleep.

He continues on his journey. In hellish agony, he drives through the hills and valleys, past miles of fence posts and rotting dairy barns. Since the sky is overcast and unmarked by the first faint smudges of daylight, he cannot distinguish east from west. He scans the shoulder for a familiar landmark that might direct him to the nearest interstate, but in the hazy beams of his headlights, he spots only a wooden cross that has been hammered into the soft earth and, farther along, a dead dog. Highways, he thinks, are a lot like graveyards.

Twenty minutes later, he comes upon an unambiguous sign of his son's presence. He pulls into the parking lot of the Hinnom Motel, and for the rest of the morning, he stands next to Batya's car. Although Devin is a man of science (he must continually remind himself of this), he is also a jealous lover just as Tom's God is a jealous God, and he can no more control his emotions than the beating of his own heart. Like everything else about human nature, jealousy is genetic, as immutable as a mathematical equation, an indifferent evolutionary force hard-wired into the species to protect and prolong the intimate association of love.

It burns him to think of it, but inside one of those rooms, in the flickering blue glow of the television, unholy and unpardonable things are going on. Should he pound on the door, demand that his son come outside and return home with him? After careful consideration, Devin chuckles sardonically at the misnomer. A home is supposed to offer sanctuary from the cares of the day, or so he has been led to believe, but this has turned out to be a terrible lie, one that has been perpetuated through the ages. Call it the propaganda of family life.

The truth is that there will never be a place on earth where mere mortals can feel completely safe. Maybe his son has already come to this realization, even as he sleeps in the arms of a woman who has vanquished his childhood faith, a woman who in the end will prove utterly incapable of protecting him from the horrible forces that rule the world.

PART THREE

Antiquing

꽃

I

They are lost, well, maybe not quite *lost*, how can they be, there are only so many roads out here, impossibly long ribbons of crushed stone that roll across immense tracts of untilled farmland, bisecting one another at ninety degree angles every two or three square miles, a thousand nameless lines plotted with monstrous logic on a grid in the middle of this vast November desolation. The leaves have already peaked, many of the trees are practically bare now, and few things compete for their attention—the rusted hulks of plows and tractors, the skeleton of an old windmill, a collapsed grain silo, a decaying barn with a hex sign near the peak of its gambrel roof, a length of barbed wire that stretches from fence post to fence post, marking either the beginning or the end of a wilderness—it's difficult to tell which.

They drive on. As they crest the rocky summit of a hog-back ridge, they smell old campfires and see a thin spire of silver smoke rising from the floor of a lonesome river valley. They hear swales of twisted yellow grass swish back and forth, whispering wetly in the mist and fog, and from time to time they glimpse painted ponies loping and cantering in the dead meadows. Except for the insatiable buzzards squatting among the big bales of hay and poking at the scattered bones of rodents, most of these farms look uninhabited. The birds watch the passing car, raise their hooked beaks, and, with long, plaintive cries of hunger, implore the travelers to provide them with the ripened innards of road kill.

Claude straightens up, suddenly serious, business-like, and takes a contemplative sip of his cold coffee. "Think of the erosion," he murmurs. "I bet the coffins will eventually slide down that steep slope. Like bobsleds. Just give it a little more time."

Elsie turns her bleary eyes to him and scowls. "What are you *talking* about?"

He points.

Dozens of shattered headstones, their inscriptions faded by a century of wind and rain and snow, erupt from a distant hillside like the skewed teeth of an exhumed skull, the last signs of a town long since deserted, its weary settlers happily returned to the anonymity of dust. Shuddering with a kind of grim pleasure, Claude imagines coffins, hundreds of them, rank and fetid and bursting with the bones of a black-clad parson and his irredeemable flock, hurtling down the muddy escarpment into oblivion.

"The soil must get pretty thin," he says. "The earth begins to crumble away. Imagine this place after a heavy downpour. I wouldn't be surprised to find a pile of remains down there in the gulch. Maybe we should check it out. You've always wanted a memento mori, right? You could probably use one as a paperweight, or maybe as a bookend."

The car swerves a little, and Elsie grips the sides of her seat. "Please pay attention to the road!"

She closes her eyes again and sighs. Except when money becomes the topic of conversation, she rarely listens to anything he has to say. She has grown accustomed to "a certain lifestyle," a fact she had to impress upon him after they spent a long sleepless night at the Hinnom Motel, where they endured the ecstatic yelps of a couple in the adjacent room. "True Olympians those two," Claude joked. "Gold medal winners." Elsie was furious. She'd been expecting a romantic resort, an enchanted cabin in the woods, or, at the very least, a quaint bed-and-breakfast that smelled of fresh-cut flowers, warm cinnamon rolls, and espresso, not some fleabag motel with mysterious stains on the pillowcases and mildew on the shower curtain.

Claude tries to reassure her that there is nothing to worry about, that he can find enough money to treat her well and still make the minimum payments to his creditors, everything is under control, but then he recalls, with the mounting panic that more and more has come to define his life, that he is two months behind on his car loan. Of course, this fact hasn't deterred him from embarking on yet another pointless excursion with his lover. How much money has he spent? No, he won't think about that just yet. He's having too much fun.

The sedan screeches around a sudden bend. Glancing back at the toppled headstones, Claude says, "Maybe I'd be better off buried up there." Self-pity comes so naturally to him. Over the years he has mastered its gratifying tone of despair; it gives him so much pleasure that he sometimes feels like a hedonist, shamelessly wallowing in the sharp sting of a self-inflicted wound. "I'd be the first new tenant in a hundred years, probably more. Gotta be cheap for a plot. Save on the funeral costs."

Elsie smirks. "Claude, darling, you couldn't get credit for a pine box."

Her voice takes on an omniscient quality. It never goes away, that voice, not entirely. During the long afternoons when Claude dozes in his cubicle at work and at night when he falls asleep in Elsie's arms after an hour of forbidden delights, the voice comes to him, shrill and acrimonious, berating him for the most inconsequential of his failings, and now he hears it again, a coiling phantasm that rattles and hisses in the claustrophobic confines of the car. Lately, he has built up an immunity to its venom and finds that it actually soothes him, lulls him into passivity, makes him think of bright blue skies, crystal clear waters, a gentle crescent of tropical beach with miles of white sugary sand.

They speed toward a red brick schoolhouse set upon by seething stalks of corn. Claude reaches for his cup of coffee and from the corner of his eye catches the schoolhouse door open and close, open and close. On the rooftop, a flock of grackles marches back and forth with a slow, dignified gait, but at the sound of an approaching car the birds suddenly take wing, converging high over the frozen fields, so high they look like an infestation of locusts come too late to destroy the fall harvest. Claude, clinging to some distant memory, watches them disappear over the horizon and recalls how lovely the world can sometimes be.

II

What finally snaps him out of his debilitating stupor isn't Elsie's abrupt scream or the searing pain of her fingernails digging deep into his forearm, but the loud thud and wet slap of matted fur against the grille, the gruesome crunch of bones beneath the spinning tires, the horrific howls of pain that echo across the immeasurable emptiness of peat bogs and paddocks and the disquieting calm of the treeless hills rising above the plain. In the rearview mirror, he sees a great shaggy carcass tumbling end over end, a dazzling shock of scarlet against the gray stretch of pocked and rutted road. Only then does he think to hit the brakes and turn on the hazards.

Elsie claws him with her long nails. "What are you *doing*?"

He yanks his arm away. "That hurts!"

"Just keep driving."

"I can't. I'm sure I have some kind of, you know, legal obligation."

"For chrissake, Claude, please don't get the law involved."

"No need to worry. It was an accident. When the time comes, I'll explain it all to the police."

She turns around and points to the thing in the road. "How do you intend to explain *that*?"

He scratches at the stubble on his chin. He hasn't shaved since they left the city, and he can see the first flecks of gray growing among the coarse black hairs. He glances at his watch and then at the receding sun reflected faintly in the milky gray puddles. It seems like they've been driving these roads for years. The days have started to blend together, dreary and formless as the heavy clouds that seem to sink closer and closer to the earth. He tries to envision this place in the dazzling summer sunshine—the patched farmland rippling with green, equatorial heat; the lush and heady meadows blazing with goldenrod, yellow buttercups, blue sage, indigo lilacs— but he simply can't do it. He suffers from a chronic lack of imagination; that's what Elsie told him last night after they made love. "You have a fat cock, sure, but a *small* mind," she said, yanking the filthy Hinnom Motel sheets around her beautiful body.

Now she folds her hands on her lap, breathes in and out, comports herself with the stillness and austerity of a necromancer practicing the ancient art of divination, another of her fleeting interests, and one destined to bore her like all the others before it—the books written by medieval Christian mystics and New Age crackpots, the bells and crystals and chimes, the wands and tinctures and incantations. Occasionally, Claude unearths some of these books buried beneath the fashion magazines on her nightstand. Though he can't say why, he commits several passages to memory: "Thou shalt speak out of the earth, and thy speech shall be heard out of the ground, and thy voice shall be from the earth like that of the python and out of the ground thy speech shall mutter." What the hell does it mean? He asked Elsie to explain it to him, but she rolled her eyes and quipped, "Oh, *you* wouldn't understand."

Looking at the mass of bloody flesh and fur on the road, Claude finds that the mysterious text offers a small clue to the dilemma he now faces.

"A ghost," he breathes.

"What? What's that?"

"Elsie, do you believe in ghosts? Perturbed spirits?"

She shakes her head and speaks slowly to him as she might to a child or an idiot. "I'm sorry to tell you this, Claude, I really am, but I think you're fucking losing it."

"But those books you're always reading—"

"Don't lose your shit. Not now. I'm warning you."

"Fine, fine." He grips the steering wheel tightly with both hands. "Just stay right here. I'm going to take a look, see what I've done."

"You didn't *do* anything!" She tries to regain her composure, but her voice is still manic, almost desperate. Saliva gathers at the corners of her mouth. "It was already *dead* when you hit it. Dead in the middle of the road. Flies buzzing all around."

Claude has never seen her so flustered, and he rather enjoys it.

"Dead? Are you sure? I thought I saw it run right in front of the car. It came out of nowhere, Elsie. Like a phantom. An apparition."

"Don't make me repeat myself. You were daydreaming. As usual. Now drive away like I asked before I become ill."

Because he can't quite accept the reality of the situation, he kisses her hand and takes in the scent of her lotion, sweet but subtle, a magic elixir capable of purging his soul of his foul crimes, his weakness of character.

"Maybe you're right . . ."

He puts the car in drive, takes his foot off the brake, and gently presses the accelerator. The sedan eases forward, it hums and purrs as a well-maintained vehicle should, a vehicle that is free of damage from a head-on collision. But before reaching the next bend in the road, Claude dares to look back one last time at the thing at the edge of the ditch, carrion for the great birds of prey that hover always in the sky, huge creatures of prehistoric visage that swoop low over the fields and perch on the telephone lines to peck madly at the vermin burrowing deep in their black wings, and though he can't be certain, he thinks he sees the thing struggling to lift its shattered head, writhing with unimaginable suffering, doomed to take its last agonizing breath beside a pasture reeking of cow shit.

III

An hour later, the ordered patchwork of fallow fields and the deranged matrix of country roads suddenly give way to a series of concentric circles that suck Claude and Elsie ever closer to the town of Gehenna. The streets reek of burning rubber and raw sewage. A canal brimming with toxic sludge encloses a row of brick warehouses like a moat protecting the ruins of a forbidden fortress, an armada of beer cans and whiskey bottles bobbing up and down on its distended surface. On the lopsided porch of an enormous Victorian house, four or five children stare blankly into the foul mist, maybe thinking of ways to escape the fate of their parents, and throw stones at a snarling black dog chained to the oak tree in the front yard.

Claude and Elsie drive through the town square. They haven't eaten since early that morning and search the dark storefronts for a bakery, a coffee shop, a farmer's market, but they find only boarded-up windows and a sinister madhouse tavern where men in denim coveralls and steel-toed boots stand in the doorway, smoking cigarettes and double-checking the losing numbers on their lottery tickets. On Main Street, they spot a diner with a red neon sign blinking in the parking lot. At this late hour there are few options, and they decide to risk it.

After locking the car doors and activating the alarm, they go inside. Claude immediately lowers his head to avoid the scornful looks of the customers who chew mechanically and with little satisfaction on their steaming buttermilk biscuits sopping with gravy. They regard him with unmistakable loathing, as if to say, "There is something not right about you. You are destructive and depraved. Now leave us be."

Claude and Elsie both order "The Fish" (that's how it's printed on the menu, "The Fish," as though it's some culinary wonder that draws people from miles around), but when the waitress sets the plates in front of them, Elsie uses the tongs of her fork to pick at the bones and scales with the precision of a pathologist.

"Look at this thing," she says. "I bet the cook scooped it out of that canal with a net he keeps by the back door. Fried it up in a greasy skillet, too." She tosses her silverware down with a loud clatter and snaps her fingers at the waitress. "Excuse me, miss! Oh, miss. A moment of your time, please. Are you *sure* this is fish?"

The waitress leans over the table. "Sure smells like it," she notes drolly.

"Well, since the menu doesn't specify what *kind* of fish it is, perhaps *you* can tell me."

The waitress shrugs. "Catfish? Naw, catfish don't have scales. Sheephead maybe. Never had the courage to try it myself. Never asked the chef about it neither."

"The *chef*." Elsie laughs. "Yes, well, I certainly won't eat catfish. They're bottom-feeders."

"That's your prerogative, ma'am."

"Prerogative? My, my, someone's been taking night classes at the community college. I'll tell you what, sweetie. Just take 'The Fish' off our bill."

"No refunds, ma'am. Says so right there on the door. Sorry about that."

Elsie smiles. "Oh, I'm sure you are. Well, then, could you please box these rancid bones so when I leave your charming little establishment, I can toss them into the trash can? I want all of your customers to see just what I think of your 'home cooking.'"

"You want them bones in a Styrofoam box?"

"Styrofoam, yes, that would be lovely. It releases toxins into rivers and streams. And we want to make sure your little town is stocked with plenty of Frankenstein fish, don't we?"

"Sure, lady. Sounds great."

"It sounds *delectable*!"

During this exchange, Claude tries to keep his eyes focused on his plate, but the need to inspect, to study, to supply his dwindling libido with some kind of fuel, however meager, proves far too tempting. Though not particularly pretty, the waitress is young, much younger than Elsie, no more than nineteen or twenty years old, and she is also slender, with a disproportionately ample bust. Normally other women do not catch his eye, but for three days now he has been forced to endure the sight of morbidly obese women who trundle their hefty rolls along the cramped aisles of antique shops and force their wobbling thighs into the tiny booths of ice-cream parlors; he has listened to their raucous laughter and has smelled the stale cigarette smoke on their clothes.

He bears witness to other things, too: a middle-aged woman and teenage boy walking arm-in-arm through a flea market. A teacher and her apt pupil, he initially thought, until they began kissing near a bin of pumpkins and gourds, their tongues wet and heavy and eager. It was disturbing to watch, but several customers stopped to stare anyway, an old man whose left ear had been sliced off, a little boy whose skull was crisscrossed with angry sutures, a big black barn cat that hopped on top of an oak barrel and sat still as a witch's familiar, licking the bright festering sores on its hind legs.

The waitress is different, she looks almost normal, and Claude admires how her thin cotton blouse, which is just a little too short for her sturdy farm-girl frame, creeps up her back and reveals a pale blue butterfly tattooed only a few breathless centimeters from the glorious crack of her ass.

Elsie, who has a sixth sense about these things, grabs her purse and shouts, "Let's go, Claude!"

"But . . . the young lady hasn't brought us our check."

"She's lucky I don't speak to the manager."

Claude considers tossing a few singles on the table, the spare change in his pockets, but the risk is too great. Insubordination of that sort will cost him dearly, and so he scurries behind Elsie, once again trying to avoid the glares of the other customers, who sigh with relief that this godless and dissolute couple is finally leaving, carried off by a howling gale of neuroses and pretension.

IV

Though she never stops carping about her hunger, Elsie insists they keep driving until they find a motel where the aging proprietors might regale them with a vending machine filled with bags of pretzels and cans of warm soda, maybe even a mini fridge stocked with small bottles of booze, but the longer she speaks, the more her voice fades in and out like a weak radio signal crackling with the sermons of bombastic preachers who describe the agonies of hellfire until they are so hoarse that all that remains is a single, unwavering note—a buzz, a hiss, an alien humming that allows Claude to indulge in his fantasies of the waitress, a skinny country girl with nothing to do on a Saturday night but drink cheap beer and get high and screw her good-for-nothing boyfriend. The bruises on her arms tell the story of rough fingers pressed into tender flesh, lots of dirty talk, vivid instruction, a motel room reeking of marijuana, a thin bedspread sullied with sweat and semen.

Claude sees a barn with a faded octagonal hex sign painted on its warped planks and, a bit farther down the road, a red-brick schoolhouse abandoned to the elements.

Elsie crosses her arms. "Didn't we pass that barn a couple hours ago? We're going in circles, aren't we?"

"I gotta piss," he announces.

"Oh, goddammit . . ."

He pulls over to the shoulder and puts the car in park. He hops the wirefence and stomps through the mud and hissing grass. Behind the great decomposing barn door, he stands with his prick dangling limply in his hand, closes his eyes, and envisions the waitress, naked, bent over a table, the blue butterfly swiveling along the base of her spine as she swings her hips. Something tells him that she probably has ugly tits, large areolas like slices of baloney, asymmetrical and pink as the drooping belly of a prize-winning sow. Razor burns on the inside of her thighs, fingernails chewed and jagged. These details do not turn him off. With ferocious self-loathing he strokes his penis until it begins to stiffen.

He listens to the stridulating weevils in the wood and the gnomic response of an owl in the rafters, but then he hears, in the distance, the cough and rumble of an old engine and the angry grind of gears. The noise makes it difficult for him to concentrate. Through the gaps in the rimed planks of wood, he glimpses a pickup truck barreling down the road, its rusty tailpipe drooping like his own defeated member. Desperate for some kind of catharsis, he varies the rhythm and pumps

away, faster, faster, but it's no use, and with a grunt of resignation, he stuffs his disobedient prick back into his pants.

The truck slows to a crawl and pulls to the shoulder in
front of his car. The man who emerges from the cab doesn't
look particularly menacing—he is elderly, rail-thin, trembling
with what might be the onset of Parkinson's, and when he removes his felt hat, he reveals a head free of hair and covered
with liver spots. A gentleman farmer, perhaps, on his way
home from church, a song of praise on his lips, a Bible opened
beside him on the seat, the pages turned to a damning passage
from Leviticus. The Jesus fish on his back bumper gives him
away. So does his sober black suit. But Claude is reluctant to
leave the barn, maybe because the man, despite his outward
appearance of infirmity and meekness, cradles a shotgun in
his arms.

Claude looks for an escape route. Hiding in here won't be
easy, but Claude can always bury himself under a pile of straw
and remain quiet as a mouse until the old man, should he be
hell-bent on senseless slaughter, finishes his business with Elsie and then drives away into the gloaming. But Claude also
understands that the longer he lingers in the barn, the longer he will have to endure Elsie's taunts. "You were *hoping* he
would kill me, weren't you? That would make you so happy,
wouldn't it?"

After a few moments of serious reflection, he emerges
from the barn and goes forth to accept his fate.

V

At first the old man says nothing at all, only nods with grim
severity. He regards Claude with clear eyes that belie his

wind-ravaged face, and when he speaks, his voice is slow and deliberate, the voice of a village elder prepared to pass judgment on the wicked.

"I believe you're the folks that ran over my dog." He points to the bed of the truck and lowers the tailgate. The hinges shriek in the cold and the wet. "You wanna take a look, see if you know him?"

Claude scrambles up the slippery embankment and peers inside. "God almighty . . ."

The thing is still alive, a big, brindled, nub-eared mutt, its head crushed like a rotten apple, its snout crusted over with blood, its reeking organs and entrails bubbling and foaming from the angry wound on its enormous, heaving belly. Claude stares, can't help but stare, and when the thing lifts an accusatory paw toward him, he stumbles backward and begins to cough on the fumes spewing from the tailpipe.

"Ain't right, you know," says the man, "to leave a animal in that condition. Maybe you folks never had no family pet?"

"I don't think that makes any difference . . ." Claude begins.

Elsie cranes her head from the passenger side window of the sedan. "Oh, sir. Sir!"

"Please, Elsie, let me handle this."

"The gentleman asked us a question, Claude, and I think he's entitled to an honest answer. He wants to know about Gonzago."

Claude laughs nervously. "I really don't think he's interested, Elsie. You're not interested, are you?"

"Gonzago was a demonic creature," she says. "A hellhound. He kept digging up my garden, eating the hostas and daises. And I'll tell you this, sir. He enjoyed watching us, yes, watching us while we were *in flagrante delicto*."

"Elsie!"

"That dog would pant and moan and lick itself feverishly. Things got so bad that Claude took him out to the backyard one night and, well, go on, tell him, Claude. Tell him how you took care of business. Tell him how instead of digging up my daisies, Gonzago is now pushing them up."

"Damn you, Elsie."

"Right now, Gonzago is probably playing fetch with Saint Peter."

"It was *your* idea, remember!" he shouts at her. "You told me . . ."

"Oh, I say all sorts of things, you know that, Claude. But, sir, let me ask you a question. Are you listening, sir? What kind of person is capable of actually carrying out such a monstrous deed?"

The old man's forehead creases with perplexity, and he seems to regret his decision to stop these odd people. "Well, I don't know about none of that. What I come here to say is that since it was you who run down my dog, I figured you should put him out of his misery. It'd be the decent thing to do. The Christian thing."

Claude gestures to the rifle. "I've never handled one of those before, but if you show me how . . ."

"Ain't nothin' to it. Just point and squeeze the trigger. It's already loaded. Here."

Claude accepts the rifle. It feels heavy in his hands and smells of oil. The black barrel glimmers faintly under a sun buried under clouds, inflexible and motionless. The old man positions the dog's head so it hangs over the tailgate, giving Claude a clear shot. Claude steps forward, pauses a moment, waits for a message imparted fleetingly on the wind, some kind of secret wisdom, an acknowledgement that what he is about to do is important, transformative, crucial to his understanding of the cosmos, but the silence is utterly vapid, banal, indifferent. He hears no message, no secret wisdom. The rusted weathervane spins on the peak of the barn, and on the bed of the truck the rain taps out a gentle song of suffering played in a minor key, *largo, morendo*. Claude looks to the sky, wondering when the snow will come and when the hand of God will stamp them all out like irritating bugs.

He looks back at the car. Elsie has shut her eyes and clamped her hands over her ears. Claude lifts the rifle and points. When he finally musters the courage to squeeze the trigger, he recoils from the powerful blast and counts the plangent echoes ricocheting off the ugly hillocks of shale and clay on the far horizon, a sound gradually hammered down and flattened by the dumb immensity of the land.

The old man bows his head.

Claude feels compelled to say something. "I don't believe in God, haven't seen the inside of a church since I was a schoolboy, but I'll be sure to say a prayer for your dog anyway."

After checking the safety on the rifle, the man plods over to the cab and tosses it through the open window. He leans against the door, his hands spread across the rough surface, fingers picking absently at the loose flakes of crimson paint. Then with a small groan of discomfort he climbs inside the truck, where he sits behind the wheel and stares at the road. He wipes the rain from his forehead, the tears from his cheeks, and with a frown as intractable and harsh as the desolation all around, turns slowly to Claude and says, "Don't believe in God? Then, my friend, you will burn, you will *burn*."

Had it been a dry day, the kind of day when the sun

scorches the fields and blisters the backs of the migrant workers who come to gather the corn and rye and wheat, Claude
would have felt the sharp sting of gravel against his face as the
man stomped on the accelerator and sped away, but it is autumn now, the road is pliant, and the tires of the truck do not
spin with the speed and force the old man would have liked,
and so Claude feels only the soft splatter of mud against his
shoes and the cuffs of his pants.

He watches the truck rise and fall on the ribbons of road,
like a tiny boat carried high and low by the swells of a tumultuous sea, and he keeps watching for what must be miles and
miles because there are no other roads out here in the center of
this mindless wasteland, and even though Elsie urges him to
get back into the car—she is in a hurry, the antique shops close
early today—Claude stands very still and waits to see if the old
man will pull over to bury his dog in the graveyard on top of
that distant, corpse-bloated knoll.

Merde at the Place de la Contrescarpe

I

After he makes bail and collects his personal effects from the crooked-nosed corrections officer working behind the bullet-proof glass, Edward de Vere limps from the county jail and takes a seat outside on one of the benches that faces the broken fountain in the center of the sprawling, concrete plaza. It's morning now. A cold wind lashes his face. Black exhaust from a passing bus stings his eyes. When the smoke finally clears, he sees the woman from last night gliding gracefully across the slick pavement. In her purple dress she looks like a phantom freed from cumbersome flesh, the agony of existence. He wonders if she has been waiting for him the entire time, keeping vigil out here in the cold. With a furtive glance over his shoulder to make sure the cops aren't observing him, he stands up and approaches the woman. If they catch him speaking to her, they will almost certainly charge him again with solicitation.

It's the first time de Vere has seen her in broad daylight, and he studies her features carefully. She might be thirty, she might be fifty, it's impossible to say, but unlike the usual castaways he chances upon in hotel bars and restaurants—those lonely, ruminative spinsters politely sipping cosmopolitans and hoping, even well into middle age, to have a romantic encounter with a dashing stranger but who in the end always settle for the usual scamming rogues, men like de Vere and sometimes men far worse—this woman understands that romance is nothing more than a fantasy, a sickness, a disease no different from the angry sores erupting on her arms and legs or the black nodules spreading through her lungs.

He calls her name, but she doesn't seem to hear, gives no sign. She climbs over the polished granite rim of the fountain and stares at something near the patinated bronze sphere. Using the lethal tips of her stilettos, she cracks the thin sheets of ice that have formed around the perimeter and then searches through the scattered bits of copper for the occasional glint of a silver coin. The pigeons follow her around like lost children and peck at her ankles. She tries to kick them aside and almost falls over.

De Vere decides to take a calculated risk. "Pardon me. What did you say your name was?"

She looks up and scowls. "I told you last night."

"Tamar, isn't it?"

"Why you asking if you already know it?"

Though he is mad with thirst, desperate for a glass of water, he says, "I thought maybe we could get a drink together."

"A drink?"

"Yes, if you know a joint that's open this early in the morning."

Polishing a quarter on the hem of her skirt, she says, "You're buying, right?"

"Naturally."

"Okay, come with me."

Since neither of them has a car they must travel on foot. Like children in a fairytale, banished to a forest of twisted black trees teeming with tribes of ravenous night-roaming trolls, they follow a trail of cigarette butts through the ruin and desolation of the old neighborhood. They walk beneath the steel arches of a bridge on the verge of collapse; they pass boarded-up storefronts and faded billboards for cheap liquor and high-interest loans; they slog up a gray ridge strangled by long tendrils of telephone lines; and in a weed-choked gravel lot, they battle through a cloud of buzzing flies and nearly trip over the remains of a dog, its belly bloated with corpse gas, its tongue angling toward a puddle of oily water.

"Gonzago . . ." de Vere mutters with affection.

"What you say?"

De Vere pauses to catch his breath. He rests his hands on his knees and asks, "Do you know what day it is?"

"Saturday, I think. I dunno."

"No, no, no. What *holy* day is it?"

"The fucking Epiphany. How should I know?"

"It's the Day of the Dead, my dear."

"Ain't no such holiday."

"There most certainly is. So it's only fitting that we should find ourselves wandering the streets and alleys of this wretched necropolis."

"Man, you like to talk a lot of shit, don't you?"

As he wades through the brown surges of foul odor emanating from the sewers, he decides on a different approach. In the plodding English of this devastated industrial town—his mother tongue, brusque, arrhythmic, percussive—he jokes how the city looks like Montemarte after the long-awaited apocalypse, Sacré-Coeur bulldozed to make way for a row of lamentable tenement buildings, a once magnificent view of the Eiffel Tower obstructed by the sulfur-spewing stacks of a blast furnace. De Vere knows he must stop daydreaming about the charmed life he once led and learn to accept his precipitous descent into bankruptcy and hopeless destitution. He is a barbarian returned at long last to the provinces, the city of his birth, a puissant thanatocracy where not even the specter of death offers the howling, beggared multitude a way to escape from so much pointless suffering. Indeed, the Church has always taught him that it is only *after* death that the real suffering begins.

A dozen blackbirds explode from an abandoned duplex and wheel in the sky.

"In its own weird way," he says, "this is a very pretty place."

The woman snorts. "Yeah, sure, and someone once said that hell is probably a pretty place."

Edward de Vere smiles. Yes, he thinks, life here is very different than in the City of Light. Different languages, different customs, different states of mind.

II

Famed as much for its bullet-sprayed bar as its handcrafted lagers and stouts, the brewery is part sanitarium, part hospice, part decaying church, its graffiti-covered toilet stalls a compendium of disgraceful customs and bawdy incantations culled from decades of drunken conversations, its cold ashen walls a safe haven for gangsters and hoodlums, a refuge for unemployed merchant marines and longshoremen, a retreat for heretical priests, a confessional for unrepentant sinners. Inside, a dozen or so men—bald, bearded, brutal, their teeth chipped or missing altogether, their skin translucent in the flickering light of the television, their eyes blinded by the muddy daylight trickling through the dirty windows— hunch on their stools like things not seen in the open air but only in caves that have been sealed for untold centuries. In silence they drink tall beakers of piss-colored beer and chew stale pretzels.

From the moment he walks through the door, de Vere understands that fistfighting is standard practice here. He skips over a pile of broken glass and makes his cautious way through a minefield of hostile stares. He has been beaten before, sometimes for good reason, sometimes not, and as he mentally prepares himself for the possibility of another thrashing, he flags down the ruddy Irishman tending bar and asks for a vodka tonic on the rocks (it's best to anesthetize oneself beforehand) "with a twist of lime" (he refuses to abandon his more urbane sensibilities, even in the face of danger). He notes how his drink seems to irritate these men, makes them slurp their beer with purpose and glare at him with even greater intensity. Why such malice, de Vere wonders? Is it because he is too clean-cut, his clothes too flashy, his hair too shiny, sculpted, and unnaturally dark? Maybe he should cut down on the dye, let a few gray strands grow in. He looks artificial, more mannequin than man. He uses his fading looks to disguise something ugly, but these men are not easily fooled by disguises. They sniff him out right away. He reeks of corruption, perversion, disease.

The bartender leans over and squeezes de Vere's shoulder. His forearms are thick and hairy, his knuckles raw. His tongue moistens a busted lip. He blows angry jets of smoke in de Vere's face and intentionally ashes on his shirt cuffs.

"Enjoying your cocktail, buddy? Having a good time? You know how to treat a lady? You gonna behave yourself?"

De Vere smiles sheepishly and thinks it wise to keep quiet.

The other men offer the woman a seat at the bar, hand her some cigarettes, buy her a few drinks. They ask how she's getting on. Does she have enough money, enough to eat? Does she need anything—clean clothes, a safe place to stay?

"This guy bothering you?" they want to know.

"Him?" The woman laughs. "Naw, he's a real gentleman. Can't you tell? Went to some kind of finishing school. Looks like a wax dummy, don't he?"

She throws her head back to swallow her whiskey and then nods with some vague sense of accomplishment, her eyes flashing like little strobe lights that briefly illuminate a dead, dreaming world. The booze cascades over her brain, baptizing her in a river of endless possibility. She smiles at her reflection in the dusty mirror the way a child might smile with equal parts fear and amusement at a total stranger passing on the street.

De Vere feels his guts suddenly rumble. He clutches his stomach and lets out a low groan.

"The shitter's that way if you need it," the woman tells him.

De Vere stands up, gives a little bow. "Excuse me, will you?"

"Oh, I'll be waiting, honey."

He tosses a few bills on the bar and then darts to the restroom, where he locks himself in one of the filthy stalls. While he sits on the toilet, huffing and groaning in an unsuccessful attempt to jettison the hardened stool lodged inside his colon, he reads the limericks and racial epithets and homophobic slurs on the door. Above the roll of toilet paper, someone has written a story in a small, satanic hand, chronicling the lives of the reprobates who have descended into this stinking Hades—a high school quarterback, a football coach, a guitarist in a death metal band, a failed writer, an oversexed teacher. Modern day scripture for the drunk and dispossessed.

Rocking back and forth on the seat, de Vere scans the lines but is unable to concentrate for long. He grinds his teeth, bears down until his face turns red, but it's no good. He's been constipated for days now. He pulls up his pants and buckles his belt. As he stands at the sink, scrubbing his hands, he pretends not to hear the violent clangor of chapel bells coming from the Jesuit school a few blocks away—his alma mater, hallowed ground where he first learned about the pleasures of the flesh and the awful prospect of eternal damnation.

III

Despite a few minor improvements to the hulking neo-gothic edifice, the Zanzibar Towers & Gardens appears uninhabited—and uninhabitable—by anything other than the long-tailed rats and mutant cockroaches that proliferate in the deep quarry of its basement. Some of the windows on the lower floors are shattered, some are missing altogether and covered in plastic sheets. Its brick façade is so blackened by soot from the nearby steel mills that it looks like it has been pieced together with lumps of charcoal. The weary Jesuits have labeled the place a "pest house" and have sought out ways to have it demolished, even pressuring building inspectors to fine the manager for failing to bring the property up to code, but the inspectors, realizing the cash-strapped city cannot afford the expense of clearing away another mountain of toxic rubble, always fall short of condemning the place outright.

The woman rents an apartment on the sixth floor, and by the time they climb the creaking staircase to the landing (there is no working elevator), both she and de Vere are breathing hard. She slides a key into the lock but before opening the door says, "Okay, let's get down to business."

"Fine with me."

"Two hundred oughtta cover it."

De Vere laughs. "I don't have that kind of cash."

"You a deadbeat or what?"

"I had to make bail this morning, remember?"

"I don't give a shit. We agreed on two hundred."

"When was this?"

"Last night."

"We never talked money, did we?"

"Fucking loser. Why don't you get lost?"

"Wait a minute." He counts the remaining cash in his wallet. "I have seventy bucks."

She snaps her fingers. "Hand it over." Shaking her head, she stuffs the money somewhere under her skirt and then opens the door. "In here. Let's go. Move it, move it."

He is unable to see anything too clearly, but eventually his eyes adjust to the gloom, and he takes in the remarkable squalor of the place, the piles of dirty clothes, the broken toys scattered on the filthy throw rugs and sticky hardwood floor—a bright blue ball, a small pink guitar, a deck of playing cards. He steps around the remains of a blonde baby doll that has undergone several hasty amputations only to be partially reassembled with tape and glue. There is something odd about the apartment, something that makes its claustrophobic rooms seem almost institutional, like a madhouse, or some terrible dungeon in ancient Rome where the consumptive prisoners languished for years without trial. Then he understands the problem. All the doors have padlocks on the outside.

De Vere crosses his arms and gives a whistle. "Nice place you have here."

"Screw you."

The woman walks into the kitchen, pushes aside a stack of plates that wobbles and then crashes into a sink already over-flowing with bowls of soggy cereal and sour milk. Under the shattered heap she finds two plastic cups and a bottle of cheap bourbon. She pours them both a drink.

"Bottoms up," she says.

"Cheers."

The bourbon has been diluted with water, but it seems to give the woman a second wind.

"Well," she says, "we better get on with it before the brat wakes up."

She unlocks one of the doors and leads him into a bed-room. Evidently she doesn't often sleep here. The bed is still made, the sheets not too terribly soiled. He removes his clothes and finds that the mattress is surprisingly comfortable. He buries his face in the pillows, pleased that only an occasional strand of long black hair finds its way into his mouth. As he waits for her to join him, he props himself up on one elbow and chances to see himself in the mirror above the dresser—a wrecked Adonis, the high school athlete gone to seed, his pimply shoulders glistening with sweat, a roll of flab hang-ing from his midsection. The woman strips and stretches out next to him, her arms limp at her sides, her legs spread wide, the soles of her feet black and blistered. The years have taken their toll on them both, but if his body is ugly and pathetic, hers is tragic, covered in welts and bruises and cryptic tattoos.

He turns away from the mirror and, without asking her permission, begins to do outrageous and terrible things to her. His hostess endures the rough treatment without complaint, even taunting him at times, telling him to stop being such a fucking pansy, to "do the job right, goddammit!" He thrashes and bucks and growls. He tests the limits of her endurance, violates her every orifice, laughs every time she whimpers with pain, and after one hour of relentless grinding, he shouts, "Shit, yes!" before finally rolling over and falling dead asleep.

It has been an exhausting twenty-four hours for them both.

IV

As usually happens when his belly begins to boil over with a devastating blend of booze, de Vere tosses and turns in bed and, before waking in a cold sweat, dreams in vivid detail of the good old days in Europe:

He finds himself sitting at his favorite sidewalk café below a swanky brothel at the Place de la Contrescarpe where, amidst the sentimental *chanson française* and the melodic laughter of the lovely young whores, de Vere and his fellow expatriates fête each other with great goblets of absinthe (frog-green and bitter, illegal of course, wreaks havoc on the nervous system) and spin tales of their latest excursions to the catacombs beneath the famous cathedral and the galleries at the Museé de l'Homme where, for a small fee, tourists can view Descartes' brain in the Cabinet of Curiosities.

"He thought his dog was a soulless machine," says de Vere, "completely unconscious of the world."

"Who did?" ask the whores.

"Descartes. His logic was a bit convoluted. If dogs possess consciousness then naturally they must possess souls. And if dogs possess souls then it only stands to reason that *all* animals possess souls, including oysters and sea sponges. But Descartes couldn't stomach the idea of heaven overrun by mangy mutts marking their territory, pissing on celestial harps, shitting at Saint Peter's feet, humping the legs of the dearly departed. *Ergo*, dogs do not possess souls. Ironic, since science has only confirmed what we have long suspected—that humans are animals, too. Isn't that why we're here tonight? To debase ourselves? To give in to our animal urges?"

The giggling existential whores do not agree. Sex, they insist, is not part of our animal nature; in fact, it's what makes us different from the animals. Sex is cerebral, spiritual, a most solemn ceremony, a sacred obligation, as subtle and complex as any religious ritual. There are customs to observe, roles to play, small but important gestures to make.

With a rare feeling of contentment, de Vere leans back in his chair and sips his absinthe. If only he could remain lost forever in this wondrous world of philosophical rumination, this astonishing cognitive theater, but of course these enchanting reveries must always take a nightmarish turn. As evening falls, a dirty yellow mist creeps up the hill, snaking through the cobblestone streets and obscuring the moon that hovers above the rooftops like some giant unblinking eye with broken capillaries. At the sound of approaching footsteps, an ominous hush falls over the patrons. Even the waiters, bearing bottles of Beaujolais, set their trays aside and peer into the dense fog.

Like a gargoyle plunging from the cornices of the great cathedral, the menacing figure of a Great Dane comes bounding toward de Vere, snarling and snapping at him.

"Gonzago?" de Vere says, rising from his seat. "Is that you, boy?"

But the dog does not wag its tail and lick his face. It lunges at him, latches onto his arm, drags him toward the fountain at the center of the square, where his wife, Elsie, greets him with a baneful smile. She sits on the edge of the fountain, her ankles crossed, her hands folded in her lap, and in a voice that is simultaneously sweet and masterfully manipulative and so very typical of women of her station, she says, "Edward, darling, there's a small matter we must discuss. You see, I've somehow managed to contract a nasty case of syphilis . . ."

She leads de Vere to the center of the fountain and chains him to one of the magnificent marble *putti* that pisses perfect parabolas of water into the sickening mist, and though he wants to escape into the night, he is prevented from doing so by Gonzago, who shreds his pants and claws his legs. Like some village idiot convicted of unlawful carnal knowledge, de Vere proclaims his innocence and rattles his chains and capers ridiculously around the shallow pool. The fog suddenly lifts, and tourists pour into the square to take pictures of him. Bulbs flash. Shutters automatically adjust to gather the meager lamplight. These people have traveled thousands of miles to witness this comic scene and aren't going to miss it for the world, the Eiffel Tower be damned.

Gonzago seems to be enjoying it, too. He licks his enormous swinging testicles and happily manufactures mountainous heaps of fetid, fly-swaddled shit. All of Paris is soiled by dog shit—the people here are too posh to pick up after their mutts—but now, to de Vere's disbelief, his wife stoops down and, using her bare hands, scoops up a warm pile of feces and fashions it into a ball. Without warning she flings it at his face, even massages it into his hair. The shit slides down his back and legs, but de Vere, far beyond any possibility of redemption, bows his head and endures this ferocious hailstorm with a stoic smile, his chin pressed against his chest.

He feels some vague sense of remorse for the ghastly things he has done to Elsie—the years of deception, the innumerable infidelities, and the terrible bout of syphilis that has gone undiagnosed for months and has obviously left her stark, raving mad.

V

The afternoon sun has managed to burn a small aperture through the thick clouds, briefly filling the world with a dazzling, orange light, like molten steel pouring from a foundry, forcing de Vere to shield his eyes when he wakes from his troubled dream. Momentarily blinded, he rolls over and almost knocks heads with the woman sleeping next to him. Her mouth hangs open like a Venus flytrap, better to capture the brown spiders that drop from the spinning blades of the ceiling fan. Her lips are dry and crusted over with an unidentifiable white glop, her face pale, swollen, a tapestry of despair stretched across the iciest trenches of hell. De Vere thinks of all the wicked things he can do to her right now. How many men, he wonders, have considered tying her to the bed, gagging her, slitting her throat, putting a quick end to the years of misery?

With expert precision, he slides from the sullied sheets, cringing as the cold floorboards groan like the waterlogged planks of a sinking ship. Bleary-eyed, whiskey-dicked, de Vere stumbles naked around the room, searching for his shirt and pants, but when he pinches his chin and smells the woman on his fingertips, he suddenly has a funny idea. He crouches in the middle of the room, tongue flitting in and out of his mouth like a snake trying to taste the early November air, and with a pleasure more exquisite than the wild hour of drunken lovemaking, he squeezes hard, grunting with the effort of it, and feels his bowels rumble and then suddenly, blissfully empty. Even his mind empties. A long, soft, stinking coil of crap oozes out of him, forming a terraced pyramid, and for one spectacular moment he is no longer a human being but a gigantic evacuating rectum, nothing more.

As he squats beside the bed, he takes inventory of the room—the empty bottle of bourbon on the dresser, the scented candles that line the windowsill, and, on the nightstand, a stack of paperback romances with lurid covers featuring bare-chested men ravaging women in various poses of rapture, their lips parted in anticipation of long-awaited and much-deserved love. De Vere flips to a random page and cringes at the absurdity of the narrative, the wretched sentimentality of it, the overwrought descriptions of breasts and buttocks, the syrupy prose that sounds more ludicrous than lascivious.

With mild embarrassment, he wonders what the Parisians, lounging on the park benches that line the perpendicular walkways of the Jardin du Luxembourg, might say if asked their opinion of these masturbatory epics. "Why rely on such a poor simulacrum," they would invariably answer, "when you can have the real thing? Love is everywhere. It falls from the skies."

In some ways, the French are very naïve and have a difficult time grasping the fact that Americans absolutely depend on sordid novels, pornographic films, and battery-operated toys. In the United States, any show of affection is considered taboo—hand-holding shunned, kissing on street corners and in public parks denounced as a kind of pathological disorder. Instead of spontaneity, Americans prefer long-term contracts and decadent wedding pageants, women in ridiculous, white gowns—*white*, of all colors!—a march down the aisle toward messy divorce, dysfunctional children, medicine cabinets crammed with mood-altering pharmaceuticals.

De Vere forces himself to read a few paragraphs more. Though he considers using the pages to wipe himself, he knows tearing them one by one from the book would make too much noise, so he uses the down comforter instead. He pulls on his pants and shirt, laces his shoes, but before exiting the bedroom, he spots the woman's purple dress hanging from the closet doorknob. He searches through each of its hidden compartments until he recovers the wad of fives and tens that he gave her. He intends to use the money to buy a croissant and a travel magazine at the quaint coffee shop down the street.

Skirting the lumpy memento in the middle of the room, he hurries over to the door, and, in his haste, nearly collides with a little girl in a yellow dress standing in the hallway. She is perhaps four years old, but looks younger. Her limbs are so bony, her hair so long and knotted, and her skin so tawny and smeared with dirt that she looks like one of those undernourished North African street urchins who lurk in the gloomy carpet shops along the Boulevard Barbès, waiting to accost tourists who have foolishly wandered away from Sacré-Coeur in search of the Metro. De Vere used to visit a nearby brasserie there run by a family of Berbers. The proprietor served a drink called *buzo*, the best in Paris, and sold bags of hash and, if he trusted you, an hour with one of "the new girls" smuggled into the country from Algeria. "You will find her most cooperative, *monsieur*," he promised, and he was never wrong. Intoxicants and copulation are the trades by which the world's underclass survive.

The little girl sucks her thumb and stares with indifference at the pile of shit next to the woman's bed.

"Come over here," de Vere whispers.

The little girl skitters away from him, her eyes large and dark as nighttime in the Sahara.

"We don't want to wake your mommy, do we? Are you hungry?"

She blinks again but doesn't respond. With coos and simple hand gestures, de Vere coaxes her toward the kitchen. "Watch your step," he says, kicking aside the pink guitar on the floor. He clears a space at the kitchen table and tells her to sit. After searching the drawers and cupboards, he finds a loaf of slightly moldy bread and puts two pieces into a toaster oven. Using a dirty steak knife from the sink, he lathers the toast with jelly scraped from the bottom of a jar.

"Guess I should have washed my hands first . . ." he murmurs, setting the plate in front of her. "What's your name?"

She stuffs the toast into her mouth.

"I have a child, too," he tells her. "A son. But he ran away from home. He was a bad boy. Very naughty. He stole lots of money from me. And stealing is the worst thing you can do to someone. I wonder how he's getting on. He's not used to the real world. Eventually he'll come back home. Sooner or later kids always do . . ."

As he speaks, the girl opens her mouth and lets the brown paste fall onto the table near his hands. He jumps away. She seems to find his reaction funny and pokes at the goop with her fingers, sniffs it, then rubs it across her face.

"Jesus," de Vere whispers, "what should we do with you? Let me think about this. Oh, I know just the thing. You'd better come with me. Yes, that's right, this way. Good girl. We'll have you all fixed up in no time at all . . ."

The bathroom is small and windowless with a single bulb screwed into a wall sconce for light. The black and white tiles are covered with long tentacles of coarse hair, the corners crawling with mildew so green it looks radioactive. Bras and panties hang from the towel rack. Bloody tissue paper fills the small trash can beside the toilet. De Vere opens the medicine cabinet, hoping to find Oxycontin, Vicodin, praying even for a single aspirin with codeine, but there are only vials labeled Sertraline, Amitriptyline, Duloxetine.

He instructs the girl to stand against the wall, pulls the shower curtain open, and plugs the drain in the tub. Though it takes a little effort, he manages to twist the faucets. Water trickles from the tap, cold and gray like the waters of the nearby river after a heavy rainstorm. Debris floats around the tub—nail clippings, pieces of plaster that have flaked from the ceiling, a thin sliver of blue soap.

"Raise your arms," he says. "Hold still."

De Vere lifts her dress. When he turns to check the water level he sees, framed in the cracked and spotted mirror, the woman's face. From the look in her eyes and the knife in her hand, he knows what she is thinking. Clearly she is still drunk, high, confused.

To the girl the woman says, "You clever little bitch, how'd you get out?"

"Excuse me, but you shouldn't talk that way . . ."

"Fuck you!" The woman jabs the knife at him, the blade bright red and dripping with jelly.

Obstinate in her silence, the naked girl clings tightly to de Vere's leg.

He gives her a gentle push. "Go on. Go see your mommy."

"Keep your stinking hands off my child!"

De Vere stumbles backward. "Listen, lady, I'm a million kinds of monster, but I'm not *that* kind of monster."

The woman lifts the girl off her feet and practically catapults her into the hallway. Then she turns the knife on de Vere again.

"Stay right there, motherfucker. Stay right where you are."

"Whatever you say."

Without taking her eyes from him, the woman slowly backs out of the bathroom, slams the door shut, and turns the lock.

VI

How long he is trapped there he cannot say—one hour, two? Only now does he remember leaving his watch on the nightstand in the bedroom. Eventually the woman will find it and pawn it to buy more drugs and liquor. He raps politely on the door, tries to reason with her, attempts to convince her that in time she will see him not as a monster but as an angel in disguise and that this experience may prove to be the defining moment in her life, the long-awaited and yearned for epiphany that will liberate her from all her pain and suffering. For years to come, as she drinks coffee in the church basement with the rest of the recovering addicts, she will, in a voice that is small and docile and trembling with guilt and self-reproach, vow before God never again to touch booze or men. He tells her these things, but she does not answer, and de Vere understands that there are many steps to take before his transfiguration from sinner to saint.

At some point he hears her leave the apartment and hurry

down the steps and, for a little while at least, he believes he is alone. Then he hears the strumming of the toy guitar and the little girl singing a plaintive melody in a foreign tongue. A prodigy, he thinks, until he realizes that she is repeating the same incomprehensible words and playing the same three chords over and over again. A ferocious heat seeps in under the crack near the floor, turning the bathroom into a sweltering blast furnace. The walls begin to converge, constricting his arms and legs, making it increasingly difficult for him to move, to breathe, to think clearly. He grows agitated, begs the girl to release him, to call the police, but no matter how hard he kicks and pounds and throws his body against the door, he knows the little girl will not come to his aid. She has been intentionally left behind to torment him.

As the day wears on, de Vere shudders uncontrollably and then starts to scream. Somewhere far away he hears the bells of the Jesuit school begin to toll, and above their awful cacophony he can make out the sound of distant voices, like the buzzing of wasps after their hive has been smashed to bits— agitated, frenzied, joyfully descending on their enemies with the promise of swift and pitiless annihilation. The voices grow louder, more senseless and savage, the boom and bellow of a mob that obeys no law save that of its own implacable desire for justice, retribution, blood.

From the stairwell the woman shouts, "The sonofabitch is up here! This way, men, this way!"

She leads them in a relentless march that ends just outside the bathroom. A hush falls over the deranged delegation. The ritual of death requires order, a long taunting silence. Someone knocks gently, almost playfully, not with bare knuckles but with the claws of a hammer, the rough edge of a galvanized pipe. De Vere tries to steady himself. He looks in the mirror, checks his hair, straightens his collar, adjusts his cuffs, then he slumps down on the toilet and leans forward to study the door. In the interlocking spirals of wood grain, he sees a map of Paris with its labyrinthine streets and stately boulevards. He yearns to taste the bittersweet absinthe one final time and to listen to the tender laughter of the French whores as they sit in the café near the square.

As the lock clicks and the door bursts open, Edward de Vere marvels at how fate sweeps so many people up like the unstoppable wave of a tsunami, how it hurtles them toward a wall where they are crushed and impaled by still further people. Life uses us as battering rams, one person against another, and few, if any, ever escape the catastrophe.

The Black Death of Gentile da Foligno

I

The newspaper provides the abominable details: another woman attacked while sleeping on a park bench, her dark hair and ragged clothes doused in what must have been gasoline or lighter fluid and then set ablaze with a book of matches. The old man reads the story with an indifference so alien to him that he later puzzles over it and wonders if he, too, has finally succumbed to the modern epidemic of apathy, but as he stands alone in the sacristy, preparing for that afternoon's ceremony, he suspects that something far more insidious has wormed its way into his brain, something that started off as small, larval, almost benign really, but has over the past year swollen into a voracious creature of spectacular size. Having already gorged itself on his reasoning faculties, it is now beginning to wreak havoc on his soul. The signs are obvious.

In the lopsided mirror beside the door, he studies the folds of skin that hang loosely from his withered cheeks and neck. He is wasting away to nothing at all, a Lazarus whose decomposing flesh has been commanded to rise from the grave and wander the earth while his spirit continues to languish in hell, a pit of infinite suffering with long and winding lava flows, glassy slag heaps, mountains of flinty black rock where a pitiable parade of condemned souls, in a desperate quest for salvation, trek across untold miles of blistering desert sand, leaving behind only cloven hoof prints as evidence of their wicked existence.

The old man feels suddenly dizzy. His head spins; his knees buckle. He clings to the back of a chair, but when he tries to focus on the floor, he finds that he is standing not inside the sacristy of his beloved chapel, but at the edge of a vertiginous void. He reaches out, arms flailing. He drops the newspaper and collapses into the chair. Desperate to slake his thirst, he grabs the mug on the end table and spills scalding coffee on his white vestment and green stole. A warning. The Church forbids priests to eat and drink one hour prior to administering the holy sacrament of communion.

"Oh God please help please God oh please!" he wails.

Edmund Campion comes racing into the sacristy. The boy's glasses magnify his protuberant eyes and give him a look of perpetual shock, as if everything he encounters in life is some kind of indecent spectacle. His face is featureless, doughy—a rich, creamy, vanilla pudding sculpted with gentle hands into an oval with two small indentations for nostrils. How many years will it take for that soft face to harden, for the deep lines and fissures of experience to crack its smooth surface?

"Is something wrong, Father Loomis? I thought I heard you scream . . ."

When the old man sees the look of alarm in the boy's eyes, he turns away in shame. "Oh, it's nothing. I'm afraid I've gone and made a terrible mess."

"Anything I can do?"

"Yes, get a new vestment. Over there."

"Of course."

In his haste, Edmund collides with the chair. An awkward boy, jittery, angular, uncoordinated, Edmund Campion is someone who literally stumbles through life, frequently knocking over Bibles and chalices and boxes of incense, always apologizing afterward with a snort of nervous laughter. His classmates torment him in the usual ways—trip him in the halls, steal his books, kick him, slap him. This is common knowledge, but the old man rarely offers the boy a word of advice or reprimands the others for their cruelty. Suffering has its place in the curriculum, its lessons to teach.

Edmund brings him a clean vestment and starts to count on his fingers. "Let's see now," he says. "I've arranged the votive candles around the statue of the Virgin. Filled the stoups at the entranceways with holy water. Adjusted the microphone at the pulpit. Checked the thermostat. Am I forgetting anything, Father? *Father?*"

"Eh? How's that?"

"Are you sure you're okay?"

"I'm fine, fine," murmurs the old man. "It's this news, this ungodly news. It doesn't make any sense to me . . ."

Edmund picks the newspaper off the floor and studies the headline with the same serious demeanor he would the catechism.

"Just awful, isn't it, Father?"

"Hmmm? Oh, yes, yes, terrible."

"Do you suppose someone like that can be forgiven? The madman, I mean?"

Edmund's constant need for black-and-white answers

irritates him. Too many students yearn for rigidly defined notions of good and evil, the dictates of moral absolutism, a wrathful God who descends from a thundering cloudbank to smite every evil thing that creeps upon the earth, but after forty years as an educator, the old man finds that the interrogatory inflection of their voices sounds more and more like another part of the natural order—the rustling grass, the whispering wind, the squawking black grackles nesting high in the branches of the oaks and elms. Those sounds could all suddenly go silent and, for a time, he might not notice their absence, but after a while he would begin to feel uneasy and suspect that something had gone terribly wrong with the universe.

The old man pinches his chin, tries to concentrate, but he struggles to construct a simple line of argument. His skills as a dialectician, honed after many years of waging a war of words with his fellow Jesuits, are beginning to fail him.

"A person who has committed such atrocities would need to fully comprehend the magnitude of his crimes, would need to feel genuine remorse for his sins. While I doubt this person is capable of seeking redemption, I do believe he possesses a soul. He is a human being after all, and the human soul, whether it realizes it or not, yearns for atonement with the Almighty."

These words are meant to bore the boy, to lull him into submission, but this tactic clearly hasn't worked. With a little huff of disdain, Edmund removes his glasses, polishes the thick lenses on his sleeve, and ripostes, "In the Gospel of Mark, Jesus speaks of Gehenna and . . ."

"God helps those who help themselves, eh, Edmund? That's why we must take action right now." Wanting to avoid a tedious debate, the old man relies on a cliché because, if he remembers correctly, clichés are usually enough to pacify such boys, the more idealistic ones, the ones who have abandoned the uncertainty of critical thinking for the safety and comfort of ideology. He pats Edmund on the shoulder. "Now, I believe I'll take a little stroll over to the café."

"To the café?"

The old man stares into his empty mug. "It's a weakness on my part, I know, but without caffeine, I find it difficult to focus. A small infraction, hmmm?"

"But the other boys . . ."

"Other boys?"

"Yes, they'll be here any minute."

"They will?"

"Father Loomis, it's almost one o'clock."

The old man glances at the clock on the sacristy wall. The hands are nearly touching, like the fingertips of a penitent who has come here to pray the Act of Contrition. The clock hasn't worked in years—it's always midnight in the chapel.

"Well, I won't be long, Edmund."

"But what should I tell the others?"

"Tell them . . . tell them . . ." With an almost imperceptible shudder, Father Loomis tries to summon forth from the ravaged labyrinth of his memory a comforting passage from scripture. He massages his temples, closes his eyes, but once again he feels the ravenous worm gnawing its way through his brain. "Ah, yes, tell them this: whoever has come to understand the world has found only a corpse, and whoever has found a corpse is superior to the world."

Before Edmund can ask the meaning of these cryptic

words, the old man shoves past him and into the empty chapel. As he hurries down the aisle, he shields his eyes from the rays of sunlight that struggle through the stained glass window. A choir should be in the balcony rehearsing, but no one is there, and the old man wonders what has brought him to this lonely place on a Saturday afternoon. He should be at the rectory right now, eating a late lunch with his fellow Jesuits. Sensing trouble, he stumbles into the frigid November air while behind him, the heavy double doors of the chapel slam shut with the terrible, final, reverberating crack of a judge's gavel.

II

The clouds break and the white sun washes away every trace of color from the sky and disguises the depth of things, flattening the world into two dimensions, a city without shape or contour. In his confusion, the old man does not wander these streets so much as they wander him, spinning him around like a blindfolded child at a party, turning him first left, then right, pushing and prodding him now forward, now backward, frustrating his attempts to navigate this unforgiving maze. After walking five or six blocks, he pauses at a corner and tries to get his bearings by watching the way the wind carries the amber soot from the nearby factories and deposits it on rooftops and car hoods, transforming the neighborhood into a Martian landscape, arid and reddish; but the wind is calm right now, eerily so, and the smog hangs heavy and inert above the tall stacks.

The old man continues on his way. The afternoon traffic twangs in the heavy smog and ozone. He walks past a row of orange barrels and comes perilously close to a construction site where the Jesuits are building a new auditorium. He shuts his eyes and awaits the dreaded *deus ex machina*. God will surely strike him down for his impudence, of that he is certain. Five minutes go by, but no steel girder plummets from the sky to crush him beneath a pile of twisted debris; no bulldozer comes roaring out of the massive crater to grind him under its steel tracks. Maybe the madman will suddenly race around the corner, wielding his bottle of lighter fluid and book of matches. The old man longs to feel the searing heat of the flames, a kind of Pentecostal fire that will burn up the poison bubbling inside his brain and cure him at last of his mysterious affliction. If he dies now, he can address his creator with a clear conscience, but should he live long enough to make it back to the chapel, he will be reviled as a sinner and have to answer for the terrible thing he plans to do.

From an alley, there emerges a pack of stray dogs. Like swaggering street thugs who show only contempt for God-fearing men, the dogs trot behind him and whine with hunger. During the course of their lonely travels, the animals accost strangers, begging them for scraps of food, but the old man knows what carrion they feed on late at night. The newspapers never mention these gruesome details, but he has heard stories from traumatized investigators who, after examining the half-devoured corpses that litter the parks and alleys, come to him for solace and comfort. Outraged by the presence of such beasts, the old man lifts his arms high above his head, and the dogs slink off into the shadows.

Across the street, on the loading dock of the local brewery, a dozen deliverymen huddle around a barrel. They roast sausages and warm their hands by the fire, and when they see the old man shambling along the sidewalk, they stare and point.

The old man waves to them but continues blindly along until, somehow, he ends up inside the Stone Town Café, where a young woman greets him with a smile too sincere to be trusted. Is she a Catholic? Impossible! Not with those obsidian eyes and cinnamon skin. She rests her elbows on the counter and speaks to him slowly, as she would to a child or a fool. Her accent is unusual, her words a confusing babel of consonants.

He can only nod his head and murmur, "Ah, yes, yes."

The woman patiently repeats, "You're back so soon, Father Loomis. Nothing wrong with your Irish coffee, I hope. Was it too weak perhaps? Here, I'll make you another." She leans over the counter and whispers, "This time I'll add a little more whiskey. Our little secret."

"Espresso!" he blurts.

"Are you sure, Father? I have a bottle of Jameson. Your favorite."

"Espresso!"

She shrugs, wipes her hands on a towel, fills the metal filter-basket with ground coffee, tampers it into a firm puck, and switches on the huge silver machine that shrieks and hisses and belches out a thick stream of red-brown foam. He watches the process closely and then begins to pace through the café. In the corner, a boy strums a guitar and tries to avoid eye contact.

"You!" The old man jabs a finger at him. "I *know* you. Why aren't you in class?"

The boy looks startled and stops playing. "But, Father Loomis, it's Saturday."

The old man sneers. Another well-fed, rosy-cheeked child from the suburbs sent here on a chartered bus for the privilege of receiving a classical education. In drafty classrooms the boys are compelled to recite Latin aphorisms from antique volumes, and though their curiosity never goes far beyond the words stenciled on the school's letterhead and chiseled in stone above the entranceway of the main building—*Omnia mutantur, nos et mutamur in illis*, a reminder that only God is eternal and unchanging and that all else is transitory and perishable—they sometimes take the initiative to read the school newspaper and stand at the classroom windows each morning to place their bets on which of the whores will be burned next, like witches at the stake.

Murder is one thing, incineration another, and it pains the old man that his students find amusement in the torture and slaying of so many innocent women. They would rather gamble on a human life than try to save one. Their logic sickens him: gambling is a ritual like any other, and all rituals demand that blood be spilled. So he takes it upon himself to set things straight. He has asked several boys to visit him this afternoon at the chapel, the ones who have been properly inculcated with the Church's teachings on social justice and divine retribution—the pious ones, the most devout among them (the school still produces a few now and then), six brave young men eager to do the Lord's work. To sweeten the deal, the old man has promised them a world of heavenly delights far beyond anything they have so far imagined.

Now he pounds his fist on the countertop and demands to know what's taking so long, what's keeping this woman, Miss Mahogany, Miss Madagascar, Miss Zanzibar.

"Coming right up, Father." With a quizzical look she places the espresso in front of him. "That will be two dollars."

He reaches into his coat pockets, but instead of cash he

finds several pages that he cut from a book using a ruler and penknife. He puzzles over the pages, tries to unravel their meaning. A history of some kind? He reads aloud, enunciating each word as he might a sermon that he carefully composed for a high holy day:

> *The plague ravaged all of medieval Europe, leaving large numbers of dispossessed peasants to wander the highways and neighboring villages. Without adequate food or shelter, many resorted to the most barbaric means of survival, including murder and, in rare circumstances, cannibalism, but in the Tuscan village of Gentile da Foligno, there lived a holy man, a monk who was determined to rescue a group of young prostitutes from certain death. On an autumn morning in 1389, as the plague was decimating the nearby city of Florence, the priest married off the prostitutes to several young men from affluent homes. Thus did the prostitutes escape the unremitting squalor of the brothels to live out their days in the relative safety and comfort of the landed gentry's country estates . . .*

Like a scholar who has just solved a particularly irksome mathematical proof, the old man slaps the crumpled sheets down on the counter and says, "Is this what you need?"

The woman pats his trembling hand. Her stealthy fingers pry at his soul, try to unfasten the latch to his heart.

"Father, would you like some help getting back to the rectory?"

The humiliation is unbearable. He glares at her, grabs the cup of espresso, and stomps toward the door.

The woman calls to him. "No blessing today?"

He whirls on his heels and shouts, "We sacrifice the intellect to God!"

Then he storms out of the café and into the ennobling poverty and squalor of the neighborhood where the sun swings across the sky like a pendulum through the dark dungeon of the world.

III

By the time he finds his way back to the chapel it is late in the afternoon, and a line has already formed outside the double doors. There are six women altogether, and at the old man's approach, they crush out their cigarettes, fall into a reverential hush, bless themselves, wipe away tears of gratitude.

Hardly the type given to sentimentality on such a joyous occasion, the old man looks them up and down and scowls. How many times must he explain that it is inappropriate to wear so much makeup, to chew gum, to expose the tattoos on the smalls of their backs? "Tramp stamps," the boys call them. Earlier that week, he gave the women the last of his cash and instructed them to visit the corner thrift shop to buy sober gray suits, formal hats, black flats—what he likes to call "church ensembles," tasteful attire—but they are still wearing their usual street clothes and smell strongly of liquor. Not that new outfits would have been entirely transformative. Money will never smooth over the roughness of their speech, their irritable habit of using double negatives, their smattering of casual *fuck you*s and *ain't*s. To insure that things go smoothly, he asks them to say as few words as possible. This isn't a moral judgment on his part. Elocution is a tricky business. Even he has great difficulty with words like *homoousian* and *homoiousian*, the most consequential of diphthongs.

"Follow me," he orders.

Inside the chapel, the chosen boys stand before the altar, their hair neatly combed, their ties straightened, their collars starched and pressed. They seem restless, nervous. Among them is Edmund Campion. He is first in line, his gawky demeanor superseded by a smile of such profound devotion that it strikes the old man as almost demented. What has this boy done, what sin has he committed that he feels the burning need to repent in such a way?

For a moment, the old man considers turning around and rushing back outside, but one of the women, the one the others call Tamar, blocks his path, and he understands that there is no escape. As he walks toward the altar, he checks his pockets, a repository for hints and clues and gentle reminders, but nothing more is to be found there. Vaguely he recalls something about legal certificates and that, by signing them, the boys have signed away not only their souls, which is nothing at all, for the soul is just a concept, a hopeful idea at best, but have also signed away their lives, which is the only thing a person ever has for certain, and even that is a tenuous proposition. The self, the old man now suspects, is an illusion, as impermanent as the wisps of incense that linger in the chapel.

Donning his white liturgical vestment and green stole—spiritual armor to protect him against any fiendish torments that hell might devise—the old man stands before the altar and lifts his hands. So begins the grotesque processional down the aisle. There is still time for his fellow Jesuits to burst through the door, time for them to drag him away and scold him like a mischievous student, but the church remains quiet and full of anticipation, like a great stone fortress hunkered down in silence, its sentries awaiting the arrival of distant armies with their awful engines of war.

Nothing happens. God, it seems, has decided not to intervene.

Long ago, the old man learned to accept the terrible truth that he would never have a shattering experience like the ones described by medieval mystics, no startling flash of insight, no vision of Christ with His right hand extended in a gesture of boundless love, but this fact does not deter him from trying one last time to make contact with the divine. He bows his head and concentrates with all his heart and all his soul and all his *mind*, and suddenly the impenetrable veil that for most of the day has obscured his vision is lifted, and the world reveals itself to him with such clarity, with such unflinching detail, that he can only take this as a sign of the unequivocal goodness of His plan.

After pairing off the young men and women—the awkward and buffoonish Edmund with world-weary Tamar— the old man opens the missal and utters the opening words of this most beautiful of ceremonies.

"Dearly beloved, we are gathered here today . . ."

Gehenna

I

This is what they do to him, to the old man, after a lifetime spent in quiet contemplation among books of eschatology.

They parade him before the students on high holy days, not unlike the mummified thumb or shriveled toe of a medieval saint or mystic, an artifact to be revered as a symbol of piety, celibacy, wisdom, and dread. Recently forced into retirement, the old man is given the title Instructor Emeritus, an honorific bestowed upon those priests too ancient and addle-minded to continue teaching without embarrassment or scandal in the classroom. Though rare and often ritualized, these appearances are meant to satisfy his need to be among the students, his proverbial "lost flock," whose intellectual curiosity seems to dwindle with each passing year.

The problem is just this: the old man, when given an opportunity to address the students, tends to say things that fly in the face of orthodoxy. The Jesuits believe (and have practically made it a matter of doctrine) that God in his munificence has traced an invisible circle around the campus, and all who enter this sacred sphere are, through divine grace, absolved of sin and henceforth immunized from the wickedness of the world. Here God walks in the cool of the evening, and here the serpent is rebuked and banished to the alleys and tenement buildings at the circle's grim periphery. At the center of the circle stands the Tree of Life, and the Jesuits urge the students to gather each morning under its sheltering limbs. But if some of the boys find these clichés convincing, it is only because they are unaware of what life holds in store for them—they will finish high school, go to college, get married, beget children, grow old; in short, they will be miserable in a million predictable ways, and it saddens the old man to think of the myriad banalities and disappointments that await. Such a life doesn't have a happy ending because it was never a happy proposition from the start.

Sensing their impassivity to their own fate, the old man dares the boys to sample the repellent fruit from that other tree, the one forbidden to them. With an admonitory wave of his hand and a loud rap of his cane, he shouts, "Wake up! Open your eyes! The overripe fruit has fallen from the branches and is rotting on the ground all around you. Go on, pick it up, taste it. For eons it has been fermenting, and its effects are quite sublime."

He paces the room, from front to back, leaning heavily on the desks for support.

"Blessed is he who can understand a metaphor. This image of a mystical circle, and the invisible wall of protection it reputedly offers, is a fantasy, an obvious fabrication for the weak of mind and spirit. In reality the circle does not exist, has never existed. This must be so because God is all-encompassing and without boundaries. He dwells inside and outside any circle that ever was or even can be. And the same is true of Good and Evil, which, like God, are in a continuous state of flux and thus indistinguishable from one another. God does not walk in the Garden but swims in this protean sea of Creation. And all men, whether they are aware of it or not, flail about and gasp for air in its cold and tempestuous waters. You do and I do. We are drenched in it. Soaked to the bone in Good and Evil."

Against their better judgment, the Jesuits allow him to finish his lecture, but later that same day, when they overhear several boys contemplating these dangerous ideas in the cafeteria, the priests, fearing a schism, an insurrection, a possible drop in enrollment, call an emergency meeting. In the gloom of the principal's office, a secret vote is taken, and the priests unanimously decide that the old man, because he may have already defiled the minds of these impressionable boys, must never again speak in the classroom.

Keeping him away from the students—this is one of the many things they do to him, but it is not the worst thing.

II

Feeding, bathing, and dressing him pose significant challenges, but bringing him to Mass each morning is particularly trying. During the Lord's Prayer, he recites soliloquies from *Hamlet* and recounts the strange, eventful histories of Saxo Grammaticus; during the Te Deum, he whistles an Irish hornpipe and dances a slap jig; during the celebration of the Eucharist, he shakes his head slowly back and forth as though in bitter disagreement, or is it in stark disbelief? The Jesuits are never quite sure and are reluctant to ponder the possibility that the old man has fallen prey to the allure of that wine-drenched harlot, Heresy.

Despite suffering from rheumatoid arthritis and having lost a great deal of weight since the onset of his illness, the old man is still agile, more so than some of his septuagenarian colleagues burdened with the responsibility of keeping watch over him, and he develops a remarkable talent for sneaking out of the chapel while the other priests are deep in meditation.

For hours the old man haunts the city streets, a forlorn figure in black that can easily pass for a ghost, a derelict, a holy fool clothed in sackcloth and ashes. At nightfall, when packs of stray dogs emerge from their fetid dens to forage for putrid meat in dark alleys, the old man, as if by instinct, finds his way inside a corner café, where he chats with the lovely barista. After ordering his usual mug of Irish coffee, he makes his way to the back tables to commiserate with the luckless poets who scribble blank verse in their prodigious notebooks, play chess, and obsess over their personal failings. Though most claim to be freethinkers and practitioners of the more esoteric philosophies of the Far East, these men, burdened with years of guilt, feel an inexplicable urge to confess their countless sins, sometimes doing so in spectacular detail. They revel in self-debasement, which they mistake for virtue, and sometimes shed a few cathartic tears for good measure.

As he tries to judge whether they are deserving of redemption, the old man relishes the pleasant heat from his whiskey and the exquisite numbness that creeps through his limbs. A few sips is all it takes to liberate him from the imprisonment of flesh and bone, and for a few wonderful moments, he slips out of his body and floats freely through the café, a diluted presence, insubstantial as the wisps of steam that rise from the golden domed espresso machine and coil around the blinking neon sign in the front window.

"I dare say, booze is more magical than the Blood," he proffers. Then he encourages the men to set aside their coffee and join him in a proper drink. He snaps his fingers and calls to the barista, "Whiskeys all around!"

The old man is incoherent by the time the Jesuits find him, his arms dangling at his sides, his jaw hanging open. The priests hoist him from the chair and struggle to carry him through the streets, slick with rain. At the rectory, they put him to bed and lock his door.

Keeping the old man away from the café—this is another thing they do to him, but still, it is not the worst thing.

III

In the morning, before classes begin, some of the boys, the more incorrigible among them, loiter in the alley behind the gymnasium, where they smoke cigarettes and sip from flasks and try to make sense of their teen angst. They joke about their sexual conquests and cast doubt on the wisdom of their elders, but when they hear the arduous scrape of heavy shoes along the broken bricks, they hastily stomp out their cigarettes and rehearse their expressions of innocence.

The old man hobbles around the corner, his eyes lost in some twilight reverie, but upon spotting the boys, he suddenly straightens up, tucks the cane under his arm, and with a kind of regal bearing, marches toward them. The boys are well aware of his apostasy, but they are unsure if he intends to impart some heretical platitude or reprimand them for their bad behavior. With the ashes and glowing embers of their cigarettes still swirling around their ankles, they address the old man with feigned respect.

"Why, good morning, Father Loomis!"

The old man grunts, turns a quizzical eye to the lavender alliums that have survived the first unforgiving blasts of freezing autumn air. He reaches down, gently removes the partially withered head from its stem, and twirls it in front of their eyes.

"You continually ask yourself, 'What is the meaning of life?' And this is what I say to you: What is the meaning of this flower I'm holding? What is the meaning of this fly crawling on my sleeve? What is the meaning of this conversation we're having? All the answers to all the mysteries of this universe and the next can be found in the delicate petals of a flower. But few people comprehend the simplicity of the message. Most people look for answers elsewhere."

He points to the pained expressions of martyrs on the chapel's stained glass windows.

"A catalogue of torments," he says. "Just look at them, the poor misguided souls. The disciples once asked Jesus, 'Master, when will the Kingdom come?' And do you know how he replied? Hmmm?"

The boys shake their heads, try to suppress their smiles.

"He said, 'It will not come by watching for it. The Kingdom of the Father is spread out upon the earth . . . *but people do not see it.*'"

The old man surrenders the flower to the wind and watches it fly apart and vanish.

"Eternal life," he murmurs, "the resurrection of the flesh." He looks up as though startled out of a dream. With spittle flying from his lips, he lets out an epiphanic cry: "To die and not be forgotten! That is the best any of us can hope for, gentlemen, the only immortality we shall ever know."

Ignoring their smirks and snide laughter, the old man lifts his cane and waves it over their heads like a magic wand.

Mantled in the soft autumn light, he continues on his sad, directionless promenade, muttering blasphemies and puzzling oaths. He can no longer control himself. By now this is quite plain to everyone.

That evening, before saying grace and breaking bread, the priests crush an assortment of black-and-white pills into a fine powder and stir it into his mashed potatoes and gravy. As missionaries sent by the Church to proselytize in remote mountain villages, the Jesuits have borne witness to a thousand unspeakable nightmares, but despite battling rare diseases and risking life and limb, not for medals or glory or honor but to tell the uncomprehending bumpkins and their brood of squalling children that contraceptives are morally suspect and that God wants them to be fruitful and multiply—despite all of this, the priests find that they have no appetite for the old man's profane banter, and they pray that the medication will temporarily solve the problem until nature decides upon a permanent solution.

Keeping him in a perpetual drug-induced stupor—this is another thing they do to him, but still it is not the worst thing.

IV

With its anarchy of adjoining corridors and antechambers and quiet galleries, the school is a labyrinth of forked paths that follows a mysterious logic that no one, save perhaps God, can fathom. Even after teaching at the school for nearly fifty years, the old man will sometimes lose his bearings in its fun-house geometries. Tottering along on his wooden cane, he passes through an arched threshold and into a hallway that seems to stretch on and on until it tapers away to a cruciform of ghostly white light. Under the high vaulted ceilings, he wanders like some hapless denizen in a rococo palace swarming with sculptures and mirrors and tapestries. There is a kind of sordidness about the place; it exudes decadence and frivolity.

At last he comes to a spiral staircase and stops to peer over the railing. Somewhere in that gaping darkness, he hears conspiring voices. They speak of a party and make lewd predictions about its outcome. Carefully clinging to a wrought-iron balustrade, the old man descends the twisted helix and makes his way to the basement, where the limestone walls are lined not with the skulls of long-deceased Jesuits or with worm-bored coffins smelling of must and decay, but with dozens of shiny new kegs of handcrafted ale recently delivered from the local brewery. There he finds two boys rolling one of the kegs toward a ramp at the back of the building.

"You! I say, you there! What do you think you're doing?"

The old man sucks in his breath and begins to shake with rage. The epic hellfire and brimstone sermon that has been bottled up in his heart for so long now threatens to erupt from his sputtering lips.

"You reprehensible . . . you impertinent . . . Do you have any idea who . . ." His words become small and faint like those of a frightened child who has been abandoned in a wilderness. "That's strange . . . I was on my way back to the rectory and . . ." Massaging his forehead, he offers the boys an apologetic smile. "Where is the rectory, gentlemen? I've lived here for so long, but I can't seem to remember . . ."

Using tones of quiet cajolery, the boys pretend to comfort the old man. "Follow us, Father Loomis. We're happy to show you the way."

Tears well up in his eyes. "Bless you. You're very kind."

"It's our pleasure."

"I'm sorry to be such a nuisance."

"No trouble at all, Father. Really."

"It's no picnic getting old, boys, let me tell you."

"Oh, we can imagine."

"I keep having these senior moments . . . And . . . Wait a minute, now . . . Are you certain this is the right way?"

"Of course."

"But this is a most unusual route."

"Circuitous. Isn't that the right word, Father?"

"I beg your pardon?"

"A very Latinate word, circuitous. Watch your step now."

"Please, let go of me."

The old man tries to break free, but it's no use. With their powerful hands, the boys take his cane and prod him toward an open door. The closet has the awful dimensions of a sarcophagus; it reeks of tobacco and formaldehyde and the rich, alluvial muck of the nearby river that rises from the sewers and floods the basement after a heavy rain. In the corner there is a mouse nest, a mop, a bucket filled with gray water, an ashtray crammed with cigarette butts.

"Here you are, Father."

"But you can't, you shouldn't . . ."

"In you go!"

They shove him inside and swing the door shut. He sobs, begs for mercy, hammers on the door until his knuckles are raw and begin to bleed. The boys turn the lock and then return to their thievery.

For the next thirty minutes, the old man listens to them roll kegs toward the ramp, and then all at once, there is silence. The hours pass slowly, and he has the sensation, an uncanny one, that the entire universe is made of the thinnest fabric.

The things that seem concrete and imperishable are nothing more than a projection on a screen, flickering images that will soon go dark forever. Trapped within that hideous blackness, the old man grows more and more terrified until, in his panic and delirium, he recognizes the death pangs of consciousness, the final stratum of reality slipping away into oblivion. From his larynx, a scream rises with terrible urgency, but his voice is so ragged and shrill that only a fugitive cry of humiliation escapes his lips and dies long before it ever reaches the staircase.

Early the next morning, compelled to visit the basement to retrieve an untapped keg for the priests' luncheon, the housekeeper, Ms. Higginson, hears a faint but persistent scratching and opens the closet door to discover a nearly unrecognizable creature curled up in the corner, a cadaverous thing of plutonic origins that, in its madness, drools and quivers and, with trembling fingers, smears its own excrement over the cold, wet stones.

"Why do we cling to our fear? Beyond our fear there is nothing. Nothing at all. We must learn to surrender to the darkness."

It's only after the pale specter opens its toothless mouth and speaks in a sibilant whisper that the housekeeper unleashes a terrible howl that rouses the Jesuits from the sweet serenity of sleep.

His own students have done this deplorable thing to him, boys he has mentored for years, but even this isn't the worst of it.

V

The priests carry him to the rectory, where they force him to stand under a spray of scalding water. Next, they set up a hospital bed in the library because, they feel, it will be easier to keep an eye on him there and because they believe the mere sight of these books will provide him with some comfort in his final days. He was once a great scholar, a polymath with wide-ranging interests—history, science, obscure religious movements. Some of the priests can still remember how, long ago, shortly after his ordination, he dreamed of writing full-time, but the act of writing takes a great deal of self-discipline, and the old man has always preferred to read about things rather than write about them. He once tried his hand at fiction, but the experience left him shaken and consumed with self-doubt. He decided that there were too many books in the world and that it wasn't for him to add one more to the already insurmountable pile.

Lying quietly in bed, it now occurs to him that writers, like the leaves lighting on the windowpane, are practically infinite in number; they accumulate outside the library, desperate to get in, and threaten to crush humanity under their collective weight. He dreads joining their ranks, an author indistinguishable from a million others, and it is for this reason that he became not only a teacher but the official keeper of these rare volumes—to bar the door and allow in only the finest works of the human imagination. But if the years have taught him anything, it is that he is a humble servant to these books, not their keeper.

He has no other intimacies, having taken a vow of celibacy when he was barely more than a boy, but he has been perfectly content with a life of the mind, which is rich and varied and full of small wonders. This attitude contrasts markedly from that of his colleagues, many of whom often wonder if they made the correct decision in life. As young seminarians they were taught that the Word of God could be heard most clearly in our love for one another—in a mother's love for her child, a father's pride in his son—but the priests had no chance for love of that kind. They were trained to profess their love for their Church, but that wasn't love, that was neurosis, because no one can love a bureaucracy. Books, the old man soon discovered, were a far superior substitute for coping with loneliness; the trick was to transform his interior monologue into a dialogue in which he conversed at length with the authors of these volumes. But now, because of his failing eyesight, he can no longer peruse the dusty spines that line the walls from floor to ceiling. Losing hope that he will live long enough to read from his favorite books a final time, the old man falls into a deep depression.

The Jesuits send a boy to sit beside his bed, but the boy has no intention of reading to him. He has not come here for that purpose. With eyes that are black and small and stupid, he smirks and asks, "Would you like to see something, Father?" From his book bag he removes a deck of pornographic playing cards and fans them out beside the pillow. "Sinful, isn't it, Father?"

The old man lifts his head and whispers, "Oh God please help please God help God please . . ."

"Relax, you rattlebag of bones. It will all be over soon, yes, very soon now."

Intentionally depriving him of his books—this is another thing they do to him, but still it is not the worst thing.

VI

The afternoon of the Great Blizzard.

His heart beats slowly now, faintly. His breathing is shallow but not labored. From his bed he can gaze out the window and observe the students leaving school for the day. After the long hours spent conjugating Greek and Latin verbs in crowded classrooms, the boys look thin, ashen-faced, glassy-eyed, old men in the making, but now that the day is over and the weekend has finally arrived, they start to bounce back to life, loosen their ties, smile up at the receding sun.

All ignore the vast wall of clouds gathering on the far horizon, tremendous lead-colored things that, from a distance, look like the craggy granite peaks of a vast mountain range. As the cold front gains momentum, the clouds start to wheel wildly across the sky and metamorphose into a hundred phantasmagoric shapes—anvils and chariots and monster movie insects that leap across the lake and decimate the city with their snapping pincers. A rumbling blast of icy air barrels through the bleak canyons of abandoned factories and empty warehouses. Discarded newspapers take flight like mutant bats flapping their gigantic wings before swirling away in a cyclone of sordid celebrity gossip and astrological twaddle. Rows of telephone lines snap one by one, silencing a thousand yammering voices, all of them buying and selling and dissembling with unparalleled expertise. The marble *putti*, prancing impertinently in the nearby fountain, douse the boys with angelic effervescence, but the boys refuse to abandon their benches until the snow explodes from the clouds. Before dashing back into the main building, some of them stop to face the brutal winds, brave soldiers readying themselves for a catastrophe of grand proportions, a nuclear winter maybe. They open their mouths and claim to feel the anger of vibrating molecules on the tips of their tongues and taste the final, unadorned truth of the cosmos in the heavy, white flakes.

With preternatural speed, the snow accumulates into dirty,

yellow dunes, turning the neighborhood into a vast urban tundra, a blinding, windswept wasteland that stretches from the lake to the doors of the rectory. Soon the humps of cars parked along the curb are barely visible. There is no sign of the police or paramedics or city snowplows. Inside the library, the lights flicker and then go out altogether, and the room quickly turns cold. The Jesuits build a fire, but within an hour they use up the last of the logs, and once more, the rectory becomes as bitter as the tomb.

"He won't last the night," they concur.

They kneel beside his bed and speak to their creator, the greatest librarian of them all, but God, while capable of retaining and synthesizing vast amounts of information, has perhaps learned that in the end, it is best to ignore the pleas of mere mortals, who too often request that he radically re-write the final pages of this absurd melodrama for their personal benefit.

Sensing God's indifference, the old man raises his head and speaks to his colleagues as though they are acolytes at the feet of a master: "Each of us is a character in some facile and purposeless tale. And just as we are fictions, so too is God a fiction. This is the essence of the one true gospel."

The priests drown him out with their humble petition to heaven: "O Lord, grant Thy healing, that the soul of Thy servant, at the hour of its departure from the body, may by the hands of Thy holy angels be presented without spot unto Thee!"

When darkness falls, the Jesuits, in their desperation, decide to use some of the books as fuel and select those titles that have contributed to the old man's apostasy, first editions of scholarly tomes that have long been out of print, books about the Black Death, the Gnostic gospels, medieval heresies. Without compunction, they cast these contentious books into the flames, and the old man, gasping for breath, endures this final vision: the secret songs and sermons of Cathars and Manichaeans and Borgesians smoldering on the popping and hissing embers, vanishing from this world forevermore in a conflagration of human folly.

Destroying his books, some will argue, is the worst thing they do to him. But even this is not the very worst thing.

VII

A government desk clerk, with small nervous hands and thinning gray hair, completes the necessary paperwork and has it signed in triplicate by the principal. An ambulance comes for the body and transports it to the county morgue, where the coroner performs a routine and rather perfunctory autopsy. From there the body is taken to a public cemetery, where a mortician prepares it for burial. His assistants place the corpse in a cheap pinewood box, hammer down the lid, and then leave it beside several other unremarkable caskets that await burial.

Through the tree-lined lanes of the sprawling necropolis, past the improbable skyline of rain-worn obelisks and the aberrant architecture of marble monuments, two grave diggers convey the body to a hilltop that overlooks the expressway. The men remove their hats, trade a few dirty jokes, and, having muttered obsequies of damning indifference, hastily lower the casket into the hole. They take up their shovels, fill the pit with clumps of frozen soil, then make their lazy way back to the basement of the small stone building near the cemetery gates to collect the next box.

The old man's family and dearest friends have preceded

him into death, and no one comes to his final resting place to say farewell or to scatter flowers over his lonely grave—no colleagues, no intercessors, no former pupils, no one at all. No vigil is held for him in the school chapel, no Mass said in his name, no mournful requiem played on the organ, and in the ensuing years no priest appears from out of the rain or snow or dazzling summer sunshine to say a simple prayer for the forgotten dead.

And this, let it be known, is the worst thing they do to him, the very worst thing.

ACKNOWLEDGMENTS

After the most remarkable, tumultuous, and emotional year of my life, I would like to take a moment to extend my sincere thanks and express my gratitude to the following people for providing me with help large and small. First and always, to my wife, Catherine Scanlon, and my daughter, Rose, for enduring my moody disposition during the writing of this novel and the next. Thanks to Dan Cleary, Robert Dudash, Robert Beckstrom, and Nancy Kelly in Elyria. Thanks to Michael Garriga, Ted Harakas, Michael Dolzani, and Sheila Drain in Berea. Thanks to the great Jane Dugan for providing a ray of light to so many people struggling every day in the salt mines. Thanks to Aaron Paulson, J. W. Schnarr, and Martin Rose, who championed early drafts of this work. Huge thanks to my agent, David Patterson, and to Tim O'Connell, my editor at Vintage Books and Pantheon, for giving me this amazing opportunity to showcase my work. Heartfelt thanks to Karl Taro Greenfeld, without whose help this whole improbable adventure may never have gotten underway. Equal thanks to Cynthia Reeser, whose Aqueous Books provides such an invaluable service for dedicated writers yearning to see their work in print and reach an audience. Finally, thanks to my friends and family for putting up with my shameless self-promotion, for buying my book (and, in some cases, reading it—Brian, Mike, and Fran), for all of your kind words of encouragement, your assurances, and your continuing support. This book is for all of you, too.